P9-CBQ-654

The Black Widowers are at it again.

● A greeting card collector finds himself the target for a mysterious message. . . .

● A Russian visitor to New York thinks he has uncovered a sinister murder plot. . . .

● A mad scientist's locked-up secrets create a desperate race to unlock his safe—but first the combination must be deciphered. . . .

● A man smokes a cigarette and loses a job—and his company loses a million dollars. . . .

But things aren't always what they seem. Here is your chance to test your detective skills against the very best—"The Black Widowers."

Fawcett Books by Isaac Asimov:

THE EARLY ASIMOV, *Book One* X2850 $1.75
THE EARLY ASIMOV, *Book Two* 23700-1 $1.95
PEBBLE IN THE SKY 23423-1 $1.75
THE STARS, LIKE DUST 23595-5 $1.75
THE CURRENTS OF SPACE 23507-6 $1.50
THE CAVES OF STEEL 23782-6 $1.75
THE END OF ETERNITY 23704-4 $1.75
I, ROBOT Q2829 $1.50
THE MARTIAN WAY 23783-4 $1.75
THE NAKED SUN 23805-9 $1.75
EARTH IS ROOM ENOUGH 23383-9 $1.75
NINE TOMORROWS 23618-8 $1.75
NIGHTFALL AND OTHER STORIES 23672-2 $1.95
THE GODS THEMSELVES 23756-7 $1.95
THE BEST OF ISAAC ASIMOV 23653-6 $1.95
TALES OF THE BLACK WIDOWERS 23788-5 $1.75
MORE TALES OF THE BLACK WIDOWERS 23806-7 $1.75
THE BICENTENNIAL MAN AND OTHER
  STORIES 23573-4 $1.75

More Tales
Of The
Black Widowers

ISAAC ASIMOV

FAWCETT CREST • NEW YORK

MORE TALES OF THE BLACK WIDOWERS

THIS BOOK CONTAINS THE COMPLETE TEXT OF THE ORIGINAL HARDCOVER EDITION.

Published by Fawcett Crest Books, a unit of CBS Publications, the Consumer Publishing Division of CBS Inc., by arrangement with Doubleday and Company, Inc.

Copyright © 1976 by Isaac Asimov

All rights reserved

ISBN: 0-449-23806-7

All the characters in this book are fictitious, and any resemblance to actual persons living or dead is purely coincidental.

Selection of the Detective Book Club

Acknowledgments

"WHEN NO MAN PURSUETH" originally published in EQMM. Copyright © 1974 by Isaac Asimov

"QUICKER THAN THE EYE" originally published in EQMM. Copyright © 1974 by Isaac Asimov

"THE IRON GEM" originally published in EQMM. Copyright © 1974 by Isaac Asimov

"THE THREE NUMBERS" originally published in EQMM under the title of "ALL IN THE WAY YOU READ IT." Copyright © 1974 by Isaac Asimov

"NOTHING LIKE MURDER" originally published in Fantasy and Science Fiction. Copyright © 1974 by Mercury Press, Inc.

"NO SMOKING" originally published in EQMM under the title of "CONFESSIONS OF AN AMERICAN CIGARETTE SMOKER." Copyright © 1974 by Isaac Asimov

"THE ONE AND ONLY EAST" originally published in EQMM. Copyright © 1975 by Isaac Asimov

"EARTHSET AND EVENING STAR" originally published in Fantasy and Science Fiction. Copyright © 1975 by Mercury Press, Inc.

"FRIDAY THE THIRTEENTH" originally published in Fantasy and Science Fiction. Copyright © 1975 by Mercury Press, Inc.

Printed in the United States of America

10   9   8   7   6   5   4   3   2

To   *Donald Bensen*
     Gilbert Cant
     Lin Carter
     John D. Clark
     L. Sprague de Camp
     Lester del Rey

Contents

Introduction

I don't think there's much more to say about the Black Widowers than I've already said in *Tales of the Black Widowers*. That was the first book in this series and the one you're now holding is the second.

In that first introduction, I explained that the Black Widowers was inspired by a real club, to which I belong, which is called the Trap Door Spiders. I won't tell you any more about that here because if you've read *Tales of the Black Widowers* you'd just be bored by the repetition, and if you haven't read it I'd rather leave you in the agony of curiosity so that you will then be driven to buy the first book and repair the omission.

Once the *Tales* was published, by the way, I handed a copy to each member of the Trap Door Spiders. One and all carefully masked their real feelings under the pretense of pleasure, and naturally, I accepted that pretense at face value.

That's all I have to say now, but lest you rejoice too quickly at being rid of me, I must warn you that I will appear again in a short afterword following each of the stories.

1

When No Man Pursueth

Thomas Trumbull scowled with only his usual ferocity and said, "How do you justify your existence, Mr. Stellar?"

Mortimer Stellar lifted his eyebrows in surprise and looked about the table at the six Black Widowers whose guest he was for that evening.

"Would you repeat that?" he said.

But before Trumbull could, Henry, the club's redoubtable waiter, had moved in silently to offer Stellar his brandy and Stellar took it with an absently murmured "Thank you."

"It's a simple question," said Trumbull. "How do you justify your existence?"

"I didn't know I had to," said Stellar.

"Suppose you did have to," said Trumbull. "Suppose you were standing before God's great judgment seat."

"You sound like an editor," said Stellar, unimpressed.

And Emmanuel Rubin, host for the evening, and a fellow writer, laughed and said, "No, he doesn't, Mort. He's ugly but he's not ugly enough."

"You stay out of it, Manny," said Trumbull, pointing a forefinger.

"All right," said Stellar. "I'll give you an answer. I hope that, as a result of my stay on Earth, I will have left some people a little more informed about science than they would have been if I had never lived."

"How have you done that?"

"By the books and articles I write on science for the layman." Stellar's blue eyes glinted from behind his heavily black-rimmed glasses and he added with no perceptible trace of modesty, "Which are probably the best that have ever been written."

"They're pretty good," said James Drake, the chemist, stubbing out his fifth cigarette of the evening and coughing as though to celebrate the momentary pulmonary release. "I wouldn't put you ahead of Gamow, though."

"Tastes differ," said Stellar coldly. "I would."

Mario Gonzalo said, "You don't write only about science, do you? It seems to me I read an article by you in a television weekly magazine and that was just humor." He had propped up the caricature he had drawn of Stellar in the course of the meal. The black-rimmed glasses were prominent and so was the shoulder-length, fading brown hair, the broad grin, and the horizontal lines across the forehead.

"Good Lord," said Stellar. "Is that me?"

"It's the best Mario can do," said Rubin. "Don't shoot him."

"Let's have some order," said Trumbull testily. "Mr. Stellar, please answer the question Mario put to you. Do you write only about science?"

Geoffrey Avalon, who had been sipping gently at his brandy, said in his deep voice which could, whenever he chose, utterly dominate the table, "Aren't we wasting time? We've all read Mr. Stellar's articles. It's impossible to avoid him. He's everywhere."

"*If* you don't mind, Jeff," said Trumbull, "it's what I'm trying to get at in a systematic way. I've seen his articles and Manny says he has written a hundred-and-something books on all sorts of subjects and the point is why and how?"

The monthly banquet of the Black Widowers was in its concluding phase—that of the grilling of the guest. It was a process that was supposed to be conducted along the simple, ordinary lines of a judicial cross-examination but never was. The fact that it so often dissolved into chaos was a matter of deep irritation to Trumbull, the club's code expert, whose dream it was to conduct the grilling after the fashion of a drumhead court-martial.

"Let's get into that, then, Mr. Stellar," he said. "Why the hell do you write so many books on so many subjects?"

Stellar said, "Because it's good business. It pays to be unspecialized. Most writers are specialists; they've got to be. Manny Rubin is a specialist; he writes mysteries—when he bothers to write at all."

Rubin's sparse beard lifted and his eyes widened with indignation behind his thick-lensed glasses. "I happen to have published over forty books, and they're not all mysteries. I've published"—he began ticking off his fingers—"sport stories, confessions, fantasies—"

"Mostly mysteries," amended Stellar smoothly. "Me, I try not to specialize. I'll write on any subject that strikes my fancy. It makes life more interesting for me so that I never go through a writer's block. Besides, it makes me independent of the ups and downs of fashion. If one kind of article loses popularity, what's the difference? I write others."

Roger Halsted passed his hand over the smooth balding forepart of his head and said, "But how do you do it? Do you have set hours to write in?"

"No," said Stellar. "I just write when I feel like. But I feel like all the time."

"Actually," said Rubin, "you're a compulsive writer."

"I've never denied it," said Stellar.

Gonzalo said, "But steady composition doesn't seem to be consistent with artistic inspiration. Does it just pour out of you? Do you revise at all?"

Stellar's face lowered and for a moment he seemed to be staring at his brandy glass. He pushed it to one side and said, "Everyone seems to worry about inspiration. You're an artist, Mr. Gonzalo. If you waited for inspiration, you'd starve."

"Sometimes I starve even when I don't," said Gonzalo.

"I just write," said Stellar, a bit impatiently. "It's not so difficult to do that. I have a simple, straightforward, unornamented style, so that I don't have to waste time on clever phrases. I present my ideas in a clear and orderly way because I have a clear and orderly mind. Most of all, I have security. I know I'm going to sell what I write, and so I don't agonize over every sentence, worrying about whether the editor will like it."

"You didn't always know you would sell what you wrote," said Rubin. "I assume there was a time when you were a beginner and got rejection slips like everyone else."

"That's right. And in those days writing took a lot longer and was a lot harder. But that was thirty years ago. I've been literarily secure for a long time."

Drake twitched his neat gray mustache and said, "Do you really sell everything you write now? Without exception?"

Stellar said, "Just about everything, but not always first crack out of the box. Sometimes I get a request for revision and, if it's a reasonable request, I revise, and if it's unreasonable, I don't. And once in a while—at least once a year, I think—I get an outright rejection." He shrugged. "It's part of the free-lance game. It can't be helped."

"What happens to something that's rejected, or that you won't revise?" asked Trumbull.

"I try it somewhere else. One editor might like what another editor doesn't. If I can't sell it anywhere I put it aside; a new market might open up; I might get a request for something that the rejected article can fill."

"Don't you feel that's like selling damaged goods?" said Avalon.

"No, not at all," said Stellar. "A rejection doesn't necessarily mean an article is bad. It just means that one particular editor found it unsuitable. Another editor might find it suitable."

Avalon's lawyer-mind saw an opening. He said, "By that reasoning, it follows that if an editor likes, buys, and publishes one of your articles, that is no necessary proof that the article is any good."

"None at all, in any one case," said Stellar, "but if it happens over and over again, the evidence in your favor mounts up."

Gonzalo said, "What happens if *everyone* rejects an article?"

Stellar said, "That hardly ever happens, but if I get tired of submitting a piece, chances are I cannibalize it. Sooner or later I'll write something on a subject that's close to it, and then I incorporate parts of the rejected article into a new piece. I don't waste *anything*."

"Then everything you write sees print, one way or another. Is that right?" And Gonzalo shook his head slightly, in obvious admiration.

"That's about right." But then Stellar frowned. "Except, of course," he said, "when you deal with an idiot editor who buys something and then doesn't publish it."

Rubin said, "Oh, have you run into one of those things? The magazine folded?"

"No, it's flourishing. Haven't I ever told you about this?"

"Not as far as I remember."

"I'm talking about Bercovich. Did you ever sell anything to him?"

"Joel Bercovich?"

"Are there likely to be two editors with that last name? Of *course*, Joel Bercovich."

"Well, sure. He used to edit *Mystery Story* magazine some years ago. I sold him a few items. I still have lunch with him occasionally. He's not in mysteries any more."

"I know he isn't. He's editing *Way of Life* magazine. One of those fancy new slick jobs that appeal to the would-be affluent."

"Hold it. *Hold it*!" cried out Trumbull. "This thing's degenerating. Let's go back to the questioning."

"Now wait," said Stellar, waving his hand at Trumbull in clear annoyance. "I've been asked a question as to whether everything I write sees print and I want to answer that because it brings up something I'm pretty sore about and would like to get off my chest."

"I think he's within his rights there, Tom," said Avalon.

"Well, go head, then," said Trumbull discontentedly, "but don't take forever."

Stelar nodded with a sort of grieved impatience and said, "I met Bercovich at some formal party. I don't even remember the occasion for it, or very much who was involved. But I remember Bercovich because we did some business as a result. I was there with Gladys, my wife, and Bercovich was there with his wife and there were maybe eight other couples. It was an elaborate thing.

"In fact, it was very elaborate, and deadly. It was formal. It wasn't black tie; they stopped short of that; but it was formal. The serving was slow; the food was bad; the conversation was constipated. I hated it. —Listen, Manny, what do you think of Bercovich?"

Rubin shrugged. "He's an editor. That limits his good points, but I've known worse. He's not an idiot."

"He isn't? Well, I must admit that at the time he seemed all right. I had vaguely heard of him, but he knew me, of course."

"Oh, of course," said Rubin, twirling his empty brandy glass.

"Well, he did," said Stellar indignantly. "It's the whole point of the story that he knew me, or he wouldn't have asked me for an article. He came up to me after dinner and told me that he read my stuff and that he admired it, and I nodded and smiled. Then he said, 'What do you think of the evening?'

"I said cautiously, 'Oh well, sort of slow,' because for all I knew he was the hostess' lover and I didn't want to be needlessly offensive.

"And he said, 'I think it's a bomb. It's too formal and that doesn't fit the American scene these days.' Then he went on to say, 'Look, I'm editor of a new magazine, *Way of Life*, and I wonder if you couldn't write us an article on formality. If you could give us, say, twenty-five hundred to three thousand words, that would be fine. You could have a free hand and take any approach you want, but be lighthearted.'

"Well, it sounded interesting and I said so, and we discussed price a little, and I said I would try and he asked if I could have it in his office within three weeks, and I said maybe. He seemed very anxious."

Rubin said, "When was all this?"

"Just about two years ago."

"Uh-huh. That was about when the magazine started. I look at it occasionally. Very pretentious and not worth the money. I didn't see your article, though."

Stellar snorted. "Naturally you haven't."

"Don't tell me you didn't write it," said Gonzalo.

"Of course I wrote it. I had it in Bercovich's office within a week. It was a very easy article to do and it was good. It was lightly satirical and included several examples of stupid formality at which I could fire my shots. In fact, I even described a dinner like the one we had."

"And he rejected it?" asked Gonzalo.

Stellar glared at Gonzalo. "He didn't reject it. I had a check in my hands within another week."

"Well then," said Trumbull impatiently, "what's all this about?"

"He never printed it," shouted Stellar. "That idiot has been sitting on it ever since, for nearly two years. He hasn't published it; he hasn't even scheduled it."

"So what," said Gonzalo, "as long as he's paid for it?"

Stellar glared again. "You don't suppose a one-time sale is all I'm after, do you? I can usually count on reprints here and there for additional money. And then I publish collections of my articles; and I can't include that one until it's published."

"Surely," said Avalon, "the money involved is not very important."

"No," admitted Stellar, "but it's not utterly unimportant either. Besides, I don't understand why the delay. He was in a hurry for it. When I brought it in he slavered. He said, 'Good, good. I'll be able to get an artist on it right away and there'll be time to do some strong illustrations.' And then nothing happened. You would think he didn't like it; but if he didn't like it, why did he buy it?"

Halsted held up his coffee cup for a refill and Henry took care of it. Halsted said, "Maybe he only bought it to buy your good will, so to speak, and make sure you would write other articles for him, even though the one you wrote wasn't quite good enough."

Stellar said, "Oh no. . . . Oh no. . . . Manny, tell these innocents that editors don't do that. They never have the budget to buy bad articles in order to buy good will. Besides, if a writer turns out bad articles you don't want his good will. And what's more, you don't earn good will by buying an article and burying it."

Trumbull said, "All right, Mr. Stellar. We listened to your story and you'll note I didn't interrupt you. Now, why did you tell it to us?"

"Because I'm tired of brooding over it. Maybe one of *you* can figure it out. Why doesn't he publish it? —Manny, you said you used to sell him. Did he ever hold up anything of yours?"

"No," said Manny, after a judicious pause. "I can't recall that he did. —Of course, he's had a bad time."

"What kind of a bad time?"

"This dinner took place two years ago, you said, so that was his first wife you met him with. She was an older woman, wasn't she, Mort?"

Stellar said, "I don't remember her. That was the only time we ever met."

"If it was his second wife, you'd remember. She's about thirty and very good-looking. His first wife died about a year and a half ago. She'd been ill a long time, it turned out, though she'd done her best to hide it and I never knew, for instance. She had a heart attack and it broke him up. He went through quite a period there."

"Oh! Well, I didn't know about that. But even so, he's married again, right?"

"Sometime last year, yes."

"And she's a good-looking person and he's consoled. Right?"

"The last time I saw him, about a month ago—just in passing—he looked all right."

"Well then," said Stellar, "why is he still holding out?"

Avalon said thoughtfully, "Have you explained to Mr. Bercovich the advantages of having your article published?"

Stellar said, "He *knows* the advantages. He's an editor."

"Well then," said Avalon, just as thoughtfully, "it may be that on second reading he found some serious flaw and feels it is not publishable as it stands. Perhaps he's embarrassed at having bought it and doesn't know how to approach you."

Stellar laughed but without humor. "Editors don't get embarrassed and they're not afraid to approach you. If he found something wrong on second reading, he'd have called me and asked for a revision. I've been asked for revisions many times."

"Do you revise when they ask for it?" said Gonzalo.

"I told you. . . . Sometimes, when it sounds reasonable," said Stellar.

James Drake nodded as though that were the answer he would have expected and said, "And this editor never asked for any revision at all?"

"*No,*" said Stellar explosively, and then almost at once he added, "Well, once! One time when I called him to ask if it were scheduled—I was getting pretty edgy about it by then—he asked if it would be all right if he cut it a little, because it seemed diffuse in spots. I asked where the hell it was diffuse in spots, because I knew it wasn't, and he was vague and I was just peeved enough to say, no, I didn't want a word touched. He could print as it was or he could send it back to me."

"And he didn't send it back to you, I suppose," said Drake.

"No, he didn't. Damn it, I offered to *buy* it back. I said, 'Send it back, Joel, and I'll return the money.' And he said, 'Oh, come, Mort, that's not necessary. I'm glad to have it in my inventory even if I don't use it right away.' Damn fool. What good does it do either him or me to have it in his inventory?"

"Maybe he's lost it," said Halsted, "and doesn't want to admit it."

"There's no reason not to admit it," said Stellar. "I've got a carbon; two carbons, in fact. Even if I wanted to keep the carbons—and they come in handy when it's book time—it's no problem these days to get copies made."

. There was a silence around the table, and then Stellar's brow furrowed and he said, "You know, he did ask once if I had a carbon copy. I don't remember when. It was one of the more recent times I called him. He said, 'By the way, Mort, do you have a carbon copy?'—just like that, 'By the way,' as if it were an afterthought. I remember thinking he was an idiot; does he expect a man of my experience *not* to have a carbon copy? I had the notion, then, that he was getting round to saying he had mislaid the manuscript, but he never said a word of the kind. I said that I had a carbon copy and he let the subject drop."

"Seems to me," said Trumbull, "that all this isn't worth the trouble you're taking."

"Well, it isn't," said Stellar, "but the thing bothers me. I keep careful files of my articles; I've got to; and this one has been in the 'to be published' file for so long I can recognize the card by the fact that its edges are dark from handling. It's a sort of irritation. —Now why did he ask me if I had a carbon copy? If he'd lost the manuscript, why not say so? And if he hadn't lost it, why ask about the carbon?"

Henry, who had been standing at the sideboard, as was his custom after the dinner had been served and the dishes cleared away, said, "May I make a suggestion, gentlemen?"

Trumbull said, "Good Lord, Henry, don't tell me that this nonsense means something to you?"

Henry said, "No, Mr. Trumbull, I'm afraid I no more understand what it's all about than anyone else in the room. It merely strikes me as a possibility that Mr. Bercovich may have been prepared to tell Mr. Stellar that the manuscript was mislaid—but perhaps only if Mr. Stellar had said that he had no carbon. It might have been the fact that Mr. Stellar *did* have a carbon that made it useless to lose, or possibly, destroy the manuscript."

"*Destroy* it?" said Stellar in high-pitched indignation.

"Suppose we consider what would happen if he published the manuscript, sir," said Henry.

"It would appear in print," said Stellar, "and people would read it. That's what I *want* to happen."

"And if Mr. Bercovich had rejected it?"

"Then I would have sold it somewhere else, damn it, and it would still have appeared in print and people would have read it."

"And if he returned it to you now, either because you refused revision or because you bought it back, then again you would sell it somewhere else and it would appear in print and be read."

"Damn right."

"But suppose, Mr. Stellar, the editor bought the article as he did and does *not* publish it. Can you sell it elsewhere?"

"Of course not. It's not mine to sell. *Way of Life* has bought first serial rights, which means they have the full and sole right to publish it before any other use is made of it. Until they publish it, or until they formally relinquish the right to do so, I can't sell it anywhere."

"In that case, Mr. Stellar, does it not seem to you that the only conceivable way in which Mr. Bercovich can keep the article from being generally read is to do exactly as he has done?"

"Are you trying to tell me, Henry," said Stellar, with naked incredulity in his voice, "that he doesn't want it read? Then why the hell did he ask me to write it?"

Henry said, "He asked you to write *an* article, sir. He did not know the exact article you would write till he saw it. Isn't it possible that, once he read the article you *did* in actual fact write, he realized that he didn't want it read and therefore took the only action possible to keep it unpublished, perhaps forever unpublished? He probably did not expect you to be the kind of writer who would hound an editor over such a matter."

Stellar spread out his hands, palms upward, and looked about at the faces of the Black Widowers in a kind of semi-humorous exasperation. "I never heard of anything so ridiculous."

Avalon said, "Mr. Stellar, you don't know Henry as we do. If this is his opinion, I suggest you take it seriously."

"But why should Joel want to destroy the thing or bury it? It's a perfectly harmless article."

Henry said, "I merely advance a possible explanation for what has gone on for two years."

"But yours is not an explanation that explains, Henry. It doesn't explain *why* he wants the article to be left unread."

"You had said, sir, that he asked for permission to cut the article a little and you refused. If you had agreed, he would perhaps have changed it so as to render it really innocuous and then he would have published it."

"But what did he want cut?"

"I'm afraid I can't say, Mr. Stellar, but I gather that *he* wanted to do the cutting. That may have been in order not to call your attention to the precise passage he wanted altered."

Stellar said, "But if he made the cuts himself, I'd still see what he had done once the article appeared."

Henry said, "Would you be likely to read the article once published and compare it sentence by sentence with the original manuscript, sir?"

"No," admitted Stellar reluctantly.

"And even if you did, sir, there might be a number of small changes and you would have no reason to suppose that one change was more significant than the others."

Stellar said, "You know, this is a more peculiar mystery than the first, Henry. What could I have said to bother him?"

"I cannot say, Mr. Stellar," said Henry.

Avalon cleared his throat in his best lawyer-like fashion and said, "It is rather a pity, Mr. Stellar, that you didn't bring the carbon copy of your manuscript with you. You could have read it to us and perhaps we could then spot the critical passage. At the very least, I'm sure we would have been entertained."

Stellar said, "Who thought this sort of thing would come up?"

Gonzalo said eagerly, "If your wife is at home, Mr. Stellar, we might call her and have her read the article to Henry on the phone. The club could afford the charge."

Henry seemed to be lost in thought. Now he said slowly as though the thinking had surfaced but was still a private colloquy he was holding with himself, "Surely it couldn't be anything impersonal. If the tenets of good taste had been broken, if the policy of the magazine had been violated, he would have seen that at once and asked for specific changes. Even if he had bought it after a hasty reading and then discovered these impersonal errors afterward, there would have been no reason to hesitate to ask for specific changes, surely. Could it be that some superior officer in the publishing firm had vetoed the article and Mr. Bercovich is embarrassed to tell you that?"

"No," said Stellar. "An editor who isn't given a free hand by the front office is very likely to quit. And even if Bercovich didn't have the guts to do that he would be only too glad to use upstairs interference as an excuse to return the manuscript. He certainly wouldn't just hold onto it."

"Then," said Henry, "it must be something personal; something that has meaning to him, an embarrassing meaning, a horrifying meaning."

"There's nothing of the kind in it," insisted Stellar.

"Perhaps there is no significance in the passage to you or to anyone else; but only to Mr. Bercovich."

"In that case," interrupted Drake, "why should Bercovich care?"

"Perhaps," said Henry, "because, if attention were called to it, it would *come* to have significance. That is why he dared not even tell Mr. Stellar what passage he wanted cut."

"You keep inventing perhapses," muttered Stellar. "I just don't believe it."

Gonzalo said abruptly, "*I* believe it. Henry has been right before and I don't hear anyone suggesting any other theory to account for the fact that the article isn't being published."

Stellar said, "But we're talking about nothing. What is the mysterious passage that is bothering Joel?"

Henry said, "Perhaps you can recall some personal reference, since that is what we suspect it would have to be. Did you not say that included in your article was an account of a dinner rather like the one that had inspired Mr. Bercovich to ask for the article in the first place?"

"Aha," said Gonzalo, "*got* it! You described the dinner too acurately, old boy, and the editor was afraid that the host would recognize it and be offended. Maybe the host is an old and valued friend of the publisher and would get the editor fired if the article appeared."

Stellar said, with no effort to hide his contempt, "In the first place, I'm an old hand at this. I don't write anything either actionable or embarrassing. I assure you I masked that dinner so that no one could reasonably speak of a resemblance. I changed every major characteristic of the dinner and I used no names. —Besides, if I had slipped and made the damned thing too real, why shouldn't he tell me? That sort of thing I would change in a shot."

Henry said, "It might be something more personal still. He and his wife were at the dinner. What was it you said about them?"

"Nothing!" said Stellar. "Do you suppose I would make use of the editor to whom I was submitting the article? Give me that much credit. I didn't refer to him under any name or any guise; didn't refer to anything he said or did at all."

"Or anything about his wife either, sir?" asked Henry.

"Or about his wife— Well, wait, she may have inspired one small exchange in the article, but of course I didn't name her, describe her or anything of the sort. It was entirely insignificant."

Avalon said, "Nevertheless, that may be it. The memory was too poignant. She had died and he just couldn't publish an article that reminded him of—of—"

Stellar said, "If you're about to finish that sentence with 'the dear departed,' I walk out. That's tripe, Mr. Avalon. With all respect—no, without too damn much respect— that's tripe. Why wouldn't he ask me to take out a sentence or two if it aroused too keen a memory? I would do it."

Avalon said, "Just because I phrase the matter in sentimental fashion, Mr. Stellar, doesn't mean it can't have significance all the same. His failure to mention it to you might be the result of a certain shame. In our culture, such things as sorrow over lost love are made fun of. *You've* just made fun of it. Yet it can be very real."

Stellar said, "Manny Rubin said she died about a year and a half ago. That means at least half a year after I wrote the article. Time enough to have it printed by then, considering his anxiety to have me meet an instant deadline. And it's been a year and a half since and he's married a beautiful woman. —Come on, how long does one sorrow over a lost love after one has found another?"

"It might help," said Henry, "if Mr. Stellar could tell us the passage in question."

"Yes," said Gonzalo, "call your wife and have her read it to Henry."

"I don't have to," said Stellar, who had only with difficulty withdrawn the wounded stare he had been directing at Avalon. "I've read the damn thing again a couple of weeks ago—about the fifth time—and I have it reasonably fresh in my mind. What it amounts to is this: we had been served the roast at a kind of snail's pace and I was waiting for others to be served before beginning. A few weren't quite that formal and were eating. Finally I broke down and salted it and was going to eat when I noticed that Mrs. Bercovich, who was on my right, had still not been served. I looked surprised and she said she had a special request and it was delayed in getting to her and I offered her my plate and she said, 'No, thank you, it's been salted.' I told that passage, without names, just so I could get across my funny line, which I remember exactly. It went, 'She was the only one at the table who objected to the salt; the rest of us objected to the meat. In fact, several of us scraped off the salt, then ate it in a marked manner.'"

No one laughed at the funny line. Trumbull went to the trouble of simulating nausea.

Halsted said, "I certainly don't see any great sentimental value in that."

"I should say not," said Stellar, "and that's every last mention of her, without name or description, and none of Joel himself."

Henry said, "Yet Mr. Rubin said that the first Mrs. Bercovich died of a heart attack, which is rather a catch-all reference to circulatory disorders in general. She may well have had seriously high blood pressure and have been put on a low-salt diet."

"Which is why she refused Stellar's salted meat," said Gonzalo. *"Right!"*

"And why she was waiting for a special dish," said Henry. "And this is something to which Mr. Bercovich desperately wants no attention drawn. Mr. Rubin said Mrs. Bercovich had done her best to hide her condition. Perhaps few people knew she was on a low-salt diet."

Stellar said, "Why should Joel care if they know?"

"I must introduce another perhaps, sir. Perhaps Mr. Bercovich, weary of waiting and, perhaps, already attracted by the woman who is now his second wife, took advantage of the situation. He may have salted her food surreptitiously, or, if she used salt substitute, he may have replaced it, at least in part, with ordinary salt—"

"And killed her, you mean?" interrupted Avalon.

Henry shook his head. "Who can tell? She might have died

at the same moment anyway. He, however, may feel he contributed to the death and may now be in panic lest anyone find out. The mere mention of a woman refusing salt at that table may, in his eyes, be a shrieking out of his guilt—"

Stellar said, "But I didn't name her, Henry. There's no way of telling who she was. And even if somehow one were to find out that it was she, how could anyone suspect anything out of the way?"

"You are perfectly right, Mr. Stellar," said Henry. "The only reason we have come to suspect Mr. Bercovich now is because of his peculiar behavior with respect to the article and not to anything in the article itself. —But, you know, we have biblical authority to the effect that the wicked flee when no man pursueth."

Stellar paused a moment in thought, then said, "All this may be, but it's not getting my article published." He pulled out a black address book, turned to the Bs, then looked at his watch. "I've called him at his home before and it isn't ten yet."

Avalon raised his hand in an impressive stop sign. "One moment, Mr. Stellar. I trust you are not going to tell your editor about what we've said here. It is all strictly confidential in the first place, and it would be slander in the second. You would not be able to support it and you may get yourself into serious trouble."

Stellar said impatiently, "I wish all of you would take it for granted that an experienced writer is aware of what libel and slander are. —Is there a telephone handy, Henry?"

"Yes, sir," said Henry. "I can bring one to the table. —May I also suggest caution?"

"Don't worry," said Stellar as he dialed. He waited a moment, then, "Hello, Mrs. Bercovich? This is Mort Stellar, one of the writers for your husband's magazine. May I speak to Joel? —Oh, sure, I'll wait." He did not look up from the telephone as he waited. "Hello, Joel, sorry to call you at home, but I've been going over the piece on formality. You don't have it scheduled, do you? —Well, all right, I didn't feel like waiting on this because I didn't want to weaken. You can shorten it if you want. —Oh, sure, that's all right. —No, Joel, just a minute, no. I don't want you to do it. I've got some things I *want* cut out and maybe that will satisfy you. —For instance, that time I have about eating the salt, instead of the meat isn't funny, now that I think of it. —Yes, that's right. Suppose I cut out that part about the woman refusing the salted meat. Will you publish it if I cut that out?"

There was a pause at this moment and now Stellar looked up at the others, grinning. Then he said, "All right, Joel. —Sure I can do it. How about 11 A.M.? —Okay, see you then."

Stellar looked complacent. "It hit him right between the eyes. He repeated the line to me. You can't tell me that he remembered that passage, in an article he bought two years ago, right off the top of his head, unless it had special meaning to him. I'll bet you're right after all, Henry. —Well, I'll cut it. The important thing is that I'll get my article into print."

Avalon frowned and said with heavy dignity, "I should say that, from the standpoint of public morality, the really important thing is that a man may have tried to kill his wife and may even have actually done so and will get away with it."

Trumbull said, "Don't get virtuously aggrieved, Jeff. If Henry is right, then there's no way of proving that he did anything, or that if he did tamper with the salt it actually contributed to her death, so what is there to do? In fact, what do we have to do? The really important thing is that Stellar has done it all. He's given the man two years of agony, first by writing the article and then by being constantly after him to publish it."

Henry said, "The really important thing, sir, may be that Mr. Bercovich will, as a result of all this, be discouraged from attempting similar experiments in the future. After all, he has a second wife now, and he may grow tired of her too."

1 Afterword

I am sometimes asked whether any of the regular members of the Black Widowers is modeled on me. The answer is, No! Definitely not!

Some people have thought that talkative know-it-all Manny Rubin is the author in disguise. Not at all! He is actually reminiscent of someone else, someone who is a dearly loved (talkative, know-it-all) friend of mine.

In "When No Man Pursueth" (which appeared first in the March 1974 issue of *Ellery Queen's Mystery Magazine*) I took the liberty of introducing myself as the guest. Mortimer Stellar is as close as I could get to myself in appearance, profession, attitude, and so on.

I showed the story to my wife, Janet, after I had written it and asked her how well she thought I had caught the real me. She said, "But the character you drew is arrogant, vain, nasty, petty, and completely self-centered."

I said, "See how close I got?"

She said, "But you're not like Mortimer Stellar at all. You're—" And she went on to list a string of nice adjectives I won't bore you with.

"Who'd believe *that*?" I said, and let the story stand as written.

Incidentally, since I introduced myself into the story, I had better make sure no unwarranted conclusions are drawn. I *have* lived through some rotten banquets and, at an editor's suggestion, I *have* written an article entitled "My Worst Meal," but that editor is a pussycat who published the article promptly and who in no way resembles Bercovich in either word, thought, or deed.

2

'Quicker Than the Eye

Thomas Trumbull, who worked for the government as a cryptologist, was clearly uneasy. His tanned and wrinkled face was set in a carved attitude of worry. He said, "He's a man from the department; my superior, in fact. It's damned important, but I don't want Henry to feel the pressure."

He was whispering and he couldn't resist the quick look over his shoulder at Henry, the waiter at the Black Widower monthly banquets. Henry, who was several years older than Trumbull, had a face that was unwrinkled, and, as he quickly set the table, he seemed tranquil and utterly unaware of the fact that five of the Black Widowers were huddled quietly at the opposite end of the room. Or, if not unaware, then certainly undisturbed.

Geoffrey Avalon, the tall patent lawyer, had, under the best of conditions, difficulty in keeping his voice low. Still, stirring his drink with a middle finger on the ice cube, he managed to impart sufficient hoarseness. "How can we prevent it, Tom? Henry is no fool."

"I'm not sure anyone from the federal administration qualifies as a guest, Tom," said Emmanuel Rubin in a swerving non sequitur. His sparse beard bristled truculently and his eyes flashed through the thick lenses of his glasses. "And I say that even though *you're* in the category. Eighty per cent of the tax money I pay to Washington is expended in ways of which I strongly disapprove."

"You've got the vote, haven't you?" said Trumbull testily.

"And a fat lot of good that does, when the manipulation—" began Rubin, quite forgetting to keep his voice low.

Oddly enough, it was Roger Halsted, the mathematics teacher, whose quiet voice had sufficient difficulty in controlling a junior high school class, who managed to stop Rubin in mid-roar. He did it by placing his hand firmly over the smaller man's mouth. He said, "You don't sound very happy about your boss coming here, Tom."

"I'm not," said Trumbull. "It's a difficult thing. The point is that I've gotten considerable credit on two different occasions over matters that were really Henry's insights. I've *had* to take the credit, damn it, since what we say here in this room is confidential. Now something has come up and they're turning to me, and I'm as stuck as the rest of them. I've had to invite Bob here without really explaining why."

James Drake, the organic chemist, coughed over his cigarette and fingered his walrus-head bolo-tie. "Have you been talking too much about your dinners, Tom?"

"I suppose it could be viewed in that way. What bothers me is Henry, though. He enjoys the game, I know, when it *is* a game, but if there's real pressure and he won't—or can't —under that pressure—"

"Then you'll look bad, eh, Tom?" said Rubin with just a touch, perhaps, of malice.

Avalon said frigidly, "I have said before and I will say it again that what began as a friendly social get-together is becoming a strain on us all. Can't we have *one* session with just conversation?"

"I'm afraid not this one," said Trumbull. "All right, here's my boss. —Now let's carry all the load we can and put as little as possible on Henry."

But it was only Mario Gonzalo walking noisily up the stairs, uncharacteristically late, and resplendent in his long hair, a crimson jacket, and subtly matching striped shirt, to say nothing of a flowing scarf meticulously arranged to display the effect of casualness.

"Sorry I'm late, Henry—" But the proper drink was in his hand before he could say more. "Thanks, Henry. Sorry, fellows, trouble with getting a taxi. That put me in a grim mood and when the driver began to lecture me on the crimes and misdemeanors of the mayor I argued with him."

"Lord help us," said Drake.

"I always argue every tenth time I hear that kind of crap. Then he managed to get lost, and I didn't notice and it took us a long time to pull out. —I mean, he was giving me this business about welfare recipients being a bunch of lazy, free-loading troublemakers and how no decent person should expect a handout but instead they should work for what they get and earn every cent. So I said what about sick people and old people and mothers with young children and he started telling me what a hard life *he* had led and *he* had never gone to anyone for a handout.

"Anyway, I got out and the fare came to $4.80, and it was a good half dollar more than it should have been because of getting lost, so I counted out four singles and then spent some time getting the exact eighty cents change and I handed it to him. He counted it over, looked surprised, and I said, just as sweetly as I could, 'That's what you earned, driver. You looking for a handout too?' "

Gonzalo burst out laughing, but no one joined him. Drake said, "That's a dirty trick on the poor guy just because you egged him into arguing."

Avalon stared down austerely from his lean height and said, "You might have gotten beaten up, Mario, and I wouldn't blame him."

"That's a hell of an attitude you fellows are taking," said Gonzalo, aggrieved—and at that point Trumbull's boss did arrive.

Trumbull introduced the newcomer all round, looking uncommonly subdued as he did so. The guest's name was Robert Alford Bunsen and he was both heavy and large. His face was pink and his white hair was sleeked back from an old-fashioned part down the middle.

"What will you have, Mr. Bunsen?" said Avalon, with a small and courtly bend at the middle. He was the only one present who was taller than the newcomer.

Bunsen cleared his throat. "Glad to meet you all. No—no —I've had my alcoholic calories for today. Some diet drink." He snapped his fingers at Henry. "A diet cola, waiter. If you don't have that, a diet anything."

Gonzalo's eyes widened and Drake, whispering philosophically through the curling smoke of the cigarette stub he held between his tobacco-stained fingers, said, "Oh well, he's government."

"Still," muttered Gonzalo, "there's such a thing as courtesy. You don't snap your fingers. Henry isn't a peon."

"You're rude to taxi drivers," said Drake. "This guy's rude to waiters."

"That's a different thing," said Gonzalo vehemently, his voice rising. "That was a matter of principle."

Henry, who had shown no signs of resentment at being finger-snapped, had returned with a bottle of soft drink on a tray and had presented it solemnly for inspection.

"Sure, sure," said Bunsen, and Henry opened it and poured half its contents into an ice-filled glass and let the foam settle. Bunsen took it and Henry left the bottle.

The dinner was less comfortable than many in the past had been. The only one who seemed unsubdued over the fact that the guest was a high, if a not very well known, official of the government was Rubin. In fact, he seized the occasion to attack the government in the person of its surrogate by proclaiming loudly that diet drinks were one of the great causes of overweight in America.

"Because you drink a lot of them and the one calorie per bottle mounts up?" asked Halsted, with as much derision as he could pack into his colorless voice.

"They've got more than one calorie per bottle now that cyclamates have been eliminated on the basis of fallacious animal experiments," said Rubin hotly, "but that's not the point. Diet anything is bad psychologically. Anyone overweight who takes a diet drink is overcome with virtue. He has saved two hundred calories, so he celebrates by taking another pat of butter and consuming three hundred calories. The only way to lose weight is to stay hungry. The hunger is telling you that you're getting less calories than you're expending—"

Halsted, who knew very well that there was a certain softness in his abdominal region, muttered, "Oh well."

"But he's right, though," said Bunsen, attacking the veal Marengo with gusto. "The diet drinks don't do me any good, but I like the taste. And I approve of looking at matters from the psychological angle."

Gonzalo, frowning, showed no signs of listening. When Henry bent over him to fill his coffee cup, he said, "What do *you* think, Henry? I mean about the taxi driver. Wasn't I right?"

Henry said, "A gratuity is not quite a handout, Mr. Gonzalo. Personal service is customarily rewarded in a small way and to equate that with welfare is perhaps not quite just."

"You're just saying that because you—" began Gonzalo, and then he stopped abruptly.

Henry said, "Yes, I benefit in the same way as the taxi driver does, but despite that I believe my statement to be correct."

Gonzalo threw himself back in his chair and chafed visibly.

"Gentlemen," said Trumbull, tapping his empty water glass with a fork, as Henry poured the liqueur, "this is an interesting occasion. Mr. Bunsen, who is my superior at the department, has a small puzzle to present to us. Let's see what we can make of it." Again, he cast a quick glance at Henry, who had replaced the bottle on the sideboard and now stood placidly in the background.

Bunsen, wiping his mouth with his napkin and wheezing slightly, also cast an anxious glance at Henry, and Trumbull leaned over to say, "Henry is one of us, Bob."

Trumbull went on, "Bob Bunsen is going to present merely the bare bones, to keep from distorting your view of the matter with unnecessary knowledge to begin with. I will remain out of it myself since I know too much about the matter."

Halsted leaned over to whisper to Drake, "I think it won't look good for Tom in the department if this doesn't work."

Drake shrugged, and mouthed rather than said, "He brought it on himself."

Bunsen, having adjusted the position of the breadbasket unnecessarily (he had earlier prevented Henry from removing it), began. "I will give you those bare bones of a story. There's a man. Call him Smith. We want him, but not just him. He's of little account. Clever at what he does, but of little account. If we get him, we learn nothing of importance and we warn off men of greater importance. If, however, we can use him to lead us to the men of greater importance—"

"We all understand," interrupted Avalon.

Bunsen cleared his throat and made a new start. "Of course, we weren't sure about Smith to begin with. It seemed very likely, but we weren't sure. If he was indeed a link in the apparatus we were trying to break up, then we reasoned that he transferred the information at a restaurant he regularly frequented. Part of the reasoning was based on psychology, something I imagine Mr. Rubin would approve. Smith had the appearance and patina of a well-bred man about town who always did the correct social thing. On that basis, we—"

He paused to think, then he said, "No, I'm getting off the subject and it's more than you need. We laid a trap for him." For a moment he reddened as though in bashfulness and then he went on firmly, "I laid the trap and it was damned complicated. We managed to beat down his caution, never mind how, and we ended with Smith having in his hand something he had to transfer. It was a legitimate item and would be useful to them, but not too useful. It would be well worth the loss to us if we had gained what we hoped to gain."

Bunsen looked about him, clearing his throat, but no one made a sound. Henry, standing by the sideboard, seemed a quiet statue. Even the napkin he held did not move.

Bunsen said, "Smith walked into the restaurant with the object on his person. After he left the restaurant he did not have the object on his person. We know therefore that he transferred the object. What we don't know is the exact moment at which he transferred it, how, and to whom. We have not been able to locate the object anywhere. Now ask your questions, gentlemen."

Trumbull said, "Let's try this one at a time. Mario?"

Gonzalo thought a moment and then shrugged. Twiddling his brandy glass between thumb and forefinger, he said, "What did this object—as you call it—look like?"

"About an inch across and flat," said Bunsen. "It had a metallic shine so it was easy to see. It was too large to swallow easily; heavy enough to make a noise if it were dropped; too thick to place in a crack; too heavy to stick easily to anything; not iron so there could be no tricks with magnets. The object, as I still call it, was carefully designed to make the task of transferring, or hiding, difficult."

"But what did he do in the restaurant? He ate a meal, I suppose?" said Gonzalo.

"He ate a meal as he always did."

"Was it a fancy restaurant?"

"A fairly elaborate one. He ate there regularly."

"I mean, there's nothing phony about the restaurant?"

"Not as far as we know, although in general that is not enough to allow us to display a blind trust in it and, believe me, we don't."

"Who was with him at the meal?"

"No one." Bunsen shook his head gravely. "He ate alone. That was his custom. He signed the check when he was through, as he always did. He had an account in the restaurant, you see. Then he left, took a taxi, and after a while he was stopped and taken into custody. The object was no longer in his possession."

"Wait, now," said Gonzalo, his eyes narrowing. "You say he signed the check. What was it he wrote? Would you know?"

"We know quite well. We have the check. He added a tip —quite the normal amount and we could find nothing wrong with that—and signed his name. That's all. Nothing more. He used the waiter's pencil and returned that pencil. Nor did he pass along anything else, and the waiter did not escape scrutiny, I assure you."

Gonzalo said, "I pass."

Drake, stubbing out his cigarette, lifted a gray eyebrow as Trumbull's finger gestured at him. "I suppose Smith was kept under close surveillance while he was in the restaurant."

"As close as though he were a coat and we were the lining. We had two men in that restaurant, each at a table near him. They were trained men and capable ones and their entire task was to note every movement he made. He could not scratch himself without being noticed. He couldn't fumble at a button, crook a finger, shift a leg, or raise a buttock without being noted."

"Did he go to the men's room at any time?"

"No, he did not. If he had, we would have managed to follow."

"Were you there yourself, Mr. Bunsen?"

"I? No, I'm no good for that kind of surveillance. I'm too noticeable. What's needed to keep a man in view is a shadow with a good, gray face and an overwhelming lack of distinction in form and feature. I'm too big, too broad; I stand out."

Drake nodded. "Do you suppose Smith knew he was being watched?"

"He may have. People in his line of work don't last long if they don't assume at every moment that they might be watched. In fact, to be truthful, at one point I got a clear impression he felt he was being watched. I was across the street at a window, with a pair of binoculars. I could see him come out from the corner entrance of the restaurant.

"The doorman held the taxi door open for him and Smith paused for just a minute. He looked about him as though trying to identify those who might be watching. And he smiled, a tight smile, not amusement, it seemed to me, as much as bravado. At that moment, I was sure we had lost. And, as it turned out, we had."

"And you really are sure," said Drake, "that he had it on him when he walked into the restaurant and that he didn't have it on him when he left."

"We really are sure. When he walked in, there was what amounted to a pickpocketing, an inspection, and a replacement. He had it; you can take that as given. When he left and took a taxi, that taxi driver was one of our men who came, when the doorman hailed him, in a completely natural manner. Smith got in with no hint of suspicion. We are positive about that. The driver, one of our best men, then— But never mind that. The point is that Smith found himself in a kind of minor trouble that had, apparently, nothing to do with us. He was arrested, taken to the police station, and searched. Later, when it became obvious that we couldn't find the object anywhere, he was searched more thoroughly. Eventually we used X rays."

Drake said, "He might have left the object in the taxi."

"I doubt he could have done that with our man driving, and in any case, the taxi was searched. See here," said Bunsen heavily, "there's no point in thinking we are incompetent in our business. When I say we watched, I mean that we watched with professional attention. When I say we searched, I mean we searched with professional thoroughness. You won't catch us on details."

"All right," said Drake, nodding, "but you missed, didn't you? The object was there and then it wasn't there, so either we call upon the supernatural or we must admit that somewhere you failed. Somewhere you blinked when you were watching or skipped when you were searching. Right?"

Bunsen looked rather as though he had bitten into a lemon. "There's no way of avoiding that conclusion, I suppose." Then, belligerently, "But show me where."

Drake shook his head, but Halsted intervened rapidly, his high forehead pink with excitement. "Now wait, the hand is quicker than the eye. The thing you're looking for was shiny and heavy, but did it have to stay that way? Smith might have pushed it into a lump of clay. Then he had something dull and shapeless which he could push against the bottom of the table or drop on the floor. It might still be there."

Bunsen said, "The hand is quicker than the eye when you have an audience that doesn't know what to watch for. We know all the tricks and we know what to expect. Smith couldn't have put the object into clay without our men knowing he was doing something. He couldn't have placed it under the table or on the floor without our men knowing he was doing something."

"Yes," said Halsted, "but in these quicker-than-the-eye things, a diversion is usually created. Your men were looking somewhere else."

"There was no diversion, and in any case the restaurant was searched quite thoroughly as soon as he left."

"You couldn't have searched it thoroughly," protested Halsted. "There were still people eating there. Did you make them all leave?"

"We searched his table, his area, and eventually all the restaurant. We are quite certain that he did not leave the object behind anywhere. He did not leave anything behind anywhere."

Avalon had been sitting stiffly in his chair, his arms folded, his forehead creased in a portentous frown. His voice boomed out now. "Mr. Bunsen," he said, "I am not at all comfortable with this account of yours. I recognize the fact that you have told us very little and that neither places, names, occasions, nor identifications have been given.

"Nevertheless, you are telling me more than I want to know. Have you permission from your superiors to tell us this? Are you quite certain in your mind that each one of us is to be trusted? You might get into trouble as a result and that would be regrettable, but I must admit that that is not the point I am most concerned with at the moment. What *is* important is that I do not wish to become the object of questioning and investigation because you have seen fit to honor me with confidences I have not asked for."

Trumbull had vainly tried to break in and managed to say finally, "Come on, Jeff. Don't act like the rear end of a horse."

Bunsen raised a massive and pudgy hand. "That's all right, Tom. I see Mr. Avalon's point and, in a way, he's right. I *am* exceeding my authority and things *will* be sticky for me if some people decide they need a scapegoat. This little exercise of mine tonight, however, may get me off the hook if it works. To my way of thinking, it's worth the gamble. Tom assured me it would be."

"What you're saying," said Trumbull, forcing a smile, "is that if the department jumps on you, you'll jump on me."

"Yes," said Bunsen, "and I weigh a lot." He picked up a breadstick and munched on it. "One more point. Mr. Avalon asked if I were sure you could each be trusted. Aside from the fact that Tom assured me you could be—not that I consider it safe to trust to personal assurances from close friends—there has been a little bit of investigation. Nothing like a full-scale affair, you understand, but enough to give me some confidence."

It was at this point that Henry cleared his throat gently, and at once every face but that of Bunsen turned toward him. Bunsen turned only after he was aware of the shift of attention.

Trumbull said, "Have you got something, Henry?"

Bunsen turned a clearly astonished look in Trumbull's direction, but Trumbull said urgently, "Have you, Henry?"

"I only want to know," said Henry softly, "if I have been cleared also. I suspect I have not and that I should retire."

But Trumbull said, "For God's sake, nothing critical is being said."

Bunsen said, "Besides, the damage is done. Let him stay."

"It seems to me," said Henry, "that the damage is indeed done. Surely there is no longer any purpose to the investigation. The man you call Smith must know he is being watched. By the time you began to use X rays on him, he must have guessed that he had been set up for a kill. —Is he still in custody, by the way?"

"No, we had no grounds to keep him. He's released."

"Then the organization of which he is a part must undoubtedly know what has happened, and they will change their modus operandi. He will not be used further, perhaps;

others involved will disappear. Things will be entirely re-arranged."

Bunsen said impatiently, "Yes, yes. Nevertheless, knowledge is important in itself. If we find out exactly how he transferred the object, we will know something about a mode of operation we didn't know before. We will, at the least, get an insight into a system of thought. —It is *always* important to know."

Henry said, "I see."

Trumbull said, "Is that all you see, Henry? Do *you* have any ideas?"

Henry shook his head. "It may be, Mr. Trumbull, that what has happened is complex and subtle. That would not be for me."

"Bull, Henry," said Trumbull.

"But it might be for Mr. Rubin," said Henry gravely. "I believe he is anxious to speak."

"Darn right," said Rubin loudly, "because I'm annoyed. Now, Mr. Bunsen, you talk about watching carefully and searching thoroughly, but I think you'll agree with me when I say that it is very easy to overlook something which becomes obvious only after the fact. I can describe a way in which Smith could have transferred the object without any trouble and no matter how many people were watching him."

"I would love to hear that description," said Bunsen.

"Okay, then, I will describe exactly what might have happened. I don't say it *did* happen, but it *could* have happened. Let me begin by asking a question—" Rubin pushed his chair away from the table and, though he was short and small-boned, he seemed to tower.

"Mr. Bunsen," he said, "since your men watched everything, I presume they took note of the details of the meal he ordered. Was it lunch or dinner, by the way?"

"It was lunch and you are right. We did notice the details."

"Then isn't it a fact that he ordered a thick soup?"

Bunsen's eyebrows raised. "A score for you, Mr. Rubin. It was cream of mushroom soup. If you want the rest of the menu, it consisted of a roast beef sandwich with a side order of french fried potatoes, a piece of apple pie with a slice of cheese, and coffee."

"Well," muttered Drake, "we can't all be gourmets."

Rubin said, "Next, I would suggest that he finished only about half his soup."

Bunsen thought for a while, then smiled. It was the first time he had smiled that evening and he revealed white and even teeth that gave a clear indication that there was a handsome man beneath the layers of fat.

"You know," he said, "I wouldn't have thought you could ask me a single question of fact concerning that episode that I could not instantly have answered, but you've managed. I don't know, offhand, if he finished his soup or not, but I'm sure that detail is on record. But let's pretend you are right and he only finished half his soup. Go on."

"All right," said Rubin, "we begin. Smith walks into the restaurant with the object. Where does he have it, by the way?"

"Left pants pocket, when he walked in. We saw no signs whatever of his changing its position."

"Good," said Rubin. "He walks in, sits down at the table, orders his meal, reads his newspaper—was he reading a newspaper, Mr. Bunsen?"

"No," said Bunsen, "he wasn't reading anything; not even the menu. He knows the place and what it has to offer."

"Then once the first course was placed before him, he sneezed. A sneeze, after all is a diversion. Roger mentioned a diversion, but I guess he thought of someone rushing in with a gun, or a fire starting in the kitchen. But a sneeze is a diversion, too, and is natural enough to go unnoticed."

"It would not have gone unnoticed," said Bunsen calmly. "He didn't sneeze."

"Or coughed, or hiccuped, what's the difference?" said Rubin. "The point is that something happened that made it natural for him to pull out a handkerchief—from the left pants pocket, I'm sure—and put it to his mouth."

"He did no such thing," said Bunsen.

"When he took away his hand," said Rubin, overriding the other's remark, "the object that had been in the left pants pocket was in the mouth."

Bunsen said, "I don't think it would have been possible for him to place the object in his mouth without our seeing him do so, or keep it there without distorting his face noticeably, but go ahead— What next?"

"The soup is before him and he eats it. You certainly won't tell me he pushed it away untasted."

"No, I'm quite certain he didn't do that."

"Or that he drank it from the bowl."

Bunsen smiled. "No, I'm quite sure he didn't do that."

"Then there was only one thing he could do. He placed a tablespoon in the soup, brought it to his mouth, brought it back to the soup, brought it to his mouth, and so on. Correct?"

"I must agree with that."

"And on one of the occasions during which the tablespoon passed from mouth to bowl, the object was in it. It was placed in the soup and, since cream of mushroom soup is not transparent, it would not be seen there. He then drank no more of the soup and someone in the kitchen picked up the object." Rubin looked about at the others triumphantly.

There was a short silence. Bunsen said, "That is all you have to say, sir?"

"Don't you agree that's a possible modus operandi?"

"No, I don't." Bunsen sighed heavily. "Quite impossible. The hand is not quicker than the trained eye, and the object is large enough to be an uncomfortable fit in the tablespoon bowl. —Furthermore, you again underestimate our experience and our thoroughness. We had a man in the kitchen and no item came back from our man's table without being thoroughly examined. If the soup bowl came back with soup in it, you can be sure it was carefully emptied by a most careful man."

"How about the waiter?" interposed Avalon, forced into interest clearly against his will.

Bunsen said, "The waiter was not one of us. He was an old employee, and besides, he was watched too."

Rubin snorted and said, "You might have told us you had a man in the kitchen."

"I might have," said Bunsen, "but Tom told me it would be best to tell you as little as possible and let you think from scratch."

Avalon said, "If you had incorporated a tiny radio transmitter in the object—"

"Then we would have been characters in a James Bond movie. Unfortunately, we must allow for expertise on the other side as well. If we had tried any such thing, they would have tumbled to it. No, the trap had to be absolutely clean." Bunsen looked depressed. "I put a hell of a lot of time and effort into it." He looked about and the depression on his face deepened. "Well, Tom, are we through here?"

Trumbull said unhappily, "Wait a minute, Bob. Damn it, Henry—"

Bunsen said, "What do you want the waiter to do?"

Trumbull said, "Come on, Henry. Doesn't anything occur to you?"

Henry sighed gently. "Something did, quite a while back, but I was hoping it would be eliminated."

"Something quite plain and simple, Henry?" said Avalon.

"I'm afraid so, sir."

Avalon said, turning to Bunsen, "Henry is an honest man and lacks all trace of the devious mind. When we are through making fools of ourselves over complexities, he picks up the one straight thread we have overlooked."

Henry said thoughtfully, "Are you sure you wish me to speak, Mr. Bunsen?"

"Yes. Go on."

"Well then, when your Mr. Smith left the restaurant, I assume that your men inside did not follow him out."

"No, of course not. They had their own work inside. They had to make sure he had left nothing behind that was significant."

"And the man in the kitchen stayed there?"

"Yes."

"Well then, outside the restaurant, the taxi driver was your man; but it would seem fair to suppose that he had to keep his eye on the traffic so as to be able to be in a position where he could maneuver himself to the curb just in time to pick up Smith; no sooner, no later."

"And a very good job he did. In fact, when the doorman hailed him, he neatly cut out another cab." Bunsen chuckled softly.

"Was the doorman one of your men?" asked Henry.

"No, he was a regular employee of the restaurant."

"Did you have a man on the street at all?"

"If you mean actually standing on the street, no."

"Then surely there was a moment or two after Smith had left the restaurant, and before he had enterd the taxi, when he was not being watched—if I may call it so—professionally."

Bunsen said with a trace of contempt, "You forget that I was across the street, at a window, with a pair of binoculars. I saw him quite well. I saw the taxi man pick him up. From the door of the restaurant to the door of the taxi took, I should say, not more than fifteen seconds, and I had him in view at every moment."

Rubin suddenly interrupted. "Even when you were distracted watching the taxi man maneuver to the curb?"

He was universally shushed, but Bunsen said, "Even then."

Henry said, "I don't forget that you were watching, Mr. Bunsen, but you have said you do not have the proper appearance for that kind of work. You do not watch, professionally."

"I have eyes," said Bunsen, and there was more than merely a trace of contempt now. "Or will you tell me the hand is quicker than the eye?"

"Sometimes even when the hand is quite slow, I think. —Mr. Bunsen, you arrived late and did not hear Mr. Gonzalo's tale. He had paid a taxi driver exactly the fare recorded on the meter, and so customary is it to pay more than that, that every one of us was shocked. Even I expressed disapproval. It is only when the completely customary is violated that the event is noticed. When it takes place, it is apt to be totally ignored."

Bunsen said, "Are you trying to tell me that something was wrong with the taxi driver? I tell you there wasn't."

"I am sure of that," said Henry earnestly. "Still, didn't you miss something that you took so entirely for granted that, even looking at it, you didn't see it?"

"I don't see what it could have been. I have an excellent memory, I assure you, and in the fifteen seconds that Smith went from restaurant to taxi he did nothing I did not note and nothing I do not remember."

Henry thought for a moment or two. "You know, Mr. Bunsen, it *must* have happened, and if you had seen it happen, you would surely have taken action. But you did *not* take action; you are still mystified."

"Then whatever it was," said Bunsen, "it did not happen."

"You mean, sir, that the doorman, a regular employee of the restaurant, hailed a cab for Smith, who was a regular patron for whom he must have performed the same service many times, and that Smith, whom you described as a well-mannered man who always did the correct social thing, did *not* tip the doorman?"

"Of course he—" began Bunsen, and then came to a dead halt.

And in the silence that followed, Henry said, "And if he tipped him, then surely it was with an object taken from the left pants pocket, an object that, from your description, happened to look something like a coin. —Then he smiled, and *that* you saw."

2   *Afterword*

"Quicker Than the Eye" first appeared in the May 1974 issue of *Ellery Queen's Mystery Magazine*.

I have to make a confession here. In writing the Black Widower stories I have always been under the impression that I was doing my best to catch the spirit of Agatha Christie, who is my idol as far as mysteries are concerned. When I presented a copy of *Tales of the Black Widowers* to Martin Gardner (who writes the "Mathematical Recreations" column in *Scientific American* and who is a recently elected member of the Trap Door Spiders) I told him this and he read it with that in mind.

When he finished, however, he sent me a note to tell me that in his opinion I had missed the mark. What I had really done, he said, was to catch some of the flavor of G. K. Chesterton's "Father Brown" stories.

You know, he's right. I was an ardent fan of those stories even though I found Chesterton's philosophy a little irritating, and in writing "Quicker Than the Eye," I was strongly influenced by the great Chestertonian classic, *The Invisible Man*.

3

The Iron Gem

Geoffrey Avalon stirred his drink and smiled wolfishly. His hairy, still dark eyebrows slanted upward and his neat graying beard seemed to twitch. He looked like Satan in an amiable mood.

He said to the Black Widowers, assembled at their monthly dinner, "Let me present my guest to you—Latimer Reed, jeweler. And let me say at once that he brings us no crime to solve, no mystery to unravel. Nothing has been stolen from him; he has witnessed no murder; involved himself in no spy ring. He is here, purely and simply, to tell us about jewelry, answer our questions, and help us have a good, sociable time."

And, indeed, under Avalon's firm eye, the atmosphere at dinner was quiet and relaxed and even Emmanuel Rubin, the ever quarrelsome polymath of the club, managed to avoid raising his voice. Quite satisfied, Avalon said, over the brandy, "Gentlemen, the postprandial grilling is upon us, and with no problem over which to rack our brains. —Henry, you may relax."

Henry, who was clearing the table with the usual quiet efficiency that would have made him the nonpareil of waiters even if he had not proved himself, over and over again, to be peerlessly aware of the obvious, said, "Thank you, Mr.

Avalon. I trust I will not be excluded from the proceedings, however."

Rubin fixed Henry with an owlish stare through his thick glasses and said loudly, "Henry, this blatantly false modesty does not become you. You know you're a member of our little band, with all the privileges thereto appertaining."

"If that is so," said Roger Halsted, the soft-voiced math teacher, sipping at his brandy and openly inviting a quarrel, "why is he waiting on table?"

"Personal choice, sir," said Henry quickly, and Rubin's opening mouth shut again.

Avalon said, "Let's get on with it. Tom Trumbull isn't with us this time so, as host, I appoint you, Mario, as griller in chief."

Mario Gonzalo, a not inconsiderable artist, was placing the final touches on the caricature he was making of Reed, one that was intended to be added to the already long line that decorated the private room of the Fifth Avenue restaurant at which the dinners of the Black Widowers were held.

Gonzalo had, perhaps, overdrawn the bald dome of Reed's head and the solemn length of his bare upper lip, and made over-apparent the slight tendency to jowl. There was indeed something more than a trace of the bloodhound about the caricature, but Reed smiled when he saw the result, and did not seem offended.

Gonzalo smoothed the perfect Windsor knot of his pink and white tie and let his blue jacket fall open with careful negligence as he leaned back and said, "How do you justify your existence, Mr. Reed?"

"Sir?" said Reed in a slightly metallic voice.

Gonzalo said, without varying pitch or stress, "How do you justify your existence, Mr. Reed?"

Reed looked about the table at the five grave faces and smiled—a smile that did not, somehow, seriously diminish the essential sadness of his own expression.

"Jeff warned me," he said, "that I would be questioned after the dinner, but he did not tell me I would be challenged to justify myself."

"Always best," said Avalon sententiously, "to catch a man by surprise."

Reed said, "What can serve to justify any of us? But if I must say something, I would say that I help bring beauty into lives."

"What kind of beauty?" asked Gonzalo. "Artistic beauty?" And he held up the caricature.

Reed laughed. "Less controversial forms of beauty, I should hope." He pulled a handkerchief out of his inner jacket pocket and, carefully unfolding it on the table, exposed a dozen or so gleaming, deeply colored bits of mineral.

"All men agree on the beauty of gems," he said. "That is independent of subjective taste." He held up a small deep red stone and the lights glanced off it.

James Drake cleared his throat and said with his usual mild hoarseness just the same, "Do you always carry those things around with you?"

"No, of course not," said Reed. "Only when I wish to entertain or demonstrate."

"In a handkerchief?" said Drake.

Rubin burst in at once. "Sure, what's the difference? If he's held up, keeping them in a locked casket won't do him any good. He'd just be out the price of a casket as well."

"Have you ever been held up?" asked Gonzalo.

"No," said Reed. "My best defense is that I am known never to carry much of value with me. I strive to make that as widely known as possible, and to live up to it, too."

"That doesn't look it," said Drake.

"I am demonstrating beauty, not value," said Reed. "Would you care to pass these around among yourselves, gentlemen?"

There was no immediate move and then Drake said, "Henry, would you be in a position to lock the door?"

"Certainly, sir," said Henry, and did so.

Reed looked surprised. "Why lock the door?"

Drake cleared his throat again and stubbed out the pitiful remnant of his cigarette with a stained thumb and forefinger. "I'm afraid that, with the kind of record we now have at our monthly dinners, those things will be passed around and one will disappear."

"That's a tasteless remark, Jim," said Avalon, frowning.

Reed said, "Gentlemen, there is no need to worry. These stones may all disappear with litle loss to me or gain to anyone else. I said I was demonstrating beauty and not value. This one I am holding is a ruby—quite so—but synthetic. There are a few other synthetics and here we have an irreparably cracked opal. Others are riddled with flaws. These will do no one any good and I'm sure Henry can open the door."

Halsted said, stuttering very slightly in controlled excitement, "No, I'm with Jim. Something is just fated to come up. I'll bet that Mr. Reed has included one very valuable item—quite by accident, perhaps—and that one will turn up missing. I just don't believe we can go through an evening without some puzzle facing us."

Reed said, "Not that one. I know every one of these stones and, if you like, I'll look at each again." He did so and then pushed them out into the center of the table. "Merely trinkets that serve to satisfy the innate craving of human beings for beauty."

Rubin grumbled, "Which, however, only the rich can afford."

"Quite wrong, Mr. Rubin. Quite wrong. These stones are not terribly expensive. And even jewelry that is costly is often on display for all eyes—and even the owner can do no more than look at what he owns, though more frequently than others. Primitive tribes might make ornaments as satisfying to themselves as jewelry is to us out of shark's teeth, walrus tusks, sea shells, or birch bark. Beauty is independent of material, or of fixed rules of aesthetics, and in my way I am its servant."

Gonzalo said, "But you would rather sell the most expensive forms of beauty, wouldn't you?"

"Quite true," said Reed. "I am subject to economic law, but that bends my appreciation of beauty as little as I can manage."

Rubin shook his head. His sparse beard bristled and his voice, surprisingly full-bodied for one with so small a frame, rose in passion. "No, Mr. Reed, if you consider yourself a purveyor of beauty only, you are being hypocritical. It's rarity you're selling. A synthetic ruby is as beautiful as a natural one and indistinguishable chemically. But the natural ruby is rarer, more difficult to get, and therefore more expensive and more eagerly bought by those who can afford it. Beauty it may be, but it is beauty meant to serve personal vanity.

"A copy of the 'Mona Lisa,' correct to every crack in the paint, is just a copy, worth no more than any daub, and if there were a thousand copies, the real one would still remain priceless because it alone would be the unique original and would reflect uniqueness on its possessor. But that, you see, has nothing to do with beauty."

Reed said, "It is easy to rail against humanity. Rareness does enhance value in the eyes of the vain, and I suppose that something that is sufficiently rare and, at the same time, notable would fetch a huge price even if there were no beauty about it—"

"A rare autograph," muttered Halsted.

"Yet," said Reed firmly, "beauty is always an enhancing factor, and I sell only beauty. Some of my wares are rare as well, but nothing I sell, or would care to sell, is rare without being beautiful."

Drake said, "What else do you sell besides beauty and rarity?"

"Utility, sir," said Reed at once. "Jewels are a way of storing wealth compactly and permanently in a way independent of the fluctuations of the market place."

"But they can be stolen," said Gonzalo accusingly.

"Certainly," said Reed. "Their very values—beauty, compactness, permanence—make them more useful to a thief than anything else can be. The equivalent in gold would be much heavier; the equivalent in anything else far more bulky."

Avalon said, with a clear sense of reflected glory in his guest's profession, "Latimer deals in eternal value."

"Not always," said Rubin rather wrathfully. "Some of the jeweler's wares are of only temporary value, for rarity may vanish. There was a time when gold goblets might be used on moderately important occasions but, for the real top of vanity, the Venetian cut glass was trotted out—until glass-manufacturing processes were improved to the point where such things were brought down to the five-and-ten level.

"In the 1880s, the Washington Monument was capped with nothing less good than aluminum and, in a few years, the Hall process made aluminum cheap and the monument cap completely ordinary. Then, too, value can change with changing legend. As long as the alicorn—the horn of a unicorn—was thought to have aphrodisiac properties, the horns of narwhals and rhinoceroses were valuable. A handkerchief of a stiffish weave which could be cleaned by being thrown into the fire would be priceless for its magical refusal to burn—till the properties of asbestos became well known.

"Anything that becomes rare through accident—the first

edition of a completely worthless book, rare because it *was* worthless—becomes priceless to collectors. And synthetic jewelry of all sorts may yet make your wares valueless, Mr. Reed."

Reed said, "Perhaps individual items of beauty might lose some of their value, but jewelry is only the raw material of what I sell. There is still the beauty of combination, of setting, the individual and creative work of the craftsman. As for those things which are valuable for rarity alone, I do not deal with them; I will not deal with them; I have no sympathy with them, no interest in them. I myself own some things that are both rare and beautiful—own them, I mean, with no intention of ever selling them—and nothing, I hope, that is ugly and is valued by me only because it is rare. Or almost nothing, anyway."

He seemed to notice for the first time that the gems he had earlier distributed were lying before him. "Ah, you're all through with them, gentlemen?" He scooped them toward himself with his left hand. "All here," he said, "each one. No omissions. No substitutions. All accounted for." He looked at each individually. "I have showed you these, gentlemen, because there is an interesting point to be made about each of them—"

Halsted said, "Wait. What did you mean by saying 'almost nothing'?"

"Almost nothing?" said Reed, puzzled.

"You said you owned nothing ugly just because it was rare. Then you said 'almost nothing.'"

Reed's face cleared. "Ah, my lucky piece. I have it here somewhere." He rummaged in his pocket. "Here it is. —You are welcome to look at it, gentlemen. It is ugly enough, but actually I would be more distressed at losing it than any of the gems I brought with me." He passed his lucky piece to Drake, who sat on his left.

Drake turned it over in his hands. It was about an inch wide, ovoid in shape, black and finely pitted. He said, "It's metal. Looks like meteoric iron."

"That's exactly what it is as far as I know," said Reed.

The object passed from hand to hand and came back to him. "It's my iron gem," said Reed. "I've turned down five hundred dollars for it."

"Who the devil would offer five hundred dollars for it?" asked Gonzalo, visibly astonished.

Avalon cleared his throat. "A collector of meteorites might, I suppose, if for any reason this one had special scientific value. The question really is, Latimer, why on Earth you turned it down."

"Oh," and Reed looked thoughtful for a while. "I don't really know. To be nasty, perhaps. I didn't like the fellow."

"The guy who offered the money?" asked Gonzalo.

"Yes."

Drake reached out for the bit of black metal and, when Reed gave it to him a second time, studied it more closely, turning it over and over. "Does this have scientific value as far as you know?"

"Only by virtue of its being meteoric," said Reed. "I've brought it to the Museum of Natural History and they were interested in having it for their collection if I were interested in donating it without charge. I wasn't. —And I don't know the profession of the man who wanted to buy it. I don't recall the incident very well—it was ten years ago—but I'm certain he didn't impress me as a scientist of any type."

"You've never seen him since?" asked Drake.

"No, though at the time I was sure I would. In fact, for a time I had the most dramatic imaginings. But I never saw him again. It was after that, though, that I began to carry it about as a luck charm." He put it in his pocket again. "After all, there aren't many objects this unprepossessing I would refuse five hundred for."

Rubin, frowning, said, "I scent a mystery here—"

Avalon exploded. "Good God, let's have no mystery! This is a social evening. Latimer, you *assured* me that there was no puzzle you were planning to bring up."

Reed looked honestly confused. "I'm not bringing up any puzzle. As far as I'm concerned, there's nothing to the story. I was offered five hundred dollars; I refused; and there's an end to it."

Rubin's voice rose in indignation. "The mystery consists in the reason for the offer of the five hundred. It is a legitimate outgrowth of the grilling and I demand the right to prove the matter."

Reed said, "But what's the use of probing? I don't know why he offered five hundred dollars unless he believed the ridiculous story my great-grandfather told."

"There's the value of probing. We now know there is a ridiculous story attached to the object. Go on, then. What was the ridiculous story your great-grandfather told?"

"It's the story of how the meteorite—assuming that's what it is—came into the possession of my family—"

"You mean it's an heirloom?" asked Halsted.

"If something totally without value can be an heirloom, this is one. In any case, my great-grandfather sent it home from the Far East in 1856 with a letter explaining the circumstances. I've seen the letter myself. I can't quote it to you, word for word, but I can give you the sense of it."

"Go ahead," said Rubin.

"Well—to begin with, the 1850s were the age of the clipper ship, the *Yankee Clipper*, you know, and the American seamen roamed the world till first the Civil War and then the continuing development of the steamship put an end to sailing vessels. However, I'm not planning to spin a sea yarn. I couldn't. I know nothing about ships and couldn't tell a bowsprit from a binnacle, if either exists at all. However, I mention it all by way of explaining that my great-grandfather—who bore my name; or rather, I bear his —managed to see the world. To that extent his story is conceivable. Between that and the fact that his name, too, was Latimer Reed, I had a tendency, when young, to want to believe him.

"In those days, you see, the Moslem world was still largely closed to the men of the Christian West. The Ottoman Empire still had large territories in the Balkans and the dim memory of the days when it threatened all Europe still lent it an echo of far-off might. And the Arabian Peninsula itself was, to the West, a mystic mixture of desert sheiks and camels.

"Of course, the old city of Mecca was closed to non-Moslems and one of the daring feats a European or American might perform would be to learn Arabic, dress like an Arab, develop a knowledge of Moslem culture and religion, and somehow participate in the ritual of the pilgrimage to Mecca and return to tell the story. —My great-grandfather claimed to have accomplished this."

Drake interrupted. "Claimed? Was he lying?"

"I don't know," said Reed. "I have no evidence beyond this letter he sent from Hong Kong. There was no apparent reason to lie since he had nothing to gain from it. Of course, he may merely have wanted to amuse my great-grandmother and shine in her eyes. He had been away from home for three years and had only been married three years prior to his sailing, and family legend has it that it was a great love match."

Gonzalo began, "But after he returned—"

"He never returned," said Reed. "About a month after he wrote the letter he died under unknown circumstances and was buried somewhere overseas. The family didn't learn of that till considerably later of course. My grandfather was only about four at the time of his father's death and was brought up by my great-grandmother. My grandfather had five sons and three daughters and I'm the second son of his fourth son and there's my family history in brief."

"Died under unknown circumstances," said Halsted. "There are all sorts of possibilities there."

"As a matter of fact," said Reed, "family legend has it that his impersonation of an Arab was detected, that he had been tracked to Hong Kong and beyond, and had been murdered. But you know there is no evidence for that whatever. The only information we have about his death was from seamen who brought a letter from someone who announced the death."

"Does that letter exist?" asked Avalon, interested despite himself.

"No. But where and how he died doesn't matter—or even *if* he died, for that matter. The fact is he never returned home. Of course," Reed went on, "the family has always tended to believe the story, because it is dramatic and glamorous and it has been distorted out of all recognition. I have an aunt who once told me that he was torn to pieces by a howling mob of dervishes who detected his imposture in a mosque. She said it was because he had blue eyes. All made up, of course; probably out of a novel."

Rubin said, "Did he have blue eyes?"

"I doubt it," said Reed. "We all have brown eyes in my family. But I don't really know."

Halsted said, "But what about your iron gem, your lucky piece?"

"Oh, that came with the letter," said Reed. "It was a small package actually. And my lucky piece was the whole point of the letter. He was sending it as a memento of his feat. Perhaps you know that the central ceremony involved in the pilgrimage to Mecca is the rites at the Kaaba, the most holy object in the Moslem world."

Rubin said, "It's actually a relic of the pre-Moslem world. Mohammed was a shrewd and practical politician, though, and he took it over. If you can't lick them, join them."

"I dare say," said Reed coolly. "The Kaaba is a large, irregular cube—the word 'cube' comes from 'Kaaba' in fact —and in its southeast corner about five feet from the ground is what is called the Black Stone, which is broken and held together in metal bands. Most people seem to think the Black Stone is a meteorite."

"Probably," said Rubin. "A stone from heaven, sent by the gods. Naturally it would be worshiped. The same can be said of the original statue of Artemis at Ephesus—the so-called Diana of the Ephesians—"

Avalon said, "Since Tom Trumbull is absent, I suppose it's my job to shut you up, Manny. *Shut up*, Manny. Let our guest speak."

Reed said, "Anyway, that's about it. My iron gem arrived in the package with the letter, and my great-grandfather said in his letter that it was a piece of the Black Stone which he had managed to chip off."

"Good Lord," muttered Avalon. "If he did that, I wouldn't blame the Arabs for killing him."

Drake said, "If it's a piece of the Black Stone, I dare say it would be worth quite a bit to a collector."

"Priceless to a pious Moslem, I should imagine," said Halsted.

"Yes, yes," said Reed impatiently, "*if* it is a piece of the Black Stone. But how are you going to demonstrate such a thing? Can we take it back to Mecca and see if it will fit into some chipped place, or make a very sophisticated chemical comparison of my lucky piece and the rest of the Black Stone?"

"Neither of which, I'm sure," said Avalon, "the government of Saudi Arabia would allow."

"Nor am I interested in asking," said Reed. "Of course, it's an article of faith in my family that the object *is* a chip of the Black Stone and the story was occasionally told to visitors and the package was produced complete with letter and stone. It always made a sensation.

"Then sometime before World War I there was some sort of scare. My father was a boy then and he told me the story when I was a boy, so it's all pretty garbled. I was impressed with it when I was young, but when I considered it after reaching man's estate, I realized that it lacked substance."

"What was the story?" asked Gonzalo.

"A matter of turbaned strangers slinking about the house, mysterious shadows by day and strange sounds by night," said Reed. "It was the sort of thing people would imagine after reading sensational fiction."

Rubin, who, as a writer, would ordinarily have resented the last adjective, was too hot on the spoor on this occasion to do so. He said, "The implication is that they were Arabs who were after the chip of the Black Stone. Did anything happen?"

Avalon broke in. "If you tell us about mysterious deaths, Latimer, I'll know you're making up the whole thing."

Reed said, "I'm speaking nothing but the truth. There were no mysterious deaths. Everyone in my family since Great-grandfather died of old age, disease, or unimpeachable accident. No breath of foul play has ever risen. And in connection with the tale of the turbaned strangers, nothing at all happened. Nothing! Which is one reason I dismiss the whole thing."

Gonzalo said, "Did anyone ever attempt to steal the chip?"

"Never. The original package with the chip and the letter stayed in an unlocked drawer for half a century. No one paid any particular heed to it and it remained perfectly safe. I still have the chip as you saw," and he slapped his pocket.

"Actually," he went on, "the thing would have been forgotten altogether but for me. About 1950, I felt a stirring of interest. I don't have a clear memory why. The nation of Israel had just been established and the Middle East was much in the news. Perhaps that was the reason. In any case, I got to thinking of the old family story and I dredged the thing out of its drawer."

Reed took out his iron gem absently and held it in the palm of his hand. "It did look meteoritic to me but, of course, in my great-grandfather's time meteorites weren't as well known to the general public as they are now. So, as I said earlier, I took it to the Museum of Natural History. Someone said it *was* meteoritic and would I care to donate it. I said it was a family heirloom and I couldn't do that, but—and this was the key point for me—I asked him if there were any signs that it had been chipped off a larger meteorite.

"He looked at it carefully, first by eye, then with a magnifying glass, and finally said he could see no sign of it. He said it must have been found in exactly the condition I had it. He said meteoritic iron is particularly hard and tough because it has nickel in it. It's more like alloy steel than iron and it couldn't be chipped off, he said, without clear signs of manhandling.

"Well, that settled it, didn't it? I went back and got the letter and read it through. I even studied the original package. There was some blurred Chinese scrawl on it and my grandmother's name and address in a faded angular English. There was nothing to be made of it. I couldn't make out the postmark but there was no reason to suppose it wasn't from Hong Kong. Anyway, I decided the whole thing was an amiable fraud. Great-grandfather Latimer had picked up the meteorite somewhere, and probably had been spending time in the Arab world, and couldn't resist spinning a yarn."

Halsted said, "And then a month later he was dead under mysterious circumstances."

"Just dead," said Reed. "No reason to think the death was mysterious. In the 1850s, life was relatively brief. Any of a number of infectious diseases could kill. —Anyway, that's the end of the story. No glamour. No mystery."

Gonzalo objected vociferously at once. "That's not the end of the story. It's not even the beginning. What's the bit about the offer of five hundred dollars?"

"Oh, *that*!" said Reed. "That happened in 1962 or 1963. It was a dinner party and there were some hot arguments on the Middle East and I was taking up a pro-Arab stance as a kind of devil's advocate—it was well before the Six-Day War, of course—and that put me in mind of the meteorite. It was still moldering away in the drawer and I brought it out.

"I remember we were all sitting about the table and I passed the package around and they all looked at it. Some tried to read the letter, but that wasn't so easy because the handwriting is rather old-fashioned and crabbed. Some asked me what the Chinese writing was on the package and of course I didn't know. Just to be dramatic, I told them about the mysterious turbaned strangers in my father's time and stressed Great-granddad's mysterious death, and didn't mention my reasons for being certain it was all a hoax. It was just entertainment.

"Only one person seemed to take it seriously. He was a stranger, a friend of a friend. We had invited a friend, you see, and when he said he had an engagement, we said, well, bring your friend along. That sort of thing, you know. I don't remember his name any more. All I do remember about him personally is that he had thinning red hair and didn't contribute much to the conversation.

"When everybody was getting ready to go, he came to me hesitantly and asked if he could see the thing once more. There was no reason not to allow it, of course. He took the meteorite out of the package—it was the only thing that seemed to interest him—and walked to the light with it. He studied it for a long time; I remember growing a little impatient; and then he said, 'See here, I collect odd objects. I wonder if you'd let me have this thing. I'd pay you, of course. What would you say it was worth?'

"I laughed and said I didn't think I'd sell it and he stammered out an offer of five dollars. I found that rather offensive. I mean, if I were going to sell a family heirloom it surely wouldn't be for five dollars. I gave him a decidedly brusque negative and held out my hand for the object. I took such a dislike to him that I remember feeling he might steal it.

"He handed it back reluctantly enough and I remember looking at the object again to see what might make it attractive to him, but it still seemed what it was, an ugly lump of iron. You see, even though I knew its point of interest lay in its possible history and not in its appearance, I was simply unable to attach value to anything but beauty.

"When I looked up, he was reading the letter again. I held out my hand and he gave me that too. He said, 'Ten dollars?' and I just said, 'No!' "

Reed took a sip of the coffee that Henry had just served him. He said, "Everyone else had left. This man's friend was waiting for him, the man who was *my* friend originally, Jansen. He and his wife were killed in an auto accident the next year, driving the very car at whose door he stood then, waiting for the man he had brought to my house. What a frightening thing the future is if you stop to think of it. Luckily, we rarely do.

"Anyway, the man who wanted the object stopped at the door and said to me hurriedly, 'Listen, I'd really like that little piece of metal. It's no good to you and I'll give you five hundred dollars for it. How's that? Five hundred dollars. Don't be hoggish about this.'

"I can make allowances for his apparent anxiety, but he was damned offensive. He did say 'hoggish'; I remember the word. After that, I wouldn't have let him have it for a million. Very coldly I told him it wasn't for sale at any price, and I put the meteorite, which was still in my hand, into my pocket with ostentatious finality.

"His face darkened and he growled that I would regret that and there would be those who wouldn't be so kind as to offer money, and then off he went— The meteorite has stayed in my pocket ever since. It is my ugly luck piece that I have refused five hundred dollars for." He chuckled in a muted way and said, "And that's the whole story."

Drake said, "And you never found out why he offered you five hundred dollars for that thing?"

"Unless he believed it was a piece of the Black Stone, I can't see any reason why he should," said Reed.

"He never renewed his offer?"

"Never. It was over ten years ago and I have never heard from him at all. And now that Jansen and his wife are dead, I don't even know where he is or how he could be located if I decided I wanted to sell."

Gonzalo said, "What did he mean by his threat about others who wouldn't be so kind as to offer money?"

"I don't know," said Reed. "I suppose he meant mysterious turbaned strangers of the kind I had told him about. I think he was just trying to frighten me into selling."

Avalon said, "Since a mystery has developed despite everything, I suppose we ought to consider the possibilities here. The obvious motive for his offer is, as you say, that he believed the object to be a piece of the Black Stone."

"If so," said Reed, "he was the only one there who did. I don't think anyone else took the story seriously for a moment. Besides, even if it were a chip of the Black Stone and the guy were a collector, what good would it be to him without definite proof? He could take any piece of scrap iron and label it 'piece of the Black Stone' and it would do him no less good than mine."

Avalon said, "Do you suppose he might have been an Arab who knew that a chip the size of your object had been stolen from the Black Stone a century before and wanted it out of piety?"

"He didn't seem Arab to me," said Reed. "And if he were, why was the offer not renewed? Or why wasn't there an attempt at taking it from me by violence?"

Drake said, "He studied the object carefully. Do you suppose he saw something there that convinced him of its value—whatever that value might be?"

Reed said, "How can I dispute that? Except that, whatever he might have seen, I certainly never have. Have you?"

"No," admitted Drake.

Rubin said, "This doesn't sound like anything we can possibly work out. We just don't have enough information. —What do you say, Henry?"

Henry, who had been listening with his usual quiet attention, said, "I was wondering about a few points."

"Well then, go on, Henry," said Avalon. "Why not continue the grilling of the guest?"

Henry said, "Mr. Reed, when you showed the object to your guests on that occasion in 1962 or 1963, you say you passed the package around. You mean the original package in which the letter and the meteorite had come, with its contents as they had always been?"

"Yes. Oh yes. It was a family treasure."

"But since 1963, sir, you have carried the meteorite in your pocket?"

"Yes, always," said Reed.

"Does that mean, sir, that you no longer have the letter?"

"Of course it doesn't mean that," said Reed indignantly. "We certainly do have the letter. I'll admit that after that fellow's threat I was a little concerned so I put it in a safer place. It's a glamorous document from the family standpoint, hoax or not."

"Where do you keep it now?" asked Henry.

"In a small wall safe I use for documents and occasional jewels."

"Have you seen it recently, sir?"

Reed smiled broadly. "I use the wall safe frequently, and I see it every time. Take my word for it, Henry, the letter is safe; as safe as the luck piece in my pocket."

Henry said, "Then you don't keep the letter in the original package any more."

"No," said Reed. "The package was more useful as a container for the meteorite. Now that I carry that object in my pocket, there was no point in keeping the letter alone in the package."

Henry nodded. "And what did you do with the package, then, sir?"

Reed looked puzzled. "Why, nothing."

"You didn't throw it out?"

"No, of course not."

"Do you know where it is?"

Slowly, Reed frowned. He said at last, "No, I don't think so."

"When did you last see it?"

The pause was just as long this time. "I don't know that either."

Henry seemed lost in thought.

Avalon said, "Well, Henry, what do you have in mind?"

Henry said, "I'm just wondering"—quietly he circled the table removing the brandy glasses—"whether that man wanted the meteorite at all."

"He certainly offered me money for it," said Reed.

"Yes," said Henry, "but first such small sums as would offer you no temptation to release it, and which he could well afford to pay if you called his bluff. Then a larger sum couched in such offensive language as to make it certain you would refuse. And after that, a mysterious threat which was never implemented."

"But why should he do all that," said Reed, "unless he wanted my iron gem?"

Henry said, "To achieve, perhaps, precisely what he did, in fact, achieve—to convince you he wanted the meteorite and to keep your attention firmly fixed on that. He gave you back the meteorite when you held out your hand for it; he gave you back the letter—but did he give you back the original package?"

Reed said, "I don't remember him taking it."

Henry said, "It was ten years ago. He kept your attention fixed on the meteorite. You even spent some time examining it yourself and during that time you didn't look at him, I'm sure. —Can you say you've seen the package since that time, sir?"

Slowly, Reed shook his head. "I can't say I have. You mean he fastened my attention so tightly on the meteorite that he could walk off with the package and I wouldn't notice?"

"I'm afraid you didn't. You put the meteorite in your pocket, the letter in your safe, and apparently never gave another thought to the package. This man, whose name you don't know and whom you can no longer identify thanks to your friends' death, has had the package for ten years with no interference. And by now you could not possibly identify what it was he took."

"I certainly could," said Reed stoutly, "if I could see it. It has my great-grandmother's name and address on it."

"He might not have saved the package itself," said Henry.

"I've got it," cried out Gonzalo suddenly. "It was that Chinese writing. He could make it out somehow and he took it to get it deciphered with certainty. The message was important."

Henry's smile was the barest flicker. "That is a romantic notion that had not occurred to me, Mr. Gonzalo, and I don't know that it is very probable. I was thinking of something else. —Mr. Reed, you had a package from Hong Kong in 1856 and at that time Hong Kong was already a British possession."

"Taken over in 1848," said Rubin briefly.

"And I think the British had already instituted the modern system of distributing mail."

"Rowland Hill," said Rubin at once, "in 1840."

"Well then," said Henry, "could there have been a stamp on the original package?"

Reed looked startled. "Now that you mention it, there was something that looked like a black stamp, I seem to recall. A woman's profile?"

"The young Victoria," said Rubin.

Henry said, "And might it possibly have been a rare stamp?"

Gonzalo threw up his arms. "Bingo!"

Reed sat with his mouth distinctly open. Then he said, "Of course, you must be right. —I wonder how much I lost."

"Nothing but money, sir," murmured Henry. "The early British stamps were not beautiful."

3   Afterword

"The Iron Gem" appeared in the July 1974 issue of *Ellery Queen's Mystery Magazine* under the title "A Chip of the Black Stone." Ordinarily, all things being equal, I go for the shorter title, so I'm changing it back to my original title in this case. (I don't always refuse to accept changes. The first story in this collection was called "No Man Pursueth" when I wrote it. The magazine changed it to "When No Man Pursueth" and I accept the extra word as an improvement.)

I wrote this story on board the *Canberra*, which took me over the ocean to the coast of Africa and back in the summer of 1973, to view a total solar eclipse—the first total solar eclipse I had ever seen. Heaven knows, they filled my time, for I was on board as a lecturer, and I gave eight lectures on the history of astronomy, to say nothing of the time it took to be charming and suave to all twelve hundred women on board. (You should see me being charming and suave. Some of them have trouble getting away.)

Just the same, I did find time to hide out in my cabin now and then to write "The Iron Gem" in longhand. What puzzles me now that I look back on it, however, is why the story didn't have anything to do with a solar eclipse when that (and the twelve hundred women) was all I was thinking of on the cruise.

4

The Three Numbers

When Tom Trumbull arrived—late, of course—to the Black Widowers' banquet, and called for his scotch and soda, he was met by James Drake, who was wearing a rather hang-dog expression on his face.

Drake's head made a gentle gesture to one side.

Trumbull followed him, unpeeling his coat as he went, his tanned and furrowed face asking the question before his voice did. "What's up?" he said.

Drake held his cigarette to one side and let the smoke curl bluely upward. "Tom, I've brought a physicist as my guest."

"So?"

"Well, he has a problem and I think it's up your alley."

"A code?"

"Something like that. Numbers, anyway. I don't have all the details. I suppose we'll get those after the dinner. But that's not the point. Will you help me if it becomes necessary to hold down Jeff Avalon?"

Trumbull looked across the room to where Avalon was standing in staid conversation with the man who was clearly the guest of the evening since he was the only stranger present.

"What's wrong with Jeff?" said Trumbull. There didn't seem

anything wrong with Avalon, who was standing straight and tall as always, looking as though he might splinter if he relaxed. His graying mustache and small beard were as neat and trim as ever and he wore that careful smile on his face that he insisted on using for strangers. "He looks all right."

Drake said, "You weren't here last time. Jeff has the idea that the Black Widowers is becoming too nearly a puzzle session each month."

"What's wrong with that?" asked Trumbull as he passed his hands over his tightly waved off-white hair to press down the slight disarray produced by the wind outside.

"Jeff thinks we ought to be a purely social organization. Convivial conversation and all that."

"We have that anyway."

"So when the puzzle comes up, help me sit on him if he gets grouchy. You have a loud voice and I don't."

"No problem. Have you talked to Manny?"

"Hell, no. He'd take up the other side to be contrary."

"You may be right. —Henry!" Trumbull waved his arm. "Henry, do me a favor. This scotch and soda won't be enough. It's cold outside and it took me a long time to get a taxi so—"

Henry smiled discreetly, his unlined face looking twenty years younger than his actual sixtyishness. "I had assumed that might be so, Mr. Trumbull. Your second is ready."

"Henry, you're a diamond of the first water" —which, to be sure, was a judgment concurred in by all the Black Widowers.

"I'll give you a demonstration," said Emmanuel Rubin. He had quarreled with the soup which, he maintained, had had just a shade too much leek to make it fit for human consumption, and the fact that he was in a clear minority of one rendered him all the more emphatic in his remaining views. "I'll show you that any language is really a complex of languages. —I'll write a word on each of these two pieces of paper. The same word. I'll give one to you, Mario— and one to you, sir."

The second went to Dr. Samuel Puntsch, who had, as was usually the case with guests of the Black Widowers, maintained a discreet silence during the preliminaries.

Puntsch was a small, slim man, dressed in a funereal color scheme that would have done credit to Avalon. He looked at the paper and lifted his unobtrusive eyebrows.

Rubin said, "Now neither of you say anything. Just write down the number of the syllable that carries the stress. It's a four-syllable word, so write down either one, two, three, or four."

Mario Gonzalo, the Black Widowers' tame artist, had just completed the sketch of Dr. Puntsch, and he laid it to one side. He looked at the word on the paper before him, wrote a figure without hesitation, and passed it to Rubin. Puntsch did the same.

Rubin said, with indescribable satisfaction, "I'll spell the word. It's u-n-i-o-n-i-z-e-d, and Mario says it's accented on the first syllable."

"*Yoo*-nionized," said Mario. "Referring to an industry whose working force has been organized into a labor union."

Puntsch laughed. "Yes, I see. I called it un-*eye*-onized; referring to a substance that did not break down into ions in solution. I accent the second syllable."

"Exactly. The same word to the eye, but different to men in different fields. Roger and Jim would agree with Dr. Puntsch, I know, and Tom, Jeff, and Henry would probably agree with Mario. It's like that in a million different places. Fugue means different things to a psychiatrist and a musician. The phrase 'to press a suit' means one thing to a nineteenth-century lover and another to a twentieth-century tailor. No two people have exactly the same language."

Roger Halsted, the mathematics teacher, said with the slight hesitation that was almost a stammer but never quite, "There's enough overlap so that it doesn't really matter, does it?"

"Most of us can understand each other, yes," said Rubin querulously, "but there's less overlap than there ought to be. Every small segment of the culture develops its own vocabulary for the sake of forming an in-group. There are a million verbal walls behind which fools cower, and it does more to create ill feeling—"

"That was Shaw's thesis in *Pygmalion*," growled Trumbull.

"No! You're quite wrong, Tom. Shaw thought it was the result of faulty education. I say it's *deliberate* and that this does more to create the proper atmosphere for world collapse than war does." And he tackled his roast beef with a fierce cut of his knife.

"Only Manny could go from unionized to the destruction

of civilization in a dozen sentences," said Gonzalo philosophically, and passed his sketch to Henry for delivery to Puntsch.

Puntsch smiled a little shakily at it, for it emphasized his ears more than a purist might have thought consistent with good looks. Henry put it on the wall with the others.

It was perhaps inevitable that the discussion veer from the iniquities of private language to word puzzles and Halsted achieved a certain degree of silence over the dessert by demanding to know the English word whose pronunciation changed when it was capitalized. Then, when all had given up, Halsted said slowly, "I would say that 'polish' becomes 'Polish,' right?"

Avalon frowned portentously, his luxuriant eyebrows hunching over his eyes. "At least that isn't as offensive as the usual Polish jokes I can't avoid hearing sometimes."

Drake said, his small gray mustache twitching, "We'll try something a little more complicated after the coffee."

Avalon darted a suspicious glance in the direction of Puntsch and, with a look of melancholy on his face, watched Henry pour the coffee.

Henry said, "Brandy, sir?"

Puntsch looked up and said, "Why, yes, thank you. That was a very good meal, waiter."

"I am glad you think so," said Henry. "The Black Widowers are a special concern to this establishment."

Drake was striking his water glass with a spoon.

He said, trying to elevate his always fuzzily hoarse voice, "I've got Sam Puntsch here partly because he worked for the same firm I work for out in New Jersey, though not in the same division. He doesn't know a damn thing about organic chemistry; I know that because I heard him discuss the subject once. On the other hand, he's a pretty fair-to-middling physicist, I'm told. I've also got him here partly because he's got a problem and I told him to come down and entertain us with it, and I hope, Jeff, that you have no objections."

Geoffrey Avalon twirled his brandy glass gently between two fingers and said grimly, "There are no bylaws to this organization, Jim, so I'll go along with you and try to enjoy myself. But I must say I would like to relax on these evenings; though perhaps it's just the old brain calcifying."

"Well, don't worry, we'll let Tom be griller in chief."

Puntsch said, "If Mr. Avalon—"

Drake said at once, "Pay no attention to Mr. Avalon."

And Avalon himself said, "Oh, it's all right, Dr. Puntsch. The group is kind enough to let me pout on occasion."

Trumbull scowled and said, "Will you all let me get on with it? Dr. Puntsch— how do you justify your existence?"

"Justify it? I suppose you could say that trying to have our civilization last for longer than a generation is a sort of justification."

"What does this trying consist of?"

"An attempt to find a permanent, safe, and non-polluting energy source."

"What kind?"

"Fusion energy. —Are you going to ask me the details?"

Trumbull shook his head. "No, unless they're germane to the problem that's disturbing you."

"Only very tangentially; which is good." Puntsch's voice was reedy, and his words were meticulously pronounced as though he had at one time had ambitions to become a radio announcer. He said, "Actually, Mr. Rubin's point was a rather good one earlier in the evening. We all do have our private language, sometimes more so than is necessary, and I would not welcome the chance to have to go into great detail on the matter of fusion."

Gonzalo, who was wearing a costume in various complementing tones of red, and who dominated the table visually more than was usually true, muttered, "I wish people would stop saying that Rubin is right."

"You want them to lie?" demanded Rubin, head thrown up at once and his sparse beard bristling.

"Shut up, you two," shouted Trumbull. "Dr. Puntsch, let me tell you what I know about fusion energy and you stop me if I'm too far off base. —It's a kind of nuclear energy produced when you force small atoms to combine into larger ones. You use heavy hydrogen out of the ocean, fuse it to helium, and produce energy that will last us for many millions of years."

"Yes, it's roughly as you say."

"But we don't have it yet, do we?"

"No, as of today, we don't have it."

"Why not, Doctor?"

"Ah, Mr. Trumbull, I take it you don't want a two-hour lecture."

"No, sir, how about a two-minute lecture?"

Puntsch laughed. "About two minutes is all anyone will sit still for. The trouble is we have to heat up our fuel to a minimum temperature of forty-five million degrees Centigrade, which is about eighty million Fahrenheit. Then we have to keep the fusion fuel—heavy hydrogen, as you say, plus tritium, which is a particularly heavy variety—at that temperature long enough for it to catch fire, so to speak, and we must keep it all in place with strong magnetic fields while this is happening.

"So far, we can't get the necessary temperature produced quickly enough, or hold the magnetic field in being long enough, for the fusion fuel to ignite. Delivering energy by laser may be another bet, but we need stronger lasers than we have so far, or stronger and better-designed magnetic fields than we now have. Once we manage it and *do* ignite the fuel, that will be an important breakthrough, but God knows there will remain plenty of engineering problems to solve before we can actually begin to run the Earth by fusion energy."

Trumbull said, "When do you think we'll get to that first breakthrough; when do you think we'll have ignition?"

"It's hard to say. American and Soviet physicists have been inching forward toward it for a quarter of a century. I think they've almost reached it. Five years more maybe. But there are imponderables. A lucky intuition might bring it this year. Unforeseen difficulties may carry us into the twenty-first century."

Halsted broke in. "Can we wait till the twenty-first century?"

"Wait?" said Puntsch.

"You say you are trying to have civilization last more than a generation. That sounds as though you don't think we can wait for the twenty-first century."

"I see. I wish I could be optimistic on this point, sir," said Puntsch gravely, "but I can't. At the rate we're going, our petroleum will be pretty much used up by 2000. Going back to coal will present us with a lot of problems and leaning on breeder fission reactors will involve the getting rid of enormous quantities of radioactive wastes. I would certainly feel uncomfortable if we don't end up with working fusion reactors by, say, 2010."

"*Après moi, le déluge,*" said Avalon.

Puntsch said with a trace of acerbity, "The deluge may well come after your time, Mr. Avalon. Do you have any children?"

Avalon, who had two children and several grandchildren, looked uncomfortable and said, "But fusion energy may stave off the deluge and I take it your feelings about the arrival of fusion are optimistic."

"Yes, there I tend to be optimistic."

Trumbull said, "Well, let's get on with it. You're working at Jim Drake's firm. I always thought of that as one of these drug supply houses."

"It's a hell of a lot more than that," said Drake, looking dolefully at what was left of a cigarette package as though wondering whether he ought to set fire to another one or rest for ten minutes.

Puntsch said, "Jim works in the organic chemistry section. I work on plasma physics."

Rubin said, "I was down there once, visiting Jim, and took a tour of the plant. I didn't see any Tokamaks."

"What's a Tokamak?" asked Gonzalo at once.

Puntsch said, "It's a device within which stable magnetic fields—pretty stable anyway—can be set up to confine the super-hot gas. No, we don't have any. We're not doing anything of the sort. We're more or less at the theoretical end of it. When we think up something that looks hopeful, we have arrangements with some of the large installations that will allow it to be tried out."

Gonzalo said, "What's in it for the firm?"

"We're allowed to do some basic research. There's always use for it. The firm produces fluorescent tubes of various sorts and anything we find about the behavior of hot gases—plasma, it's called—and magnetic fields may always help in the production of cheaper and better fluorescents. That's the practical justification of our work."

Trumbull said, "And have you come up with anything that looks hopeful? —In fusion, I mean, not in fluorescents."

Puntsch began a smile and let it wipe off slowly. "That's exactly it. I don't know."

Halsted placed his hand on the pink area of baldness in the forepart of his skull and said, "Is that the problem you've brought us?"

"Yes," said Puntsch.

"Well, then, Doctor, suppose you tell us about it."

Puntsch cleared his throat and pursed his lips for a moment, looking about at the men at the banquet table and leaning to one side in order to allow Henry to refill his coffee cup.

"Jim Drake," he said, "has explained that everything said in this room is confidential; that everyone"—his eye rested briefly on Henry—"is to be trusted. I'll speak freely, then. I have a colleague working at the firm. His name is Matthew Revsof and Drake knows him."

Drake nodded. "Met him at your house once."

Puntsch said, "Revsof is halfway between brilliance and madness, which is sometimes a good thing for a theoretical physicist. It means, though, that he's erratic and difficult to deal with at times. We've been good friends, mostly because our wives have gotten along together particularly well. It became one of those family things where the children on both sides use us almost interchangeably as parents, since we have houses in the same street.

"Revsof is now in the hospital. He's been there two months. I'll have to explain that it's a mental hospital and that he had a violent episode which put him into it and there's no point in going into the details of that. However, the hospital is in no hurry to let him go and that creates a problem.

"I went to visit him about a week after he had been hospitalized. He seemed perfectly normal, perfectly cheerful; I brought him up to date on some of the work going on in the department and he had no trouble following me. But then he wanted to speak to me privately. He insisted the nurse leave and that the door be closed.

"He swore me to secrecy and told me he knew exactly how to design a Tokamak in such a way as to produce a totally stable magnetic field that would contain a plasma of moderate densities indefinitely. He said something like this, 'I worked it out last month. That's why I've been put here. Naturally, the Soviets arranged it. The material is in my home safe; the diagrams, the theoretical analysis, everything.'"

Rubin, who had been listening with an indignant frown, interrupted. "Is that possible? Is he the kind of man who could do that? Was the work at the stage where such an advance—"

Puntsch smiled wearily. "How can I answer that? The

history of science is full of revolutionary advances that required small insights that anyone might have had, but that, in fact, only one person did. I'll tell you this, though. When someone in a mental hospital tells you that he has something that has been eluding the cleverest physicists in the world for nearly thirty years, and that the Russians are after him, you don't have a very great tendency to believe it. All I tried to do was soothe him.

"But my efforts to do that just excited him. He told me he planned to have the credit for it; he wasn't going to have anyone stealing priority while he was in the hospital. I was to stand guard over the home safe and make sure that no one broke in. He was sure that Russian spies would try to arrange a break-in and he kept saying over and over again that I was the only one he could trust and as soon as he got out of the hospital he would announce the discovery and prepare a paper so that he could safeguard his priority. He said he would allow me coauthorship. Naturally, I agreed to everything just to keep him quiet and got the nurse back in as soon as I could."

Halsted said, "American and Soviet scientists are co-operating in fusion research, aren't they?"

"Yes, of course," said Puntsch. "The Tokamak itself is of Soviet origin. The business of Russian spies is just Revsof's overheated fantasy."

Rubin said, "Have you visited him since?"

"Quite a few times. He sticks to his story. —It bothers me. I don't believe him. I think he's mad. And yet something inside me says: What if he isn't? What if there's something in his home safe that the whole world would give its collective eyeteeth for?"

Halsted said, "When he gets out—"

Puntsch said, "It's not that easy. Any delay is risky. This is a field in which many minds are eagerly busy. On any particular day, someone else may make Revsof's discovery —assuming that Revsof has really made one—and he will then lose priority and credit, and a Nobel Prize for all I know. And, to take the broader view, the firm will lose a considerable amount of reflected credit and the chance at a substantial increase in its prosperity. Every employee of the firm will lose the chance of benefiting from what general prosperity increase the firm might have experienced. So you see, gentlemen, I have a personal stake in this, and so has Jim Drake, for that matter.

"But even beyond that— The world is in a race that it may not win. Even if we do get the answer to a stable magnetic field, there will be a great deal of engineering to work through, as I said before, and, at the very best, it will be years before fusion energy is really available to the world— years we might not be able to afford. In that case, it isn't safe to lose any time at all waiting for Revsof to get out."

Gonzalo said, "If he's getting out soon—"

"But he *isn't*. That's the worst of it," said Puntsch. "He may never come out. He's deteriorating."

Avalon said in his deep, solemn voice, "I take it, sir, that you have explained the advantages of prompt action to your friend."

"That I have," said Puntsch. "I've explained it as carefully as I could. I said we would open the safe before legal witnesses, and bring everything to him for his personal signature. We would leave the originals and take copies. I explained what he himself might possibly lose by delay. —All that happened was that he—well, in the end he attacked me. I've been asked not to visit him again till further notice."

Gonzalo said, "What about his wife? Does she know anything about this? You said she was a good friend of your wife's."

"So she is. She's a wonderful girl and she understands perfectly the difficulty of the situation. She agrees that the safe should be opened."

"Has *she* talked to her husband?" asked Gonzalo.

Puntsch hesitated. "Well, no. She hasn't been allowed to see him. He—he— This is ridiculous but I can't help it. He claims Barbara, his wife, is in the pay of the Soviet Union. Frankly, it was Barbara whom he—when he was put in the hospital—"

"All right," said Trumbull gruffly, "but can't you get Revsof declared incompetent and have the control of the safe transferred to his wife?"

"First, that's a complicated thing. Barbara would have to testify to a number of things she doesn't want to testify to. She—she loves the man."

Gonzalo said, "I don't want to sound ghoulish, but you said that Revsof was deteriorating. If he dies—"

"Deteriorating mentally, not physically. He's thirty-eight

years old and could live forty more years and be mad every day of it."

"Eventually, won't his wife be forced to request he be declared incompetent?"

Puntsch said, "But when will that be? —And all this still isn't the problem I want to present. I had explained to Barbara exactly how I would go about it to protect Matt's priority. I would open the safe and Barbara would initial and date every piece of paper in it. I would photocopy it all and give her a notarized statement to the effect that I had done this and that I acknowledged all that I removed to be Revsof's work. The originals and the notarized statement would be returned to the safe and I would work with the copies.

"You see, she had told me at the very start that she had the combination. It was a matter of first overcoming my own feeling that I was betraying a trust, and secondly, overcoming her scruples. I didn't like it but I felt I was serving a higher cause and in the end Barbara agreed. We decided that if Revsof was ever sane enough to come home, he would agree we had done the right thing. And his priority *would* be protected."

Trumbull said, "I take it you opened the safe, then."

"No," said Puntsch, "I didn't. I tried the combination Barbara gave me and it didn't work. The safe is still closed."

Halsted said, "You could blow it open."

Puntsch said, "I can't bring myself to do that. It's one thing to be given the combination by the man's wife. It's another to—"

Halsted shook his head. "I mean, can't Mrs. Revsof ask that it be blown open?"

Puntsch said, "I don't think she would ask that. It would mean bringing in outsiders. It would be an act of violence against Revsof, in a way, and— Why doesn't the combination work? That's the problem."

Trumbull put his hands on the table and leaned forward. "Dr. Puntsch, are you asking us to answer that question? To tell you how to use the combination you have?"

"More or less."

"Do you have the combination with you?"

"You mean the actual slip of paper that has the combination written upon it? No. Barbara keeps that and I see her point. However, if you want it written down, that's no problem. I remember it well enough." He brought out a little notebook from his inner jacket pocket, tore off a sheet of paper, and wrote rapidly. "There it is!"

$$12R\ 27\ 15$$

Trumbull glanced at it solemnly, then passed the paper to Halsted on his left. It made the rounds and came back to him.

Trumbull folded his hands and stared solemnly at the bit of paper. He said, "How do you know this is the combination to the safe?"

"Barbara says it is."

"Doesn't it seem unlikely to you, Dr. Puntsch, that the man you described would leave the combination lying about? With the combination available, he might as well have an unlocked safe. —This row of symbols may have nothing to do with the safe."

Puntsch sighed. "That's not the way of it. It isn't as though the safe ever had anything of intrinsic value in it. There's nothing of great intrinsic value in Resof's house altogether, or in mine, for that matter. We're not rich and we're not very subject to burglary. Revsof got the safe about five years ago and had it installed because he thought he might keep papers there. He had this fetish about losing priority even then, but it wasn't till recently that it reached the point of paranoia. He did make a note of the combination for his own use so he wouldn't lock himself out.

"Barbara came across it one day and asked what it was and he said that it was the combination to his safe. She said, 'Well, don't leave it lying around,' and she put it in a little envelope in one of her own drawers, feeling he might need it someday. He never did, apparently, and I'm sure he must have forgotten all about it. But *she* didn't forget, and she says she is certain it has never been disturbed."

Rubin said, "He might have had the combination changed."

"That would have meant a locksmith in the house. Barbara says she is certain it never happened."

Trumbull said, "Is that all there was written on the page? Just six numbers and a letter of the alphabet?"

"That's all."

"What about the back of the sheet?"

"Nothing."

Trumbull said, "You understand, Dr. Puntsch, this isn't a code, and I'm not expert on combination locks. What does the lock look like?"

"Very ordinary. I'm sure Revsof could not afford a really fancy safe. There's a circle with numbers around it from 1 to 30 and a knob with a little pointer in the middle. Barbara has seen Matt at the safe and there's no great shakes to it. He turns the knob and pulls it open."

"She's never done that herself?"

"No. She says she hasn't."

"She can't tell you why the safe doesn't open when you use the combination?"

"No, she can't. —And yet it seems straightforward enough. Most of the combination locks I've dealt with—all of them, in fact—have knobs that you turn first in one direction, then in the other, then back in the first direction again. It seems clear to me that, according to the combination, I should turn the knob to the right till the pointer is at twelve, then left to twenty-seven, then right again to fifteen."

Trumbull said thoughtfully, "I can't see that it could mean anything else either."

"But it doesn't work," said Puntsch. "I turned twelve, twenty-seven, fifteen a dozen times. I did it carefully, making sure that the little pointer was centered on each line. I tried making extra turns; you know, right to twelve, then left one full turn and then to twenty-seven, then right one full turn and then to fifteen. I tried making one full turn in one direction and not in the other. I tried other tricks, jiggling the knob, pressing it. I tried everything."

Gonzalo said, grinning, "Did you say 'Open sesame'?"

"It didn't occur to me to do so," said Puntsch, not grinning, "but if it had, I would have tried it. Barbara says she never noticed him do anything special, but of course, it could have been something unnoticeable and for that matter she didn't watch him closely. It wouldn't occur to her that she'd have to know someday."

Halsted said, "Let me look at that again." He stared at the combination solemnly. "This is only a copy, Dr. Puntsch. This can't be exactly the way it looked. It seems clear here but you might be copying it just as you thought it was. Isn't it possible that some of the numbers in the original might be equivocal so that you might mistake a seven for a one, for instance?"

"No, no," said Puntsch, shaking his head vigorously. "There's no chance of a mistake there, I assure you."

"What about the spaces?" said Halsted. "Was it spaced exactly like that?"

Puntsch reached for the paper and looked at it again. "Oh, I see what you mean. No, as a matter of fact, there were no spaces. I put them in because that was how I thought of it. Actually the original is a solid line of symbols with no particular spacing. It doesn't matter, though, does it? You can't divide it any other way. I'll write it down for you without spaces." He wrote a second time under the first and shoved it across the table to Halsted.

12R2715

He said, "You can't divide it any other way. You can't have a 271 or a 715. The numbers don't go higher than thirty."

"Well now," muttered Halsted, "never mind the numbers. What about the letter R?" He licked his lips, obviously enjoying the clear atmosphere of suspense that had now centered upon him. "Suppose we divide the combination this way":

12 R27 15

He held it up for Puntsch to see, and then for the others. "In this division, it's the twenty-seven which would have the sign for 'right' so it's the other two numbers that turn left. In other words, the numbers are twelve, twenty-seven, and fifteen all right, but you turn left, right, left, instead of right, left, right."

Gonzalo protested. "Why put the R there?"

Halsted said, "All he needs is the minimum reminder. He knows what the combination is. If he reminds himself the middle number is right, he knows the other two are left."

Gonzalo said, "But that's no big deal. If he just puts down the three numbers, it's either left, right, left, or else it's right, left, right. If one doesn't work, he tries the other. Maybe the R stands for something else."

"I can't think what," said Puntsch gloomily.

Halsted said, "The symbol couldn't be something other than an R, could it, Dr. Puntsch?"

"Absolutely not," said Puntsch. "I'll admit I didn't think of associating the R with the second number, but that doesn't matter anyway. When the combination wouldn't work right, left, right, I was desperate enough not only to try it left, right, left; but right, right, right and left, left, left. In every case I tried it with and without complete turns in between. Nothing worked."

Gonzalo said, "Why not try all the combinations? There can only be so many."

Rubin said, "Figure out how many, Mario. The first number can be anything from one to thirty in either direction; so can the second; so can the third. The total number of possible combinations, if any direction is allowed for any number, is sixty times sixty times sixty, or over two hundred thousand."

"I think I'll blow it open before it comes to trying them all," said Puntsch in clear disgust.

Trumbull turned to Henry, who had been standing at the sideboard, an intent expression on his face. "Have you been following all this, Henry?"

Henry said, "Yes, sir, but I haven't actually seen the figures."

Trumbull said, "Do you mind, Dr. Puntsch? He's the best man here, actually." He handed over the slip with the three numbers written in three different ways.

Henry studied them gravely and shook his head. "I'm sorry. I had had a thought, but I see I'm wrong."

"What was the thought?" asked Trumbull.

"It had occurred to me that the letter R might have been in the small form. I see it's a capital."

Puntsch looked astonished. "Wait, wait. Henry, does it matter?"

"It might, sir. We don't often think it does, but Mr. Halsted explained earlier in the evening that 'polish' becomes 'Polish,' changing pronunciation simply because of a capitalization."

Puntsch said slowly, "But, you know, it *is* a small letter in the original. It never occurred to me to produce it that way. I always use capitals when I print. How odd."

There was a faint smile on Henry's face. He said, "Would you write the combination with a small letter, sir."

Puntsch, flushing slightly, wrote:

$$12r2715$$

Henry looked at it and said, "As long as it is a small *r* after all, I can ask a further question. Are there any other differences between this and the original?"

"No," said Puntsch. Then, defensively, "No significant differences of any kind. The matter of the spacing and the capitalization hasn't changed anything, has it? Of course, the original isn't in my handwriting."

Henry said quietly, "Is it in anyone's handwriting, sir?"

"What?"

"I mean, is the original typewritten, Dr. Puntsch?"

Dr. Puntsch's flush deepened. "Yes, now that you ask, it *was* typewritten. That doesn't mean anything either. If there were a typewriter here I would typewrite it for you, though, of course, it might not be the same typewriter that typed out the original."

Henry said, "There is a typewriter in the office on this floor. Would you care to type it, Dr. Puntsch?"

"Certainly," said Puntsch defiantly. He was back in two minutes, during which time not one word was said by anyone at the table. He presented the paper to Henry, with the typewritten series of numbers under the four lines of handwritten ones:

12r2715

Henry said, "Is this the way it looked now? The typewriter that did the original did not have a particularly unusual typeface?"

"No, it didn't. What I have typed looks just like the original."

Henry passed the paper to Trumbull, who looked at it and passed it on.

Henry said, "If you open the safe, you are very likely to find nothing of importance, I suppose."

"I suppose it too," snapped Puntsch. "I'm almost sure of it. It will be disappointing but much better than standing here wondering."

"In that case, sir," said Henry, "I would like to say that Mr. Rubin spoke of private languages early in the evening.

The typewriter has a private language too. The standard typewriter uses the same symbol for the numeral one and the small form of the twelfth letter of the alphabet.

"If you had wanted to abbreviate 'left' and 'right' by the initial letters in handwriting, there would have been no problem, since neither form of the handwritten letter is confusing. If you had used a typewriter and abbreviated it in capitals it would have been clear. Using small letters, it is possible to read the combination as 12 right, 27, 15; or possibly 12, right 27, 15; *or* as left 2, right 27, left 5. The 1 in 12 and 15 is not the numeral 1 but the small version of the letter L and stands for left. Revsof knew what he was typing and it didn't confuse him. It could confuse others."

Puntsch looked at the symbols openmouthed. "How did I miss that?"

Henry said, "You spoke, earlier, of insights that anyone might make, but that only one actually does. It was Mr. Gonzalo who had the key."

"I?" said Gonzalo strenuously.

"Mr. Gonzalo wondered why there should be one letter," said Henry, "and it seemed to me he was right. Dr. Revsof would surely indicate the directions for all, or for none. Since one letter was indubitably present, I wondered if the other two might not be also."

4 Afterword

This appeared in the September 1974 issue of *Ellery Queen's Mystery Magazine* under the title "All in the Way You Read It." Again I prefer the shorter title, so I return it to my own "The Three Numbers."

I am sometimes asked where I get my ideas; in fact, I am frequently asked that. There's no big secret. I get them from everything I experience, and you can do it, too, if you're willing to work at it.

For instance, I know I've got a possible Black Widower story if I can think of something that can be looked at two or more ways, with only Henry looking at it the right way.

So once, when I was sitting at my typewriter, wishing I had an idea for a Black Widower story (because I felt like writing one of them that day rather than working at whatever task was then facing me), I decided to look at the typewriter and see if there was some useful ambiguity I could extract from the keyboard. After some thought, I extracted one and had my story.

5

Nothing Like Murder

Emmanuel Rubin looked definitely haggard when he arrived at the monthly banquet of the Black Widowers. Whereas ordinarily he gave the clear impression of being a foot taller than the five feet five which literal minds would consider his height to be, he seemed shrunken this time into his natural limits. His thick glasses seemed to magnify less, and even his beard, sparse enough at best, straggled limply.

"You look your age," said the resplendent Mario Gonzalo. "What's wrong?"

"And you look like an overdressed D'Artagnan," said Rubin with marked lack of snap.

"All we Latins are handsome," said Gonzalo. "But, really, what's wrong?"

"I'm short about six hours' sleep," said Rubin aggrievedly. "A deadline trapped me when I wasn't looking. In fact, the deadline was two days ago."

"Did you finish?"

"Just about. I'll have it in tomorrow."

"Who done it this time, Manny?"

"You'll just damn well have to buy the book and find out." He sank down in a chair and said, "Henry!" making a long gesture with thumb and forefinger.

Henry, the perennial waiter of the Black Widowers' banquets, obliged at once and Rubin said nothing until about a quarter of the contents had been transferred into his esophagus. Then he said, "Where's everybody?" It was as though he had noticed for the first time that he and Gonzalo were the only two present.

"We're early," said Gonzalo, shrugging.

"I swear I didn't think I'd make it. You artists don't have deadlines, do you?"

"I wish the demand were great enough to make deadlines necessary," said Gonzalo grimly. "Sometimes we're driven, but we can be more independent than you word-people. They recognize the demands of creativity in art. It's not something you can hack out at the typewriter."

"Listen," began Rubin, then thought better of it and said, "I'll get you next time. Remind me to describe your cockamamie crayon scribbles to you."

Gonzalo laughed. "Manny, why don't you write a best seller and be done with it? If you're just going to write mystery novels to a limited audience you'll never get rich."

Rubin's chin lifted. "Think I can't write a best seller? I can do it any time I want to. I've analyzed it. In order to write a best seller you have to hit one of the only two markets big enough to support one. It's either the housewife or the college kids. Sex and scandal get the housewife; pseudo-intellect gets the college kids. I could do either if I wanted to but I am not interested in sex and scandal and I don't want to take the effort to lower my intellect so far as to make it pseudo."

"Try, Manny, try. You underestimate the full measure of the incapacity of your intellect. Besides," Gonzalo added hastily to stave off a retort, "don't tell me that it's only the pseudo-intellect that gets through to the college students."

"Sure!" said Rubin indignantly. "Do you know what goes big with the college crowd? *Chariots of the Gods?*, which is sheer nonsense. I'd call it science fiction except that it's not that good. Or *The Greening of America*, which was a fad book—one month they were all reading it because it's the 'in' thing to do, the next month it's out."

"What about Vonnegut's books? What about *Future Shock*, Manny? I heard you say you liked *Future Shock*."

"So-so," said Rubin. He closed his eyes and took another sip.

Gonzalo said, "Even Henry doesn't take you seriously. Look at him grinning."

Henry was setting the table. "Merely a smile of pleasure, Mr. Gonzalo," he said, and indeed his smooth and sixtyish face radiated exactly that emotion. "Mr. Rubin has recommended a number of books that have been college favorites and I have read them with pleasure usually. I suspect he likes more books than he will admit."

Rubin ignored Henry's remark and brought his weary eyes to bear on Gonzalo. "Besides, what do you mean, '*even* Henry'? He reads a hell of a lot more books than you do."

"Maybe, but he doesn't read *your* books."

"Henry!" cried Rubin.

Henry said, "I have bought and read several of Mr. Rubin's mysteries."

Gonzalo said, "And what do you think of them? Tell the truth. I'll protect you."

"I enjoy them. They are very good of their kind. Of course, I lack a sense of the dramatic and, once the dramatic is discounted, it is possible to see the solution—where the author allows it."

At that moment the others began to arrive and Henry was busied with the drinks.

It had been a very long time since the Black Widowers had had a foreigner as guest and Drake, who was host, basked in the glory of it and smiled quietly through the wreathed smoke from his eternal cigarette. Moreover, the guest was a Russian, a real Russian from the Soviet Union, and Geoffrey Avalon, who had studied Russian during World War II, had the chance to use what he could remember.

Avalon, standing tall and speaking with a severe and steady syllable-by-syllable stress, sounded as lawer-like as though he were addressing a Russian jury. The Russian, whose name was Grigori Deryashkin, seemed pleased and answered in slow, distinct phrases until Avalon ran down.

Deryashkin was a stocky man in a loose-fitting gray suit, a white shirt, and dark tie. He had blunt features, large teeth, an easy smile, and English that consisted of an adequate vocabulary, an uncertain grammar, and a marked but by no means unpleasant accent.

"Where'd you get him?" asked Thomas Trumbull of Drake in a low voice as Deryashkin turned away momentarily from

Avalon to take a large vodka on the rocks from Henry.

"He's a science writer," said Drake. "He came to visit the laboratory to get some details on our work on hormonal insecticides. We got to talking and it occurred to me that he might enjoy hobnobbing with some filthy capitalists."

That Deryashkin enjoyed the meal was certain. He ate with huge gusto, and Henry, having caught the spirit of hands across the sea—or perhaps to show off America at its most munificent—casually, and with the smooth unnoticeability that was his professional characteristic, brought him seconds of everything.

Roger Halsted watched that process wistfully but said nothing. Ordinarily, second helpings were frowned upon at the Black Widowers' banquets on the theory that a swinishly crammed stomach detracted from the brilliance of the postprandial conversation and Halsted, who taught mathematics at a junior high school and who often felt the need of caloric support in consequence, most definitely disagreed with that.

"From what part of the Soviet Union do you come, Mr. Deryashkin?" asked Trumbull.

"From Tula, hundred-ninety kilometers south of Moscow. You have heard of Tula?"

There was a moment of silence and then Avalon said magisterially, "It played a role, I believe, in the Hitlerian War."

"Yes, yes." Deryashkin seemed gratified. "In the late fall of 1941 the drive for Moscow reached out claws to the north and to the south. The advanced German forces reached Tula. In the cold and the snow we held them; they did not take Tula. They never took Tula. We called out the home guard then: boys, old men. I was sixteen years old and carried a rifle made in our own factory. We make best samovars in Russia, too; Tula is notable in war and peace. Later in the war, I was with artillery. I reached Leipzig, but not Berlin. —We were friends then, Soviet Union and America. May we stay friends." He lifted his glass.

There was a murmur of agreement and Deryashkin's good humor was further strengthened by the dessert. "What is this?" he asked, pointing with his fork, after his first mouthful.

"Pecan pie," said Drake.

"Very good. Very rich."

Henry had a second piece of pie on the table for Deryashkin almost as soon as the first had been devoured, and then, having noted Halsted's eyes following the progress of that piece, quietly placed a similar second helping before him as well. Halsted looked in either direction, found himself studiously ignored, and fell to cheerfully.

Trumbull leaned toward Drake and whispered, "Does your guest know the system of grilling?"

Drake whispered, "I tried to explain but I'm not sure he really got it. Anyway, let's not ask him the usual opener about how he justifies his existence. He may consider that an anti-Soviet remark."

Trumbull's tanned face crinkled into a silent snarl. Then he said, "Well, it's your baby. Get it started."

Henry was quietly filling the small brandy glasses when Drake coughed, stubbed out his cigarette, and tapped his water glass with his fork. "It's time," he said, "to deal with our guest from abroad, and I suggest that Manny, who has been suspiciously silent throughout the meal, undertake the—"

Deryashkin was leaning back in his chair, his jacket unbuttoned, his tie loosened. He said, "We come to the conversation now, and I suggest, with the permission of the company, that we talk about your great city of New York. I have been here for two weeks now, and I will say it is a city of the damned."

He smiled into the vacuum the remark had created and nodded his head jovially. "A city of the damned," he said again.

Trumbull said, "You're talking about Wall Street, I suppose—that nest of imperialist bloodsuckers?" (Drake kicked his shin.)

But Deryashkin shook his head and shrugged. "Wall Street? I haven't been there and it is of no interest. Considering condition of your dollar, I doubt Wall Street has much power these days. Besides, we are friends and I have no wish to speak phrases such as imperialist bloodsuckers. That is part of the newspaper cliché like 'dirty Commie rat.' Is that not so?"

"All right," said Rubin. "Let's not use ugly words. Let's just use nice words like city of the damned. Why is New York a city of the damned?"

"It is a city of terror! You have crime everywhere. You live in fear. You do not walk the streets. Your parks are power vacuums in which only hoodlums and hooligans can stroll. You cower behind locked doors."

Avalon said, "I suppose that New York shares the problems that beset all large and crowded cities these days, including, I am sure, the large cities of the Soviet Union. Still, these problems are not as bad as painted."

Deryashkin lifted both arms. "Do not misunderstand. You are my excellent hosts and I have no wish to offend. I recognize the conditions to be widespread, but in a city like New York, gorgeous in many ways, very advanced and wealthy in many places, it seems wrong, ironic, that there should be so much fear. Murders openly planned in the streets! Actual war of one segment of the population with another!"

Rubin broke in with his beard bristling combatively for the first time that evening. "I don't want to offend any more than you do, Comrade, but I think you've got a bad case of believing your own propaganda. There's crime, yes, but for the most part the city is peaceful and well off. Have *you* been mugged, sir? Have *you* been molested in any way?"

Deryashkin shook his head. "So far, not. I will be honest. So far I have been treated with all possible courtesy; not least, here. I thank you. For the most part, though, I have been in affluent sections. I have not been where your troubles are."

Rubin said, "Then how do you know there are troubles except for what you read and hear in unfriendly media?"

"Ah," said Deryashkin, "but I did venture into park— near the river. There I hear a murder planned. This is not what I read in any newspaper or what I am told by any enemy or ill-wisher of your country. It is the truth. I *hear* it."

Rubin, his glasses seeming to concentrate the fury in his eyes into an incandescent glare, pointed a somewhat trembling finger and said, "Look—"

But Avalon was on his feet and, from his better than six feet, he easily dominated the table. "Gentlemen," he said in his commanding baritone, "let's stop right here. I have a suggestion to make. Our guest, Tovarisch Deryashkin, seems to think he has heard murder planned openly in the streets. I confess I don't understand what he means by that, but I would suggest we invite him to tell us in detail what he heard and under what circumstances. After all, he could be right and it could be an interesting story."

Drake nodded his head vigorously. "I take host's privilege

and direct that Mr. Deryashkin tell us the story of the planned murder from the beginning and, Manny, you let him tell it."

Deryashkin said, "I will be glad to tell the story as accurately as I can, for what it is. There are not many details, but that it involves murder there can be no doubt. —Perhaps before I start, more brandy. —Thank you, my friend," he said amiably to Henry.

Deryashkin sipped at his brandy and said, "It happened late this morning. Zelykov and I—Zelykov is colleague, brilliant man in biology and genetics, held down a bit in day of Lysenko, but excellent. He does not speak English well and I act to interpret for him. Zelykov and I were at the Biology Department at Columbia University for a couple of hours this morning.

"When we left, we were not certain how to follow up the leads we had received. We were not entirely sure about significance of what we have heard or what we should next do. We went down toward the river—Hudson River, which is very polluted, I understand—and we looked across to other shore, which is pretty from distance, but commercialized, I am told, and at highway, which is in between, and not so pretty.

"It was a nice day. Quite cold, but cold days do not frighten a Russian from Tula. We sit and talk in Russian and it is a pleasure to do so. Zelykov has only a few words of English and even for me it is a strain to talk English constantly. It is a great language; I would not be offensive; the language of Shakespeare and your own Mark Twain and Jack London, and I enjoy it. But"—he cocked his head to one side and thrust out his lips—"it is a strain, and it is pleasant to speak one's native language and be fluent.

"But I mention that we are speaking Russian only because it plays a part in the story. You see, two young men, who don't look like hooligans, approach. They have short hair, they are shaved, they look well to do. I am not really paying attention at first. I am aware they are coming but I am interested in what I am saying and I am not really clear that they are going to speak to us till they do. I don't remember exactly what they say, but it was like, 'Do you mind if we sit?'

"Naturally, I don't mind. There is two halves to the bench,

with a metal dividing in the middle. On each half is more than enough for two people. Zelykov and I, we are in one half; these two young men can be in the other half. I say, 'Be our guests. You are welcome. Sit down and relax.' Something like that.

"But—and this is the important thing—I have just been speaking Russian to Zelykov, so when the young men asked the question I answered, without thinking, still in Russian. I would have corrected this, but they sat down at once and did not pay more attention to us, so I thought, Well, it is done and what more is necessary to say?

"You see, however"—and here he paused, and tapped his nose with his forefinger—"the significance of this?"

Rubin said at once, "No. I don't."

"They thought we were foreigners."

"And so you are," said Rubin.

"Ah," said Deryashkin, "but foreigners who could not speak English."

Trumbull interposed, "And how does that matter, Mr. Deryashkin?"

Deryashkin transferred his forefinger to the palm of his left hand, marking each emphasis. "*If* they think we speak English, they take another bench; but *since* they say to themselves, 'Aha, we have here foreigners who will not understand us,' they sit right down next to us and talk freely, and of course I listen. I talk to Zelykov, but I listen, too."

Halsted, staring at his empty brandy glass, said, "Why did you listen? Did they seem suspicious?"

"To me, yes," said Deryashkin. "They are students, since we are near Columbia University and they carry books. I know, of course, that the American student body is very activist and, in some cases, destructive."

Rubin interrupted hotly, "Three years ago. Not now."

"Of course," said Deryashkin genially, "you defend. I do not criticize. I understand that many students were motivated by hostility to war, and this I understand. Any humane idealist would be in favor of peace. Yet it is undeniable that under cover of idealism there are undesirable elements too. Besides, we are sitting in a park. It is empty and there is not someone we can count on for help if the students are armed and hostile. Also, it is well known that in New York bystanders do not interfere when a criminal action is taking place.

"I do not actually think we are in immediate danger, but it would be foolhardy to let attention wander. I keep aware of the hooligans and, without looking at them, I listen a bit."

Rubin said, "Why do you call them hooligans? They haven't done anything so far except to take a seat; and they asked permission politely before they did that much."

"The politeness," said Deryashkin, "cannot be given too much credit. That was only to check what it was we were. And I call them hooligans because that is what they were. What they were talking about was a plan for murder."

There was a distinct air of incredulity about the table as Deryashkin paused at this point for effect. Finally Avalon asked, "Are you sure of that, Mr. Deryashkin?"

"Quite sure. They used the word 'murder.' They used it several times. I did not hear all that they said clearly. They were talking in low voices—a natural precaution. I was also talking, as was Zelykov."

Rubin leaned back in his chair. "So you caught only scraps of conversation. You can't be sure there was anything wrong with it."

"I heard the word 'murder,' Mr. Rubin," said Deryashkin seriously. "I heard it several times. You know English better than I do, I'm sure, but you tell me if there is any word in the English language that is like 'murder.' If they say 'mother' I can hear the difference. I can pronounce the English *th* and I can hear it, so I do not put a *d* where it does not belong. I hear the initial letter *m* clearly, so it is not —uh—girder, let us say, which I think is word for steel beams in building construction. I hear 'murder.' What else does one talk about but killing if one speaks of murder?"

Gonzalo said, "They could be using the word in a colloquial expression. If they were discussing an upcoming football game with another college, they could say, 'We'll murder the bums!' "

Deryashkin said, "They are talking too seriously for that, my dear sir. It is not a football game they discuss. It is low tones, serious, very serious, and there is also to be taken into account what else they said."

"Well, what else did they say?" asked Trumbull.

"There was something about 'lying in the shadows,' which is something you don't do for football games. They would lie in the shadows waiting to trap someone, catch them by surprise, *murder* them."

"Did they say all that?" demanded Rubin.

"No, no. This is my interpretation." Deryashkin frowned. "They also said something about tying them up. 'Tie them up in the dark.' That they did say. I remember distinctly. There was also talk about a signal."

"What signal?" asked Avalon.

"A ring of a bell. That I heard too. It is, I think, a well-organized conspiracy. They will lie in wait at night; there will be a signal when the right person is there or when the coast is clear; one ring of some kind; then they tie up the victim or victims and murder them.

"There is no question about this in my mind," Deryashkin continued. "One hooligan is doing all the talking at first—as though he is reciting the plan—and when he is finished the other one says, 'Right! You have it perfect! We'll go over some of the other things, but you'll make it.' And he warned him against talking."

"Against talking?" said Rubin.

"Several times it was mentioned. About talking. By both of them. Very seriously."

Rubin said, "You mean they sat down next to two strangers, talked their heads off, and warned each other against talking?"

Deryashkin said rather tightly, "I said several times they assumed we could not speak English."

Trumbull said, "Look, Manny, let's not make a fight out of this. Maybe Mr. Deryashkin has something here. There are radical splinter groups among the student bodies of America. There have been buildings blown up."

"There have been no cold-blooded murders planned and carried out," said Rubin.

"Always a first time for everything," said Avalon, frowning, and clearly concerned.

Trumbull said, "Well, Mr. Deryashkin, did you do anything?"

"Do anything?" Deryashkin looked puzzled. "To hold them, you mean? It was not so easy. I am listening, trying to understand, learn as much as possible, without showing that I am listening. If they see I am listening, they will see we understand and will stop talking. We might even be in danger. So I don't look at them while I am listening and suddenly it is silent and they are walking away."

"You didn't go after them?" asked Drake.

Deryashkin shook his head emphatically. "If they are hooligans, they are armed. It is well known that handguns are sold freely in America and that it is very common for young people to carry arms. They are young and look strong, and I am myself nearly fifty and am a man of peace. A war veteran, but a man of peace. As for Zelykov, he has a bad chest and on him I cannot count. If the hooligans leave, let them leave."

"Did you report anything to the police?" asked Halsted.

"I? Of what use? What evidence have I? What can I say? I see right now that you are all skeptical and you are intelligent men who know my position and see that I am a man of responsibility, a scientific man. Yet you are skeptical. What would the policeman know but that I have heard these scattered things? And I am a Soviet citizen. Is it possible a policeman would accept the word of a Russian foreigner against American young men? And I would not wish to be involved in what could become a large scandal that would affect my career and perhaps embarrass my country. So I say nothing. I do nothing. Can you suggest anything to say or do?"

"Well, no," said Avalon deliberately, "but if we wake up one of these mornings and discover that murder has been done and that some group of college students are responsible, we would not exactly feel well. *I* would not."

"Nor I," said Trumbull, "but I see Mr. Deryashkin's position. On the basis of what he's told us, he would certainly have a hard time interesting a hard-boiled police sergeant. —Unless we had some hard evidence. Have you any idea what the students looked like, Mr. Deryashkin?"

"Not at all. I saw them for a moment as they approached. After that I did not look at them, merely listened. When they left, it was only their backs I saw. I noticed nothing unusual."

"You could not possibly identify them, then?"

"Under no conditions. I have thought about it. I said to myself, if the school authorities were to show me pictures of every young man who attended Columbia University, I could not tell which were the two who had sat on the bench."

"Did you notice their clothes?" asked Gonzalo.

"It was cold, so they wear coats," said Deryashkin. "Gray coats, I think. I did not really notice."

"Gray coats," muttered Rubin.

"Did they wear anything unusual?" said Gonzalo. "Funny hats, mittens, checked scarves?"

"Are you going to identify them that way?" said Rubin. "You mean you're thinking of going to the police and they'll say, 'That must be Mittens Garfinkel, well-known hooligan. Always wears mittens.'"

Gonzalo said patiently, "Any information—"

But Deryashkin interposed. "Please, gentlemen, I noticed nothing of that kind. I cannot give any help in clothing."

Halsted said, "How about your companion, Mr.—uh—"

"Zelykov."

"How about Mr. Zelykov?" Halsted's soft voice seemed thoughtful. "If he noticed anything—"

"No, he never looked at them. He was discussing genes and DNA. He didn't even know they were there."

Halsted placed his palm delicately on his high forehead and brushed back at non-existent hair. He said, "You can't be sure, can you? Is there any way you can call him up right now and ask?"

"It would be useless," protested Deryashkin. "I know. Believe me. When they left, I said to him in Russian, 'Can you imagine the criminality of those hooligans?' and he said, 'What hooligans?' I said, 'Those that are leaving.' And he shrugged and did not look but kept on talking. It was getting cold even for us and we left. He knows nothing."

"That's very frustrating," said Halsted.

"Hell," said Rubin. "There's nothing to this at all. I don't believe it."

"You mean I am lying?" said Deryashkin, frowning.

"No," said Rubin. "I mean it's a misinterpretation. What you heard can't involve murder."

Deryashkin, still frowning, said, "Do all you gentlemen believe that what I heard can't involve murder?"

Avalon, keeping his eyes on the tablecloth in some embarrassment, said, "I can't really say I am certain that a murder is being planned, but I think we ought to *act* as though a murder is being planned. If we are wrong we have done nothing worse than make fools of ourselves. If we are right we might save one or more lives. Do the rest of you agree with that?"

There was an uncertain murmur that seemed to be agreement, but Rubin clenched a hostile fist and said, "What the devil do you mean by acting, Jeff? What are we supposed to do?"

Avalon said, "We might go to the police. It might be difficult for Mr. Deryashkin to get a hearing; but if one of us—or more—back him—"

"How would that help?" said Rubin sardonically. "If there were fifty million of us introducing our friend here, the evidence would still boil down to the uncertain memory of one man who recalls a few scraps of conversation and who cannot identify the speakers."

"In that," said Deryashkin, "Mr. Rubin is right. Besides, I will not take part. It is *your* city, *your* country, and I will not interfere. Nothing could be done in any case, and when the murder takes place it will be too bad, but it cannot be helped."

"Nothing will happen," said Rubin.

"No?" said Deryashkin. "How then can you explain what I heard? If all else is ignored, there is yet the word 'murder.' I heard it clearly more than once and it is a word that cannot be mistaken. In the English language there is nothing like 'murder' that I could have taken for that word. And surely if people speak of murder there must be murder in the wind. You are, I think, the only one here, Mr. Rubin, who doubts it."

There was a soft cough from one end of the table. Henry, who had cleared away the coffee cups, said apologetically, "Not the only one, Mr. Deryashkin. I doubt it too. In fact, I am quite certain that what the young men said was harmless."

Deryashkin turned in his seat. He looked surprised. He said, "Comrade Waiter, if you—"

Trumbull said hastily, "Henry is a member of the Black Widowers. Henry, how can you be certain?"

Henry said, "If Mr. Deryashkin will kindly consent to answer a few questions, I think we will all be certain."

Deryashkin nodded his head vigorously and spread out his arms. "Ask! I will answer."

Henry said, "Mr. Deryashkin, I believe you said that the park was empty and that no one was in sight to help if the young men proved violent. Did I understand correctly? Were the other benches in the park area unoccupied?"

"Those we could see were empty," said Deryashkin readily. "Today was not a pleasant day for park-sitting."

"Then why do you suppose the young men came to your bench, the only one which was occupied?"

Deryashkin laughed briefly and said, "No mystery, my friend. The day was cold and our bench was the only one in the sun. It was why we picked it ourselves."

"But if they were going to discuss murder, surely they would prefer a bench to themselves even if it meant being a little on the cold side."

"You forget. They thought we were foreigners who could not speak or understand English. The bench *was* empty in a way."

Henry shook his head. "That does not make sense. They approached you and asked to sit down before you spoke Russian. They had not reason to think you couldn't understand English at the time they approached."

Deryashkin said testily, "They might have heard us talking Russian from a distance and checked it out."

"And sat down almost at once, as soon as you spoke Russian? They didn't test you any further? They didn't ask if you understood English? With murder in the wind, they were satisfied with a small Russian comment from you, guessed they would be safe, and sat down to discuss openly a hideous crime? Surely if they were conspirators they would have stayed as far away from you as possible in the first place, and even if they were irresistibly attracted to the sun, they would have put you through a much more cautious testing process. The logical interpretation of the events, at least to me, would seem to be that whatever they had to discuss was quite harmless, that they wanted a bench in the sun, and that they did not at all care whether they were overheard or not."

"And the word 'murder'?" said Deryashkin with heavy sarcasm. "That, too, then, must be quite, quite harmless."

"It is the use of the word 'murder,'" said Henry, "that convinces me that the entire conversation was harmless, sir. It seems to me, surely, that no one would use the word 'murder' in connection with their own activities; only with those of others. If you yourself are going to murder, you speak of it as 'rubbing him out,' 'taking him for a ride,' 'getting rid of him,' or if you'll excuse the expression, sir, 'liquidating him.' You might even say 'killing him' but surely no one would casually speak of murdering someone. It is too ugly a word; it demands euphemism."

"Yet they said it, Mr. Waiter," said Deryashkin. "Talk as you will, you won't argue me out of having heard that word clearly more than once."

"They did not say what you heard, perhaps."

"And how is that possible, my friend? Eh?"

Henry said, "Even with the best will in the world and with the most rigid honesty, Mr. Deryashkin, one can make mistakes in interpreting what one hears, especially—please excuse me—if the language is not native to you. For instance, you say the expression 'tie them up' was used. Might it not be said that you heard them say 'bind them' and that you interpreted that as 'tie them up'?"

Deryashkin seemed taken aback. He thought about it for a while. He said, "I cannot swear I did not hear them say 'bind them.' Since you mention it, I begin to imagine perhaps I heard it. But does it matter? 'Bind them' means 'tie them up.'"

"The meaning is approximately the same, but the words are different. And if it is 'bind them' I know what it is you must have heard if all the scraps you report are put together. Mr. Rubin knows too—better than I do, I believe—though he may not quite realize it at the moment. I think it is his sub-realization that has made him so resistant to the notion of Mr. Deryashkin having overheard an actual conspiracy."

Rubin sat up in his seat, blinking. "What do I know, Henry?"

Deryashkin said, "You have to explain 'murder.' Nothing counts if you do not explain 'murder.'"

Henry said, "I am not a linguist myself, Mr. Deryashkin, but I once heard it said that it is the vowels of a foreign language that are hardest to learn and that what is called a 'foreign accent' is mostly a mispronunciation of vowels. You might therefore not be able to distinguish a difference in vowels and, even with all the consonants unchanged, what you heard as 'murder' might really have been 'Mordor.'"

And at that Rubin threw up both hands and said, "Oh, my God."

"Exactly, sir," said Henry. "Early in the evening, I recall a discussion between yourself and Mr. Gonzalo concerning books that are popular with college students. One of them, surely, was *The Lord of the Rings* trilogy by J. R. R. Tolkien."

"Tolkien" said Deryashkin, mystified, and stumbling over the word.

Henry said, "He was an English writer of fantasy who died very recently. I am quite sure that college students form Tolkien societies. That would account for the references to 'talking' that you mentioned, Dr. Deryashkin, as part of the conversation of the young men. They were not exhorting each other to keep quiet but were speaking of the Tolkien Society that I imagine one of them wished to join.

"In order to join, it might be that the candidate must first memorize the short poem that is the theme of the entire trilogy. If the young man were indeed reciting the poem, which twice mentions 'the Land of Mordor,' then I believe every scrap of conversation you heard could be accounted for. Mr. Rubin recommended the trilogy to me once and I enjoyed it immensely. I cannot remember the poem word for word, but I suspect Mr. Rubin does."

"Do I!" said Rubin explosively. He rose to his feet, placed one hand on his chest, threw the other up to the ceiling, and declaimed grandiloquently:

Three Rings for the Elven-kings under the sky,
  Seven for the Dwarf-lords in their halls of stone,
Nine for Mortal Men doomed to die,
  One for the Dark Lord on his dark throne
In the Land of Mordor where the Shadows lie.
  One Ring to rule them all, One Ring to find them,
  One Ring to bring them all and in the darkness bind them
In the Land of Mordor where the Shadows lie.

Henry nodded. "You see that it includes not only the word Mr. Deryashkin interpreted as 'murder' but also reference to the 'one ring,' to 'lying in the shadows,' to 'tying them up in the dark.'"

There was silence for a while.

Then Deryashkin said, "You are right. Now that I hear the poem, I must admit that this is what I heard this morning. Quite right. ——But how could you know, waiter?"

Henry smiled. "I lack a sense of the dramatic, Mr. Deryashkin. You felt New York to be a jungle, so you heard jungle sounds. For myself, I prefer to suppose college students would sound like college students."

5 *Afterword*

J. R. R. Tolkien died on September 2, 1973. I was in Toronto at the time attending the 31st World Science Fiction Convention and was deeply moved at the news. —And yet on the very day I learned of his death, I won the Hugo for my science fiction novel *The Gods Themselves* and I couldn't help being happy.

Having read Tolkien's *The Lord of the Rings* three times at the time of his death (and I've read it a fourth time since) and having enjoyed it more each time, I felt that the only way I could make up for having been happy on that sad day was to write a story in memory of him. So I wrote "Nothing Like Murder."

Ellery Queen's Mystery Magazine decided, however, not to use it. The feeling was that the readers would not be well enough acquainted with Tolkien to be able to appreciate the story. So, after some hesitation, I sent it to the *Magazine of Fantasy and Science Fiction*, for which I write a monthly science column.

Rather to my surprise (for the story is neither fantasy nor science fiction), Ed Ferman, the editor of F & SF, accepted it, and it appeared in the October 1974 issue of the magazine. I then waited for angry letters from science fiction fans, but all I got was a number of very pleased comments from readers who were delighted that I was an admirer of Tolkien. So it all worked out well.

6

No Smoking

James Drake was by no means the only smoker among the small membership of the Black Widowers, but he certainly made the greatest single contribution to the pall that commonly hovered over the monthly banquets of that august body.

It was perhaps for that reason that the dour-faced Thomas Trumbull, arriving toward the end of the cocktail hour, as he usually did, and having un-parched himself with a scotch and soda that had been handed him deftly and without delay by the invaluable Henry, hunched his lapel ostentatiously in Drake's direction.

"What's that?" asked Drake, squinting through the smoke of his cigarette.

"Why the hell don't you read it and find out?" said Trumbull with somewhat more than his usual savagery. "If the nicotine has left you any eyesight with which to read, that is."

Trumbull's lapel bore a button which read: "Thank you for not smoking."

Drake, having peered at it thoughtfully, puffed a mouthful of smoke in its direction and said, "You're welcome. Always glad to oblige."

Trumbull said, "By God, I'm a member of the most oppressed minority in the world. The non-smoker has no rights any smoker feels bound to observe. Good Lord, don't I have any claim to a measure of reasonably clean and unpolluted air?"

Emmanuel Rubin drifted toward them. His sparse and straggly beard lifted upward—a sure sign that he was about to pontificate—and his eyes blinked owlishly behind the magnifying thickness of his glasses.

"If you live in New York," he said, "you inhale, in automobile exhaust, the equivalent of two packs of cigarettes a day, so what's the difference?" And he ostentatiously lit a cigarette.

"All the more reason why I don't want any more on top of the exhaust I breathe," said Trumbull, scowling.

"Don't tell me," said Drake in his softly hoarse voice, "that you believe this hogwash that—"

"Yes, I believe it," snapped Trumbull. "If you want to risk heart attacks, emphysema, and lung cancer, that's *your* business, and I wish you joy of any or all of them. I wouldn't interfere with your pleasure for the world if you want to do it off in a closed room somewhere. But why the hell should *I* breathe your foul smoke and run the risk of disease so that you might have your perverse pleasure—"

He broke off since Drake, who was visibly attempting not to, had one of his not too infrequent coughing spells.

Trumbull looked pleased. "Happy coughing," he said. "When's the last time you could breathe freely?"

Roger Halsted, who occasionally smoked but was not doing so at the moment, said, with the mild stutter with which he was sometimes afflicted, "Why are you so upset, Tom? What makes this meeting different from any other?"

"Nothing at all, but I've had enough. I've overflowed. Every time I come home after an evening with you smoldering garbage piles, my clothes smell and I have to burn them."

"What I think," said Drake, "is that he found that button when he was reaching into a subway trash can for a newspaper, and it's made a missionary out of him."

"I feel like a missionary," said Trumbull. "I would like to push a law through Congress that would place tobacco in the same category with marijuana and hashish. By God, the evidence for the physiological damage caused by tobacco is infinitely stronger than for any damage caused by marijuana."

Geoffrey Avalon, always sensitive to any reference to his own profession of law, stared down austerely from his seventy-four inches and said, "I would not advise another law legislating morality. Some of the finest men in history have tried to reform the world by passing laws against bad habits, and there is no record of any of them working. I'm old enough to remember Prohibition in this country."

Trumbull said, "You smoke a pipe. You're an interested party. Am I the only non-smoker here?"

"I don't smoke," said Mario Gonzalo, raising his voice. He was in another corner, talking to the guest.

"All right then," said Trumbull. "Come here, Mario. You're host for the evening. Set up a no-smoking rule."

"Out of order. Out of order," said Rubin heatedly. "The host can only legislate on Black Widower procedures, not on private morality. He can't order the members to take off their clothes, or to stand on their heads and whistle 'Dixie,' or to stop smoking—or to start smoking, for that matter."

"It could be done," said Halsted gently, "if the host proposed the measure and put it to a vote, but the smokers are four to two against you, Tom."

"Wait awhile," said Trumbull. "There's Henry. He's a member. What do you say, Henry?"

Henry, the perennial waiter at the Black Widowers' banquets, had nearly completed setting the table. Now he lifted his smooth and unwrinkled face which, as always, belied the fact that he was a sexagenarian, and said, "I do not myself smoke and would welcome a ban on smoking, but I do not demand it."

"Even if he did," said Rubin, "it would be four to three, *still* a majority on the side of vice."

"How about the guest?" said Trumbull doggedly, "Mr.—"

"Hilary Evans," said Avalon severely. He made it his business never to forget a guest's name, at least for the evening of the dinner.

Trumbull said, "Where do you stand, Mr. Evans?"

Hilary Evans was short and tubby, with cheeks that were plump, pink, and smooth. His mouth was small and his eyes were quick-moving behind the lightly tinted lenses of his metal-rimmed spectacles. His hair, surprisingly dark in view of the lightness of his complexion, lay back smoothly. He might have been in his middle forties.

He said in a tenor voice, "I smoke occasionally and do

not often mind if others do, but I have current reasons for sympathy with you, sir. Smoking has been the occasion for misery for me."

Trumbull, one eye nearly closing as he lifted the side of his mouth in a snarl, looked as though he would have pressed the matter further, but Rubin said at once, "Five to three. Issue settled," and Henry imperturbably announced that the dinner was served.

Trumbull scrambled to get the seat next to Gonzalo, the other non-smoker, and asked him in an undertone, "Who is this Evans?"

Gonzalo said, "He's personnel manager for a firm in whose advertising campaign I was involved. He interviewed me and, even though he's rather a queer guy, we got along. I thought he might be interesting."

"I hope so," said Trumbull, "though I don't think much of a guy who votes with the enemy even though he sympathizes with me."

Gonzalo said, "You don't know the details."

"I intend to find out," said Trumbull grimly.

The dinner conversation had trouble getting off the subject of tobacco. Avalon, who had reduced his second drink to the usual half-way mark and had then left it severely alone, remarked that cigarette smoking was the only new vice introduced by modern man.

"How about LSD and the mind-expanding drugs?" said Gonzalo at once and Avalon, having thought about that for a moment, owned defeat.

Rubin loudly demanded the definition of "vice." He said, "Anything you don't like is a vice. If you approve of it, it isn't. Many a temperance crusader was addicted to food as viciously as anyone could be addicted to drink." And Rubin, who was thin, pushed his soup away half eaten, with a look of ostentatious virtue.

Halsted, who was not thin, muttered, "Not many calories in clear turtle soup."

Trumbull said, "Listen, I don't care what you do, or whether it's a vice or a virtue, as long as you keep it to yourself and to those you practice it with. If you drink whisky and I don't want to, no alcohol gets into *my* blood; if you want to pick up a dame, there's no risk of *my* picking up anything that goes along with that. But when you drag at a cigarette *I* smell the smoke, *I* get it in my lungs, *I* run the risk of cancer."

"Quite right," said Evans suddenly. "Filthy habit," and he glanced quickly at Drake, who was sitting next to him and who shifted his cigarette to his other hand, the one farther from Evans.

Avalon cleared his throat. "Gentlemen, there are no strictures against tobacco that can be considered new. Over three and a half centuries ago James I of England wrote a book called *Counterblaste to Tobacco* in which he rehearsed every point that Tom could make, allowing for gains in scientific knowledge since then—"

"And you know what kind of a person James I was?" said Rubin with a snort. "Filthy and stupid."

"Not really stupid," said Avalon. "Henry IV of France called him the 'wisest fool in Christendom' but that merely indicated he lacked judgment rather than learning."

"I call that stupid," said Rubin.

"If lacking judgment were the criterion, few of us would escape," said Avalon.

"You'd be first in line, Manny," said Trumbull, and then allowed his expression to soften as Henry placed a generous sliver of pecan pie, laden with ice cream, before him. Trumbull approved of pecan pie as he approved of few things.

Over the last of the coffee Gonzalo said, "Gentlemen! Gentlemen! I think it's time to leave the general for the specific. Our guest is now the subject and, Tom, are you willing—"

Trumbull said with alacrity, "I am not only willing to take over the grilling, I insist on it. Let's have quiet. —Henry, you can bring the brandy at your convenience. —Mr. Evans, it is the custom of this organization to ask a guest, as our first question, how he justifies his existence. In this case, I will tell you how you may justify your existence as far as I am concerned. Please tell me why it is you have current reason to sympathize with my view on smoking, though you smoke yourself on occasions. Have you been cheated by the tobacco industry?"

Evans shook his head and smiled briefly. "It has nothing to do with the tobacco industry. I wish it had. I work for an investment firm and my reasons have to do with my activities there."

"In what way?"

Evans looked rather gloomy. "That," he said, "would be difficult to explain adequately. I might say that a matter of smoking has rather spoiled a hitherto perfect record of mine in the Sherlock Holmes way. But," and here he sighed, "I'd rather not talk about it, to be perfectly honest."

"Sherlock Holmes?" said Gonzalo delightedly. "Henry, if—"

Trumbull waved an imperious arm. "Shut *up*, Mario. I think, Mr. Evans, that the price of the meal is an honest attempt on your part to explain exactly what you mean. We have time and we will listen."

Evans sighed again. He adjusted his glasses and said, "Mr. Gonzalo, in inviting me, you told me I would be grilled. I must confess I did not think the sore spot would be probed at the very start."

Trumbull said, "Sir, I merely followed up your own remark. You have no one to blame but yourself for making it. Please do not spoil our game."

Gonzalo said, "It's all right, Mr. Evans. I told you that nothing said in this room is ever repeated outside."

"Never!" said Trumbull emphatically.

Evans said, "Not that there is anything in the least criminal or unethical about what happened to me. It is merely that I will be forced to—deflate myself. I imagine I could easily be made fun of if it were to become general knowledge that—"

"It will not get about," said Trumbull and, anticipating the other's next remark out of weary experience, went on, "Nor will our esteemed waiter be a problem to you. Of us all, Henry is the most trustworthy."

Evans cleared his throat and held his brandy glass between thumb and forefinger. "The point is that I am personnel manager. It is my job to help decide on whether this one or that one is to be hired, fired, promoted, or left behind. Sometimes I turn out to be the court of last resort, for I have proven myself to be expert at the job. —You see, since I have been assured of the confidentiality of what I say, I can afford to praise myself."

"Tell the truth even if it be self-praise," said Trumbull. "In what way have you proved yourself to be expert?"

"In hiring a man to a sensitive position," said Evans, "and many of our positions are extremely sensitive since we routinely handle very large sums of money, we, of course, rely on all sorts of reference data which the applicant, whether coming from outside or facing promotion from inside, may be unaware of. We know much about his background, his character, his personality, his experience.

"Yet that, you see, if often not enough. To know that a person has done well in a certain position is no certain augury that he will do well in another more responsible position, or one that is merely different. To know that he has done well in the past does not tell us what strains he is under that might cause him to do ill in the future. We may not know to what extent he dissimulates. The human mind is a mystery, gentlemen.

"It may happen, then, that on certain occasions there is left room for doubt, despite all the information we have, and it is then that the judgment is left up to me. For many years my judgments have been justified by subsequent experience with those I have chosen for one position or another, and in many cases by indirect experience with those I have turned away. At least this has been so until—"

Evans removed his glasses and rubbed his eyes as though aware that an inner sight had failed him. "My superiors are kind enough to say that one mistake in twenty-three years is excusable, but it doesn't help. I shall not be trusted in future as I have been before. And rightly so, for I acted too soon, and on the basis of a prejudice."

Gonzalo, who was putting the final touches on the sketch of the guest, and making him look preternaturally prim with a mouth pursed to a dot, said, "Against whom or what were you prejudiced?"

Rubin said, "Artists, I hope."

Trumbull cried out, "Let the man *talk*. —The prejudice had something to do with smoking?"

Evans replaced his glasses carefully and fixed his gaze on Trumbull. "I have a system which is impossible to describe in words, for it is based partly on intuition and partly on experience. —I am a close observer of the minutiae of human behavior. I mean the small things. I select something highly characteristic of a particular person, out of some instinctive feeling I appear to have.

"It might be smoking, for instance. If so, I note how he handles the cigarette; how he fiddles with it; the manner in which he puffs; the interval between puffs; how far down he smokes the stub; how he puts it out. There is infinite complexity in the interaction between a person and his cigarette—or anything else, his tie clasp, his fingers, the table before him. I have studied the complexity of small behavior all my adult life, first out of curiosity and amusement and, soon enough, out of serious intent."

Drake smiled narrowly and said, "You mean those little things tell you something about the people you interview?"

"Yes, they do," said Evans emphatically.

"All right. That's where the Sherlock Holmes angle comes in. And what can you tell us about ourselves, then?"

Evans shook his head. "I have been paying little professional attention to any of you. Even if I had, the conditions here are not proper for my purposes and I am without the ancillary knowledge that more standardized investigations would have placed on my desk. I can say very little about you."

Trumbull said, "This isn't a parlor game anyway, Jim. Mr. Evans can tell you're a tobacco addict who flips ashes into his soup—"

Evans looked surprised and said hastily, "As a matter of fact, Dr. Drake *did* get some ashes in his soup—"

"And I noticed it too," said Trumbull. "What are the proper conditions for you to study your victim?"

"The conditions I have standardized over the years. The person to be interviewed enters my office alone. He sits in a certain chair under a certain light. He is under a certain tension I do nothing to relieve. I take some time to choose what it is I will observe in detail, and then we start."

"What if you don't find anything you can observe? What if he's a complete blank?" asked Gonzalo.

"That never happens. Something always shows up."

Gonzalo said, "Did something show up when you interviewed me?"

Evans shook his head. "I never discuss that sort of thing with the individuals involved, but I can tell you this. There was a mirror in the room."

Gonzalo bore up under the general laughter and said, "A handsome man has his problems."

Trumbull said, "Someone must have told you that. —Mr. Evans, could you get to the crux of your story: your embarrassment."

Evans nodded and looked unhappy. He turned slightly and

said to Henry, "I wonder if I might have another cup of coffee."

"Certainly, sir," said Henry.

Evans sipped at it and said thoughtfully, "The trouble is, you see, that I have watched smoking so meticulously on so many occasions that I have developed a dislike for smokers; a prejudice, if you will; even though I smoke myself on occasion. It is not nearly as strong as yours, Mr. Trumbull, but on occasion it explodes and it did so to my own hurt on one occasion.

"The story concerns two men who had worked in a branch office of ours; we can call them—uh, Williams and Adams."

Avalon cleared his throat and said, "If I were you, Mr. Evans, I would use their real names. In the course of telling the story, you are very likely to do so anyway. Remember that you speak here in confidence."

Evans said, "I will attempt the substitution in any case. The two men were quite different in appearance. Williams was a large, bulky man with something of a stoop and with a slow way of talking. Adams was smaller, straighter, and could be very eloquent indeed.

"Both were of an age, both in their early thirties; both were equally competent, it appeared, and had fulfilled their jobs with equal satisfaction; both seemed to be qualified to fill a key opening that had become available in the home office. Both were bachelors, both rather withdrawn. Both led quiet lives and did not seem to show elements of instability in their socializing—"

Halsted interrupted. "What does that mean? Instability?"

Evans said, "Neither gambled to a dangerous extent. Neither exhibited sexual or personal habits so at variance with their social surroundings as to make them unduly conspicuous. Neither exhibited strong likes or dislikes that might twist them into unexpected actions. They had come to be friendly in a mild sort of way while working in the same office, but it was symptomatic of the lack of intensity of emotion in both men that, although it was the closest friendship either had, as far as we knew, it was merely a casual relationship."

Rubin, leaning back in his chair, said, "Well, that churns up my writer's soul. Here we have two mild buddies, going down life's pathway in parallel paths, both quiet milksops— and now they find that they are competing for the same job, a job with more money and more prestige, and suddenly the lambs become lions and turn on each other—"

"Nothing of the kind," said Evans impatiently. "There was competition between the two, of course. That couldn't be helped. But neither before nor after was there any sign that this rivalry would find a release in violence.

"Both had taken advantage of the company's policy of encouraging further education and had been involved in courses in computer technology which we supervised. Both had done very well. It was hard to choose between them. All the data we had indicated, rather surprisingly, that Williams —slow, bumbling Williams—was actually a trifle the more intelligent of the two. Yet there was hesitation; he somehow didn't *seem* more intelligent than the quick and articulate Adams. So they left it up to me, with their usual confidence in my methods—"

Trumbull said, "Do you mean to tell us that your company *knew* you judged men by how they fiddled with paper clips and so on?"

"They knew this," said Evans a little defensively, "but they also knew that my recommendations were invariably proven accurate in the aftermath. What more could they ask?"

He finished his coffee and went on. "I saw Williams first, since I rather had the suspicion that he might be the man. I would not turn down the better-qualified man simply because he was slow-spoken. I suppose," and he sighed, "everything would have been entirely different if I had seen Adams first, but we can't adjust past circumstances to suit our convenience, can we?

"Williams seemed distinctly nervous, but that was certainly not unusual. I asked some routine questions while I studied his behavior. I noticed that his right forefinger moved on the desk as though it were writing words, but that stopped when he caught me looking at his hand; I should have been more careful there. In fact I had not really settled on what I was to study, when he reached for the cigarettes and matches."

"What cigarettes?" asked Rubin.

"I keep an unopened pack of cigarettes on the desk, together with a matchbook, some paper clips, a ball-point pen, and other small objects within easy reach of the person being interviewed. There is a great tendency to handle them and that can be useful to me. The pack of cigarettes is often played with, for instance, but it is rarely opened.

"Williams, however, opened the pack and that caught me rather by surprise, I must confess. His dossier had not mentioned him to be a heavy smoker, and for someone to help himself to the interviewer's cigarettes without asking permission would require a strong addiction."

Evans closed his eyes as though he were reproducing the scene upon the inner surface of his eyelids and said, "I can see it now. I became aware of an incongruity in the proceedings when he placed a cigarette between his lips with an attempt at simulating self-possession that utterly failed. It was then that I began to watch, since the incompatibility of the arrogance that led him to take a cigarette without permission and the timorousness with which he handled the cigarette caught my attention.

"His lips were dry, so that he had to remove the cigarette briefly, and wet his lips with his tongue. He then put it back between his lips and held it there as though he were afraid it would fall out. He seemed more and more nervous and I was now watching nothing else, only his hand and his cigarette. I was sure they would tell me all I wanted to know. I heard him scratch a match to life and, still holding onto the cigarette, he lit it with the match in his left hand.

"He seemed to hesitate, taking one or two shallow puffs while I watched and then, as though somehow aware I was not impressed by his performance, he inhaled deeply, and instantly went into a prolonged and apparently dangerous fit of coughing. —It turned out that he didn't smoke."

Evans opened his eyes. "That came out at once, of course. Apparently, he felt that by smoking he would impress me as a suave and competent fellow. He knew that he had a bumbling appearance and wanted to counteract it. It did quite the reverse. It was an attempt to use me, to make a fool of me, and I was furious. I tried not to show it but I knew at once that under no circumstances would I recommend Williams for the job.

"And that was disastrous, of course. Had I seen Adams first, I would surely have interviewed him in my most meticulous fashion. As it was, with Williams out, I am afraid I treated Adams casually. I recommended him after the barest interaction. Do you wonder that my prejudice against smoking has intensified and that I am more inclined now than I was before to sympathize with your views, Mr. Trumbull?"

Trumbull said, "I take it that Mr. Adams proved incompetent at the job."

"Not at all," said Evans. "For two years he filled it in the fashion that I had predicted in my report after my inadequate examination of him. In fact, he was brilliant. In a number of cases he made decisions that showed real courage and that proved, in the aftermath, to have been correct.

"He was, in fact, in line for another promotion when one day he disappeared, and with him over a million dollars in company assets. When the situation was studied, it seemed that he had been intelligent enough and daring enough to play successful games with a computer, and his courageous decisions, which we had all applauded, had been part of the game. You see, had I examined him as thoroughly as I should have done, I would not have missed that streak of cunning and of patience. It was obvious he had been planning the job for years and had studied computer technology with that thought in mind and with the object of qualifying himself for the promotion which he finally gained. —Quite disastrous, quite disastrous."

Drake said, "Over a million is quite disastrous all right."

"No, no," said Evans. "I mean the blow to my pride and to my standing in the company. Financially, it is no great blow. We were insured and we may even get the stolen items back someday. In fact, justice has been done in a crude sort of way. Adams did not get away with it; in fact, he's dead." Evans shook his head and looked depressed.

"Rather brutally, too, I'm afraid," he went on. "He had lost himself, quite deliberately and successfully, in one of the rabbit warrens of the city, disguised himself more by a new way of life than by anything physical, lived on his savings and didn't touch his stealings, and waited patiently for time to bring him relative safety. But he got into a fight somehow and was knifed. He was taken to the morgue and his fingerprints identified him. That was about six months ago."

"Who killed him?" asked Gonzalo.

"That's not known. The police theory is this— The privacy index of a slum is low and somehow the fact that Adams had something hidden must have gotten around. Perhaps he drank a bit to forget the rather miserable life he was leading while waiting to be safely rich, and perhaps he talked a bit too much. Someone tried to cut himself in on the loot; Adams resisted; and Adams died."

"And did whoever killed him take the loot?"

Evans said, "The police think not. None of the stolen items have surfaced in the six months since Adams' murder. Adams might have the patience to sit on a fortune and lie in hiding, but the average thief would not. So the police think the hoard is still wherever Adams kept it."

Halsted made his characteristic brushing gesture up along his high forehead, as though checking to see if the hairline had yet come down to its original place, and said thoughtfully, "Could you check on the company's knowledge of the details of Adams' life and personality and work out a kind of psychological profile that would tell where the stolen goods would have been placed?"

"I tried that myself," said Evans, "but the answer we came up with is that a man like Adams would hide it most ingeniously. And that does us no good."

Avalon said with a sudden slap of his hand on the table, "I have an idea. Where is Williams? The other man, the one who lost out, I mean?"

Evans said, "He's still at his old job, and doing well enough."

Avalon said, "Well, you might consult him. They were friends. He might know something the company doesn't; something vital that he himself wouldn't dream is vital."

"Yes," said Evans dryly. "That occurred to us and he was interviewed. It was useless. You see, the friendship between the two men had been mild enough to begin with, but it had ceased completely after the incident of the interviews.

"Apparently Adams had, in apparent friendliness, advised Williams to practice smoking in order to demonstrate self-possession and nonchalance. Adams had often told the large, slow-speaking Williams that he made an unfortunate first impression and that he should do something about it.

"Adams' often-repeated advice had its effect at precisely the wrong moment for Williams. Sitting in my office and keenly aware that he made a poor appearance, he could not resist reaching for the cigarettes—with disastrous results. The poor man blamed Adams for what happened, although the action was his own and he must bear the responsibility himself. Still, it ended the friendship and we could learn nothing useful from Williams."

Gonzalo interrupted excitedly, "Wait a minute! Wait a minute! Couldn't Adams have deliberately set it up that way; sort of hypnotized Williams into the act? Couldn't he have arranged it so that Williams was sure to reach for a cigarette at some crucial point? The interview would be the crucial point; Williams would be eliminated; Adams would get the job."

Evans said, "I don't accept such Machiavellianism. How would Adams know that there would be cigarettes at hand on just that occasion? Too unlikely."

"Besides," said Avalon, "that sort of Iago-like manipulation of human beings works on the stage but not in real life."

There was a silence after that and then Trumbull said, "So that's it, I suppose. One crook, now a dead man, and one bundle of stolen goods, hidden somewhere. Nothing much we can do with that. I don't think that even Henry could do anything with that." He looked toward Henry, who was standing by the sideboard patiently. "Henry! Could you tell us, by chance, where the hiding place of the ill-gotten pelf might be?"

"I think I might, sir," said Henry calmly.

Trumbull said, "What?"

Evans said in Trumbull's direction, "Is he joking?"

Henry said, "I think it is possible, on the basis of what we have heard here this evening, to work out what may really have happened."

Evans said indignantly, "What really happened other than what I have told you? This is nonsense."

Trumbull said, "I think we ought to hear Henry, Mr. Evans. He's got a knack too."

"Well," said Evans, "let him have his say."

Henry said, "It occurs to me that because of Mr. Williams' foolish behavior at the interview you were virtually forced to recommend Mr. Adams—yet it is hard to believe that Mr. Williams could be so stupid as to imagine he could pretend to smoke when he was a non-smoker. It is common knowledge that a non-smoker will cough if he inhales cigarette smoke for the first time."

Evans said, "Williams says he was tricked into it by Adams. It was more likely, stupidity. It may be hard to believe that a person could be stupid, but under pressure some quite intelligent people do stupid things and this was one of those occasions."

"Perhaps it was," said Henry, "and perhaps we are looking

at the matter from the wrong end. Perhaps it was not Adams who tricked Williams into attempting to smoke, thus forcing you to recommend Adams for the job. Perhaps it was Williams who did it deliberately in order to force you to recommend Adams for the job."

"Why should he do that?" said Evans.

"Might the two not have been working together, with Williams the brains of the pair? Williams arranged to have Adams do the actual work while he remained in the background and directed activities. Then might not Williams, after arranging a murder as cleverly as he had arranged the theft, have taken the profits? And if all that is so, would you not expect Williams, right now, to know where the stolen goods are?"

Evans merely stared in utter disbelief and it fell to Trumbull to put the general stupefaction into words. "You've pulled that from thin air, Henry."

"But it fits, Mr. Trumbull. Adams could not have arranged the smoking attempt. He wouldn't have known the cigarettes would be there. Williams *would* know; he was sitting there. He might have had something else in mind to force Adams into the job but, seeing the cigarettes, he used those."

"But it's still out of whole cloth, Henry. There's no evidence."

"Consider," said Henry earnestly. "A non-smoker can scarcely pretend to be a smoker. He will cough; nothing will prevent that. But anyone can cough at will; a cough need never be genuine. What if Williams was, in actual fact, an accomplished smoker who had once given up smoking? It would have been the easiest thing for him to pretend he was a non-smoker by pretending to cough uncontrollably."

Evans shook his head stubbornly. "There is nothing to indicate Williams was a smoker."

"Isn't there?" said Henry. "Is it wise of you, sir, to concentrate so entirely on one particular variety of behavior pattern when you interview a prospect? Might you not miss something crucial that was not part of the immediate pattern you were studying?"

Evans said coldly, "No."

Henry said, "You were watching the cigarette, sir, and nothing else. You were not watching the match with which it was lit. You said you *heard* him scratch the match; you didn't see it."

"Yes, but what of that?"

Henry said, "These days, there is no occasion to use matches for anything but cigarettes. A non-smoker, in an age when electricity does everything and even gas stoves have pilot lights, can easily go years without striking a match. It follows that a non-smoker who cannot inhale smoke without coughing cannot handle a matchbook with any skill at all. Yet you described Williams as having held his cigarette with his right hand and having used his left hand only to light it."

"Yes."

"An unskilled smoker," said Henry, "would surely use two hands to light a cigarette, one to hold the matchbook and one to remove the match and strike it on the friction strip. A skilled smoker pretending to be unskilled might be so intent on making sure he handled the cigarette with the properly amateurish touch that he might forget to do the same for the match. In fact, forgetting the match altogether, he might, absent-mindedly, use the kind of technique that only an accomplished smoker could possibly have learned and have lit the match one-handed. I have seen Dr. Drake do such a thing."

Drake, who had, for the last minute, been laughing himself into a quiet coughing fit, managed to say, "I don't do it often any more, because I use a cigarette lighter these days, but here's how it goes." Holding a book of matches in his left hand, he bent one of the matches double with his left thumb so that the head came up against the friction strip. A quick stroke set it aflame.

Henry said, "This is what Williams must have done, and that one-handed match strike indicates an accomplished smoker far more surely than any number of coughs would indicate a non-smoker. If the police look back into his past life far enough, they'll find a time when he smoked. His act in your office will then seem exactly what it was—an act."

"Good God, yes," said Trumbull, "and you can preserve Black Widower confidentiality. Just tell the police that you remember—what you actually remember, what you've told us tonight."

"But to have not realized this," said Evans confusedly, "will make me seem more a fool than ever."

"Not," said Henry softly, "if your statement leads to a solution of the crime."

6 Afterword

"No Smoking" appeared in the December 1974 issue of *Ellery Queen's Mystery Magazine* under the title of "Confessions of an American Cigarette Smoker."

I'm growing ever more fanatical on the subject of smoking. Trumbull in this story is speaking for me. I allow no smoking in either my apartment or my office, but one is limited in one's dictatorial powers elsewhere. The meetings of the Trap Door Spiders are indeed made hideous with smoke—as are almost all other meetings I attend.

There's nothing I can do about it directly, of course, except to complain when the law is with me. (I once plucked the cigarette out of the hand of a woman who was smoking under a "No Smoking" sign in an elevator and who wouldn't put it out when I asked her, politely, to do so.) It helps a bit, though, to write a story expressing my views.

7

Season's Greetings

Thomas Trumbull, whose exact position with government intelligence was not known to the other Black Widowers, creased his face into a look of agonized contempt, bent toward Roger Halsted, and whispered, "Greeting Cards?"

"Why not?" asked Halsted, his eyebrows lifting and encroaching on the pink expanse of his forehead. "It's an honorable occupation."

Trumbull had arrived late to the monthly banquet of the Black Widowers and had been introduced to the guest of the evening even while Henry, the wonder-waiter, had placed the scotch and soda within the curve of his clutching fingers. The guest, Rexford Brown, had a markedly rectangular face, a good-humored mouth, a closely cut fuzz of white hair, a soft voice, and a patient expression.

Trumbull said discontentedly, "It's the season for it, with Christmas next week; I'll grant you that much. Still it means we'll have to sit here and listen to Manny Rubin tell us his opinion of greeting cards."

"Who knows?" said Halsted. "It may turn out that he's written greeting-card rhymes himself. Anyone who's been a boy evangelist—"

Emmanuel Rubin, writer and polymath, had, as was well known, an incredible sharpness of hearing where mention was made, however tangentially, of himself. He drifted over and said, "Written what?"

"Greeting-card rhymes," said Halsted. "You know—'There once were three travelers Magian, Who on a most festive occasion—' "

"No limericks, damn you," shouted Trumbull.

Geoffrey Avalon looked up from the other end of the room and said in his most austere baritone, "Gentlemen, I believe Henry wishes to inform us that we may be seated."

Mario Gonzalo, the club artist, had already completed his sketch of the guest with an admirable economy of strokes and said lazily, "I've been thinking about Roger's limericks. Granted, they're pretty putrid, but they can still be put to use."

"If you printed them on toilet paper—" began Trumbull.

"I mean money," said Gonzalo. "Look, these banquets cost, don't they? It would be nice if they could be made self-supporting, and Manny knows about a half dozen publishers who will publish anything if they publish *his* garbage—"

Drake, stubbing his cigarette out with one hand, put the other over Mario's mouth. "Let's not get Manny into an explosive mood."

But Rubin, who was inhaling veal at its most Italian with every indication of olfactory pleasure, said, "Let him talk, Jim. I'm sure he has an idea that will add new dimensions to the very concept of garbage."

"How about a *Black Widowers' Limerick Book*?"

"A what?" said Trumbull in a stupefied tone.

"Well, we all know limericks. I have one that goes, 'There was a young lady of Sydney Who could take it—' "

"We've heard it," said Avalon, frowning.

"And, 'There was a young fellow of Juilliard With a—' "

"We've heard that one too."

"Yes," said Gonzalo, "but the great public out there hasn't. If we included all the ones we make up and all the ones we can remember, like Jim's limerick about the young lady of Yap, the one that rhymes 'interstices' and 'worse disease'—"

"I will not," said Trumbull, "consent to have the more or less respectable name of the Black Widowers contaminated with any project of such infinite lack of worth."

"What did I tell you about garbage?" said Rubin.

Gonzalo looked hurt. "What's wrong with the idea? We

could make an honest buck. We could even include clean ones. Roger's are all clean."

"That's because he teaches at a junior high school," said Drake, snickering.

"You should hear some of those kids," said Halsted. "How many are in favor of a *Black Widowers' Limerick Book*?"

Gonzalo's hand went up in lonely splendor. Halsted looked as though he might join him; his arm quivered—but stayed down.

Rexford Brown asked mildly, "May I vote?"

"It depends," said Trumbull suspiciously. "Are you in favor or not?"

"Oh, I'm in favor."

"Then you can't vote."

"Oh well, it wouldn't change the result, anyway, but I'm for anything that will bring moments of pleasure. There aren't enough of those."

Gonzalo, speaking with his mouth full, said, "Tom never had one. How would he know?"

Rubin, with a clear effort to keep from sounding sardonic, and marking up a clear failure, said, "Is it those moments of pleasure that justify you in spending your life in the greeting-card business, Mr. Brown?"

"One of the ways," said Brown.

"Hold it, Manny," said Avalon. "Wait for the coffee."

The conversation then grew general, though Gonzalo kept sulkily silent and was observed to be fiddling with his napkin, on which he wrote, in careful Old English lettering, "There once was a group of dull bastards—" but never got to a second line.

Over the coffee, Halsted said, "Okay, Manny, you nearly got to it earlier, so why don't you start the grilling?"

Rubin, who was just holding up his hand to Henry to indicate that he had enough coffee for the moment, looked up at this, his eyes owlish behind the thick lenses of his glasses and his sparse beard quivering.

"Mr. Brown," he said, "how do you justify your existence?"

Brown smiled and said, "Very good coffee. It gives me a moment of pleasure and so does a greeting card. But wait, that's not all. There's more to it than that. You may take no pleasure from what you consider doggerel or moist sentiment or tired wit. That is *you*, but you are not everyone. The prepared greeting card is of service to those who can't write letters or who lack the time to do so or who wish only to maintain a minimal contact. It supplies the needs of those to whom doggerel is touching verse, to whom sentiment is a real emotion, to whom any wit at all is not tired."

Rubin said, "What is your function in connection with them? Do you manufacture them, ship them, design them, write the verses?"

"I manufacture them primarily, but I contribute to each of the categories, and more besides."

"Do you specialize in any particular variety?"

"Not too intensively, although I'm rather weak on the funny ones. Those are for specialized areas. I must say, though, the discussion on limericks interested me. I don't know that limericks have ever been used on greeting cards. How did yours go, Roger?"

"I was just improvising," said Halsted. "Let's see now— 'There once were three travelers Magian, Who on a most festive occasion—'."

Trumbull said, "Imperfect rhyme."

Halsted said, "That's all right. You make a virtue out of necessity and keep it up. Let's see. Let's see—"

He thought a moment and said:

"There once were three travelers Magian,
    Who on a most festive occasion
        Presented their presents
        With humble obeisance
    To the King of the Israelite nation."

"King of the Jews," muttered Avalon under his breath.

"You just tossed that off?" asked Brown.

Roger flushed a little. "It gets easy when you have the meter firmly fixed in your head."

Brown said, "I don't know that that one's usable, but I sell one or two that are not too distant from that sort of thing."

"I wish," said Avalon, with a trace of discontent on his handsome, dark-browed face, "that you had brought some samples."

Brown said, "I didn't know it would be the kind of dinner where that would be expected. If you want samples, though, my wife is the one for you. Clara is the real expert."

"Is she in greeting cards too?" asked Gonzalo, his large,

slightly protuberant eyes filled with interest.

"No, not really. She grew interested in them through me," said Brown. "She began to collect interesting ones, and then her friends began to collect them and send them to her. Over the last ten or twelve years the thing has been getting more and more elaborate. Christmastime especially, of course, since that is greeting-card time par excellence. There isn't a holiday, though, on which she doesn't receive a load of unusual cards. Just to show you, last September she got forty-two Jewish New Year cards, and we're Methodists."

Rubin said, "Jewish New Year cards are usually pretty tame."

"Usually, but people managed to find some dillies. She put them up on the mantelpiece and you never saw such a fancy collection of variations on the theme of the Star of David and the Tablets of the Law. —But it's Christmastime that counts. She practically papers the walls with cards and the apartment becomes a kind of fairyland, if I may use the term without being misunderstood.

"In fact, gentlemen, if you're really interested in seeing samples of unusual greeting cards, you're invited to my apartment. We have open house the week before Christmas. All the people who send cards come around to see where and how theirs contribute. Practically everyone from the apartment house comes too, and it's a large one—to say nothing of the repairman, doorman, postman, delivery boys, and who knows how many others from blocks around. I keep telling her we'll have to get the apartment declared a national landmark."

"I feel sorry for your postman," said Drake in his softly hoarse smoker's voice.

Brown said, "Don't be. He takes a proprietary interest and gives us special treatment. He never leaves our mail in the box—even when it would fit there. He always takes it up the elevator after all the rest of the mail has been distributed, and gives it to us personally. If no one's home, he goes back down and leaves it with the doorman."

Drake said, "That sounds as though you have to give him a healthy tip come Christmastime."

"A very healthy one," said Brown. He chuckled. "I had to reassure him yesterday on that very point."

"That you would give him a tip?"

"Yes. Clara and I were due at a luncheon and we were

late, which was annoying because I had taken time off from work to attend and we dashed out of the elevator at the ground floor just as the postman was about to step into it with our mail. Clara recognized it, of course—it's always as thick as an unabridged dictionary in December—and said, 'I'll take it, Paul, thank you,' and off she whirled. The poor old guy just stood there, so caught by surprise and so shocked that I said to him, 'It's all right, Paul, not one cent off the tip.' Poor Clara!" He chuckled again.

"Why poor Clara?" asked Trumbull.

"I know," said Gonzalo, "it wasn't your mail."

"Of *course* it was our mail," said Brown. "It's the only mail old Paul ever takes up. Listen, the days he's off they hold back the greeting-card items so he can bring them himself the next day. He's practically a family retainer."

"Yes, but why poor Clara?" asked Trumbull, escalating the decibels.

"Oh, that. We got into our car and, since it was a half-hour drive, she counted on going through the mail rapidly and then leaving it under the seat. —But the first thing she noticed was a small envelope, obviously a greeting card, sticking out from the rest of the mail, almost as though it were going to fall out. I saw it myself when she had snatched the mail from Paul. Well, we never get small greeting cards, so she took it out and said, 'What's this?'

"She flipped the envelope open and it was a Christmas card—the blankest, nothingest, cheapest Christmas card you ever saw—and Clara said, 'Who had the nerve to send me this?' I don't think she'd as much as seen a plain card in years. It irritated her so that she just put the rest of the mail away without looking at it and chafed all the way to the luncheon."

Halsted said, "It was probably a practical joke by one of her friends. Who sent it?"

Brown shrugged. "That's what we don't know. —It wasn't you, Roger, was it?"

"Me? Think I'm crazy? I sent her one with little jingle bells in it. Real ones. Listen," and he turned to the others, "you really have to knock yourself out for her. You should see the apartment on Mother's Day. You wouldn't believe how many different cards have tiny little diapers in them."

"And we don't have any children, either," said Brown, sighing.

"Wasn't there a name on that card you got?" asked Trumbull, sticking to the subject grimly.

"Unreadable," said Brown. "Illegible."

Gonzalo said, "I smell a mystery here. We ought to try to find out who sent it."

"Why?" said Trumbull, changing attitude at once.

"Why not?" said Gonzalo. "It might give Mrs. Brown a chance to get back at whoever it is."

"I assure you," said Brown, "you'll find no hint to the sender. Even fingerprints wouldn't help. We handled it and so did who knows how many postal employees."

"Just the same," said Gonzalo, "it's a pity we can't look at it."

Brown said rather suddenly, "Oh, you can look at it. I've got it."

"You've *got* it?"

"Clara was gong to tear it up, but I had just stopped for a red light and I said, 'Let me see it,' and I looked it over and then the green light came on and I shoved it in my coat pocket and I suppose it's still there."

"In that case," said Halsted, "let's see it."

"I'll get it," said Brown. He retired for a moment to the cloakroom and was back at once with a square envelope, pinkish in color, and handed it to Halsted. "You're welcome to pass it around."

Halsted studied it. It had not been carefully pasted and the flap had come up without tearing. On the back was the address in its simplest possible form:

BROWN
354 CPS 21C
NYC 10019

The handwriting was a just-legible scrawl. The stamp was a Jackson 10¢, the postmark was a black smear, and there was no return address.

The other side of the envelope was blank. Halsted removed the card from within and found it to be a piece of cardboard folded down the middle. The two outside surfaces were the same pink as the envelope and were blank. The inner surfaces were white. The left-hand side was blank and the right-hand side said "Season's Greetings" in black letters that were only minimally ornamented. Underneath was a scrawled signature beginning with what looked like a capital D followed by a series of diminishing waves.

Halsted passed it to Drake on his left and it made its way around the table till Avalon received it and looked at it. He passed it on to Henry, who was distributing the brandy glasses. Henry looked at it briefly and handed it back to Brown.

Brown looked up a little surprised, as though finding the angle of return an unexpected one. He said, "Thank you," and sniffed at his brandy delicately.

"Well," said Gonzalo, "I think the name is Danny. Do you know any Danny, Mr. Brown?"

"I know a Daniel Lindstrom," said Brown, "but I don't think his own mother ever dared call him Danny."

Trumbull said, "Hell, that's no Danny. It could be Donna or maybe a last name like Donner."

"We don't know any Donna or Donner."

"I should think," said Avalon, running his finger about the rim of his brandy glass, "that Mr. Brown has surely gone over every conceivable first and last name beginning with D in his circle of acquaintances. If he has not come up with an answer, I am certain we will not. If this is what Mario calls a mystery, there is certainly nothing to go on. Let's drop the subject and proceed with the grilling."

"No," said Gonzalo vehemently. "Not yet. Good Lord, Jeff, just because *you* don't see something doesn't mean there's nothing there to be seen." He turned in his seat. "Henry, you saw that card, didn't you?"

"Yes, sir," said Henry.

"All right, then. Wouldn't you agree with me that there is a mystery worth investigating here?"

"I see nothing we can seize upon, Mr. Gonzalo," said Henry.

Gonzalo looked hurt. "Henry, you're not usually that pessimistic."

"We cannot manufacture evidence, surely, sir."

"That's plain enough," said Avalon. "If Henry says there's nothing to be done, then there's nothing to be done. Manny, continue the grilling, won't you?"

"No, damn it," said Gonzalo, with quite unaccustomed stubbornness. "If I can't have my book of limericks, then

I'm going to have my mystery. If I can show you where this card *does* tell us something—"

"If pigs can fly," said Trumbull.

Halsted said, "Host's privilege. Let Mario talk."

"Thanks, Roger." Gonzalo rubbed his hands. "We'll do this Henry-style. You listen to me, Henry, and you'll see how it goes. We have a signature on the card and the only thing legible about it is the capital *D*. We might suppose that the *D* is enough to tell us who the signer is, but Mr. Brown says it isn't. Suppose we decided then that the *D* is the only clear part of the signature because it's the only thing that's important."

"Wonderful," said Trumbull, scowling. "Where does that leave us?"

"Just listen and you'll find out. Suppose the greeting card is a device to pass on information, and it is the D that's the code."

"What does D tell you?"

"Who knows? It tells you what column to use in a certain paper, or in what row a certain automobile is parked, or in what section to find a certain locker. Who knows? Spies or criminals may be involved. Who knows?"

"That's exactly the point," said Trumbull. "Who knows? So what good does it do us?"

"Henry," said Gonzalo, "don't you think my argument is a good one?"

Henry smiled paternally. "It is an interesting point, sir, but there is no way of telling whether it has any value."

"Yes, there is," said Avalon. "And a very easy way, too. The letter is addressed to Mr. Brown. If the D has significance, then Mr. Brown should know what that significance is. Do you, Mr. Brown?"

"Not the faintest idea in the world," said Brown.

"And," said Avalon, "we can't even suppose that he has guilty knowledge which he is hiding, because if that were the case, why show us the card in the first place?"

Brown laughed. "I assure you. No guilty knowledge. At least, not about this card."

Gonzalo said, "Okay, I'll accept that. Brown here knows nothing about the D, but what does that show? It shows that the letter went to him by mistake. In fact, that fits right in. Who would send a card like that to someone who makes her apartment into a Christmas card show place? It *had* to have gone wrong."

Avalon said, "I don't see how that's possible. It's addressed to him."

"No, it isn't, Jeff. It is not addressed to him. It is addressed to Brown and there must be a trillion Browns in the world." Gonzalo's voice rose and he was distinctly flushed. "In fact, I'll bet there's another Brown in the building and the card was supposed to go to him and *he* would know what the D means. Right now this other Brown is waiting and wondering where the devil the greeting card he's expecting is and what the letter is. He's in a spot. Maybe heroin is involved, or counterfeit money or—"

"Hold on," said Trumbull, "you're going off the diving board into a dry pool."

"No, I'm *not*," said Gonzalo. "If I were this other Brown, I would figure out that it probably went to the wrong Brown, I mean the right one, the one we've got here, and I would go up to the apartment to search for it. I would say, 'I want to look at the collection,' and I would poke around but I wouldn't find it because Brown has the card right here and—"

Brown had been listening to Gonzalo's fantasy with a rather benign expression on his face, but now it was suddenly replaced by a look of deep astonishment. He said, "Wait a minute!"

Gonzalo caught himself up. He said, "Wait a minute, what?"

"It's funny, but Clara said that someone *had* been poking around the cards today."

Rubin said, "Oh no. You're not going to tell me that Mario's nonsense has something to it. Maybe she's just imagining it."

Brown said, "I told her she was, but I wonder. She gets the mail each day and spends some time sorting it out in her —well, she calls it her sewing room, though I've never caught her sewing there—and then comes out and distributes it according to some complicated system of her own. And today she found that some of the cards had been misplaced since the day before. I don't really see her making a mistake in such a matter."

"There you are," said Gonzalo, sitting back smugly. "That's what I call working out an inexorable chain of logic."

"Who was in the house today?" said Trumbull. "I mean, besides you and your wife?"

"No one. There were no visitors. It's a little too early for open house. No one. And no one broke in, either."

"You can't be sure," said Gonzalo. "I predicted someone would be poking around and someone was. I think we've got to follow this up now. What do you say, Henry?"

Henry waited a moment before replying. "Certainly," he said, "it seems to be a puzzling coincidence."

Gonzalo said, "Not puzzling at all. It's just this other Brown. We've got to get him."

Brown sat there, frowning, as though the fun had gone out of the game for him. He said, "There is no other Brown in the building."

"Maybe the spelling is different," said Gonzalo, with no perceptible loss of confidence. "How about Browne with a final *e* or spelling it with an *au* the way the Germans do?"

"No," said Brown.

"Come on, Mr. Brown. You don't know the name of everyone in the building."

"I know quite a few, and I certainly know the Bs. You know, you look at the directory sometimes and your eyes automatically go to your own name." He thought awhile as though he were picturing the directory. Then he said with a voice that seemed to have grown pinched, "There's a Beroun, though, B-e-r-o-u-n. I think that's the spelling. No, I'm *sure* of it."

The Black Widowers sat in silence. Gonzalo waited thirty seconds, then said to Henry, "Showed them, didn't we?"

Halsted passed his hand over his forehead in the odd gesture characteristic of him and said, "Tom, you're something or other in the cloak-and-dagger groups. Is it possible there might be something to this?"

Trumbull was deep in thought. "The address," he said finally, "is 354 CPS. That's Central Park South— I don't know. I might be happier if it were CPW, Central Park West."

"It says CPS quite clearly," said Gonzalo.

"It also says Brown quite clearly," said Drake, "and not Beroun."

"Listen," said Gonzalo, "that handwriting is a scrawl. You can't tell for sure whether that's a *w* or a *u* and there could be an *e* in between the *b* and the *r*."

"No, there couldn't," said Drake. "You can't have it both ways. It's a scrawl when you want the spelling different, and it's quite clear when you don't."

"Besides," said Avalon, "you're all ignoring the fact that there's more than a name in the address, or a street either. There's an apartment number, too, and it's 21C. Is that your apartment number, Mr. Brown?"

"Yes, it is," said Brown.

"Well then," said Avalon, "it seems that the theory falls to the ground. The wrong Brown or Beroun doesn't live in 21C. The right Brown does."

For the moment Gonzalo seemed nonplused. Then he said, "No, it's all making too much sense. They must have made a mistake with the apartment number too."

"Come on," said Rubin. "The name is misspelled and the apartment number is miswritten and the two end up matching? A Mr. Brown at the correct apartment number? That's just plain asking too much of coincidence."

"It could be a small mistake," said Gonzalo. "Suppose this Beroun is in 20C or 21E. It might take just two small mistakes, one to make Beroun look like Brown and one to get 21C instead of 20C."

"No," said Rubin, "it's still two mistakes meshing neatly. Come on, Mario, even you can see how stupid it is."

"I don't care how stupid it may seem theoretically. What is the situation in actual practice? We know there is a Beroun in the same apartment house with Brown. All we have to do now is find out what Beroun's apartment number is and I'll bet it's very close to 21C, something where it is perfectly easy to make a mistake."

Brown shook his head. "I don't think so. I know there's no Beroun anywhere on my floor, on the twenty-first, that is. And I know the people who live below me in 20C and above me in 22C and neither one is Beroun or anything like it."

"Well then, where *does* Beroun live? What apartment number? All we have to do is find that out."

Brown said, "I don't know which apartment number is Beroun's. Sorry."

"That's all right," said Gonzalo. "Call your wife. Have her go down and look at the directory and then call us back."

"I can't. She's gone out to a movie."

"Call the doorman, then."

Brown looked reluctant. "How do I explain—"

Drake coughed softly. He stubbed out his cigarette, even though there was still a quarter inch of tobacco in front of the filter, and said, "I have an idea."

"What?" said Gonzalo.

"Well, look here. You have apartment 21C and if you look at the envelope you see that 21C is made in three marks. There's a squiggle for the 2 and a straight line for the 1 and a kind of arc for the C."

"So what?" said Gonzalo, looking very much as though ideas were his monopoly that evening.

"So how can we be sure that the 1 belongs to the 2 and makes the number 21? Maybe the 1 belongs to the C, and if you take them together, the guy's trying to write a K. What I'm saying is that maybe the apartment number is 2K."

"That's it," said Gonzalo excitedly. "Jim, remind me to kiss any girl sitting next to you any time there are girls around. Sure! It's Beroun, 354 CPS 2K, and the postman read it as Brown, 354 CPS 21C. The whole thing's worked out and now, Tom, you pull the right strings to get someone after this Beroun—"

"You know," said Trumbull, "you're beginning to hypnotize me with this fool thing and I'm almost ready to arrange to have this damned Beroun watched—except that, no matter how I stare at this address, it still looks like Brown, not Beroun, and like 21C, not 2K."

"Tom, it's got to be Beroun 2K. The whole thing fits."

Brown shook his head. "No, it doesn't. Sorry, Mario, but it doesn't. If Beroun lived in 2K, your theory might be impressive, but he doesn't."

"Are you sure?" asked Gonzalo doubtfully.

"It happens to be the Super's apartment. I've been there often enough."

"The Super," said Gonzalo, taken aback for a moment and then advancing to the charge again. "Maybe he'd fit even better. You know—blue-collar worker—maybe he's in the numbers racket. Maybe—Hey, of course it fits. Who would be poking around your apartment today looking over the Christmas cards? The Super, that's who. He wouldn't have to break in. He'd have the keys and could get in any time."

"Yes, but why is the card addressed to Brown, then?"

"Because the names may be similar enough. What's the Super's name, Mr. Brown?"

Brown sighed. "Ladislas Wessilewski," and he spelled it out carefully. "How are you going to write either one of those names so that it looks anything like Brown?"

Avalon, sitting bolt upright, passed a gentle finger over each half of his mustache and said sententiously, "Well, Mario, there we have our lesson for the day. Not everything is a mystery and inexorable chains of logic can end nowhere."

Gonzalo shook his head. "I still say there's something wrong there. —Come on, Henry, help me out here. Where did I go off base?"

Henry, who had been standing quietly at the sideboard for the past fifteen minutes, said, "There is indeed a possibility, Mr. Gonzalo, if we accept your assumption that the Christmas card represents a code intended to transfer information. In that case, I think it is wrong to suppose that the card was misdirected.

"If the card had been delivered to the wrong place, it is exceedingly odd that it should end up at an apartment where there is a notorious card collector, well known as such throughout the apartment house and perhaps over a much wider area."

Gonzalo said, "Coincidences do happen, Henry."

"Perhaps, but it seems much more likely that Mr. Brown's address was used deliberately. Who would pay any attention whatever to one greeting card, more or less, addressed to Mr. and Mrs. Brown, when they get so many? Since they get many greeting cards even on such unlikely holidays, for them, as the Jewish New Year and Mother's Day, it would be quite convenient to use them as a target at any time of the year, especially if all the card says is a noncommital 'Season's Greetings.' "

Brown said with sudden coldness, "Are you suggesting, Henry, that Clara and I are involved in some clandestine operation?"

Henry said, "I doubt it, sir, since, as someone said earlier, you would not have brought up the matter of the card if you were."

"Well then?"

"Assuming Mr. Gonzalo's theory to be correct, I suggest the cards were sent to you rather than to someone else, because if they actually reached you they would be unnoticeable. They may have underestimated here your wife's penchant for novel cards and her contempt for plain ones."

"But as far as I know, this is the only card of the kind we've ever received, Henry."

"Exactly, sir. It was an accident. You're not supposed to receive them. Your name on them is simply a blind, losing it in hundreds of other greeting-card envelopes similarly addressed. Only these particular cards are supposed to be intercepted."

"How?"

"By the person who well knows the quantity and kind of mail you get and could suggest that you be used for the purpose; by the person who would have the easiest opportunity to intercept, but failed this one time. Mr. Brown, how many times have you come out of the elevator just as the postman was going in, and how many times have you taken the package out of his hands on such an occasion?"

Brown said, "As far as I know, that was the only time."

"And the card in question was sticking out, almost as though it were falling out. That's how your wife noticed it at once."

"You mean *Paul—*"

"I mean it seems strange that a postman should be so insistent on dealing with your Christmas cards that he arranges to have them left in the post office an extra day when he is not on duty. Is it so that he remains sure of never missing one of the cards addressed to you that he must intercept?"

Trumbull interrupted. "Henry, I know something of this. Postmen in the process of sorting mail are under constant observation."

"I imagine so, sir," said Henry, "but there are other opportunities."

Brown said, "You don't know Paul. I've known him since we've moved into the apartment. Years! He's a phenomenally cautious man. I imagine he'd lose his job if he were ever seen pocketing a letter he was supposed to deliver. That lobby is a crowded place; there are always two postmen working. I know him, I tell you. Even if he wanted to, he would never take the chance."

Henry said, "But that is precisely the point, Mr. Brown. If this man is as you say he is, it explains why he is so insistent on taking the mail up to you. Even in this crowded city, there is one place you can count on being surely unobserved for at least a few moments and that is in an empty automatic elevator.

"There is nothing to prevent the postman, in sorting the mail and preparing the bundle, from placing one greeting card, which he recognizes by shape, color, and handwriting, in such a way that it will stick out from the rest. Then, in the elevator, which he takes only when he is sure he is the only rider, he has time to flick out the envelope and put it in his pocket, even if he remains alone only for the time it takes to travel one floor."

Brown said, "And was it Paul who was poking around in our apartment today?"

"It's possible, I should think," said Henry. "Your wife receives the mail from the postman at the door and, since it is getting close to Christmas, the arrangements she must make are getting complicated. She rushes to the sewing room without bothering to bolt the door. The postman has a chance to push the little button that makes it possible to turn the knob from outside. He might then have had a few minutes to try to find the card. He didn't, of course."

Brown said, "A man so cautious as to insist on using an empty elevator for the transfer of a letter surely would not—"

"It is perhaps a sign of the desperation of the case. He may know this to be an unusually important card. If I were you, sir—"

"Yes?"

"Tomorrow is Saturday and you may not be at work, but the postman will. Hand this card to the postman. Tell him that it can't possibly be yours and that perhaps it is Beroun's. His facial expression may be interesting and Mr. Trumbull might arrange to have the man watched. Nothing may come of it, of course, but I strongly suspect that *something* is there."

Trumbull said, "There *is* a chance. I can make the arrangements."

A look of gloom gathered on Brown's face and he shook his head. "I hate laying a trap for old Paul at Christmastime."

"Being guest at the Black Widowers has its drawbacks, sir," said Henry.

7 *Afterword*

"Season's Greetings" was rejected by *Ellery Queen's Mystery Magazine* for some reason, as it is their complete right to do, of course—even without a reason, if they don't care to advance one. What's more, there clearly isn't the shadow of an excuse for sending it on to F & SF. So I just let it stay unsold.

Actually, I like to have a few stories in the collections that have *not* appeared in the magazines. There ought to be some small bribe for the reader who has been enthusiastic enough and loyal enough to read them all when they first appeared.

Of course, I might reason that in book form you have the stories all in one bunch without the admixture of foreign components so that it doesn't matter if all were previously published—but it would also be nice to have something new. This is one of them, and it isn't the only one in this book, either.

8

The One and Only East

Mario Gonzalo, host of the month's Black Widowers' banquet, was resplendent in his scarlet blazer but looked a little disconsolate nevertheless.

He said in a low voice to Geoffrey Avalon, the patent attorney, "He's sort of a deadhead, Jeff, but he's got an interesting problem. He's my landlady's cousin and we were talking about it and I thought, Well, hell, it could be interesting."

Avalon, on his first drink, bent his dark brows disapprovingly and said, "Is he a priest?"

"No," said Gonzalo, "not a Catholic priest. I think what you call him is 'elder.' He's a member of some small uptight sect. —Which reminds me that I had better ask Tom to go a little easy on his language."

Avalon's frown remained. "You know, Mario, if you invite a man solely on the basis of his problem, and without any personal knowledge of him whatever, you could be letting us in for a very sticky evening. —Does he drink?"

"I guess not," said Mario. "He asked for tomato juice."

"Does that mean *we* don't drink?" Avalon took an unaccustomedly vigorous sip.

"Of course we drink."

"You're the host, Mario—but I suspect the worst."

The guest, standing against the wall, was dressed in a

135

somber black and wore a mournful expression which may have been merely the result of the natural downward slant of the outer corners of his eyes. His face almost glistened with a recent close shave and bore a pallor that might merely have been the contrast with his dark clothes. His name was Ralph Murdock.

Emmanuel Rubin, his spectacle-magnified eyes glaring and his sparse beard vibrating with the energy of his speech, had taken the measure of the man at once and had managed to maneuver the discussion into a sharp analysis of the nature of the Trinity almost before the meal had been fairly begun.

Murdock seemed unmoved, and his face remained as calm as that of Henry, the club waiter, who performed his functions as imperturbably as ever.

"The mistake," said Murdock, "usually made by those who want to discuss the mysteries in terms of ordinary logic is to suppose that the rules that originate from observation of the world of sense impression apply to the wider universe beyond. To some extent, they may, but how can we know where and how they do not?"

Rubin said, "That's an evasion."

"It is not," said Murdock, "and I'll give you an example within the world of sense impression. We obtain our common-sense notions of the behavior of objects from the observation of things of moderate size, moving at moderate speeds and existing at moderate temperatures. When Albert Einstein worked a scheme for a vast universe and enormous velocities, he ended with a picture that seemed against common sense; that is, against the observations we found it easy to make in everyday life."

Rubin said, "Yet Einstein deduced the relativistic universe from sense impressions and observations that anyone could make."

"Provided," said Murdock smoothly, "that instruments were used which were unknown to man some centuries earlier. The observations we can now make and the effects we can now produce would seem to mankind a few centuries ago like the result of wizardry, magic, or even, perhaps, revelation, if these things were made apparent without the proper introduction and education."

"Then you think," said Rubin, "that the revelation that has faced man with a Trinity now incomprehensible may make sense in a kind of super-relativity of the future?"

"Possibly," said Murdock, "or possibly it makes sense in a kind of super-relativity that was reached by man long ago through the short-circuiting of mere reason and the use of more powerful instruments for gaining knowledge."

With open delight, the others joined in the battle, everyone in opposition to Murdock, who seemed oblivious to the weight of the forces against him. With an unchanging expression of melancholy and with unmoved politeness, he answered them all without any sense of urgency or annoyance. It was all the more exciting in that it did not deal with matters that could be settled by reference to the club library.

Over the dessert, Trumbull, with a careful mildness of vocabulary that was belied by the ferocious wrinkling of his tanned face, said, "Whatever you can say of reasoning, it has lengthened the average human life by some forty years in the last century. The forces beyond reason, whatever they may be, have been unable to lengthen it a minute."

Murdock said, "That reason has its uses and seeming benefit no one can deny. It has enabled us to live long, but look round the world, sir, and tell me whether it has enabled us to live decently. And ask yourself further whether length without decency is so unmixed a blessing."

By the time the brandy was served and the lances of all had been shivered against Murdock's calm verbal shield, it seemed almost anticlimactic to have Gonzalo strike his water glass with his spoon to mark the beginning of the post-dinner grilling.

Gonzalo said, "Gentlemen, we have had an unusually interesting dinner, I think"—and here he made a brief gesture at Avalon, who sat on his left, one it was well for Murdock not to have seen—"and it seems to me that our guest has already been put through his hurdles. He has acquitted himself well and I think even Manny has suspicious signs of egg on his face. —Don't say anything, Manny. —As host, I am going to end the grilling then and direct Mr. Murdock, if he will, to tell us his story."

Murdock, who had ended the dinner with a large glass of milk, and who had refused Henry's offer of coffee and of brandy, said:

"It is kind of Mr. Gonzalo to invite me to this dinner and I must say I have been pleased with the courtesy extended me. I am grateful as well. It is not often I have a chance to discuss matters with unbelievers who are as ready to listen as yourselves. I doubt that I have convinced any of you, but it is by no means my mission to convince you— rather to offer you an opportunity to convince yourselves.

"My problem, or 'story' as Mr. Gonzalo has called it, has preyed on my mind these recent weeks. I have confided some of it, in a moment of agony of mind, to Sister Minerva, who is, by the reckoning of the world, a cousin of mine, but a sister by virtue of a common membership in our Church of the Disciples of Holiness. She, for reasons that seemed worth while to herself, mentioned it to her tenant, Mr. Gonzalo, and he sought me out and implored me to attend this meeting.

"He assured me that it was possible you might help me in this problem that preys upon my mind. You may or you may not; that does not matter. The kindness you have already shown me is great enough to make failure in the other matter something of little consequence.

"Gentlemen, I am an elder of the Church of the Disciples of Holiness. It is a small church of no importance at all as the world counts importance, but the world's approval is not what we seek. Nor do we look for consolation in the thought that we alone will find salvation. We are perfectly ready to admit that all may find their way to the throne by any of an infinite number of paths. We find comfort only in that our own path seems to us to be a direct and comfortable one, a path that gives us peace—a commodity as rare in the world as it is desirable.

"I have been a member of the Church since the age of fifteen and have been instrumental in bringing into the fold several of my friends and relations.

"One whom I failed to interest was my Uncle Haskell.

"It would be easy for me to describe my Uncle Haskell as a sinner but that word is usually used to describe offenses against God, and I consider that to be a useless definition. God's mercy is infinite and His love is great enough to find offense in nothing that applies to Himself only. If the offense were against man that would be far graver, but here I can exonerate my Uncle Haskell by at least the amount by which I can exonerate mankind generally. One cannot live a moment without in some way harming, damaging or, at the very least, inconveniencing a fellow man, but I am sure my Uncle Haskell never intended such harm, damage, or inconvenience. He would have gone a mile out of his way to prevent this, if he knew what was happening and if prevention were possible.

"There remains the third class of damage—that of a man against himself—and it was here, I am afraid, that my Uncle Haskell was a sinner. He was a large man, with a Homeric sense of humor and gargantuan appetites. He ate and drank to excess, and womanized as well, yet whatever he did, he did with such gusto that one could be deluded into believing he gained pleasure from his way of life, and fall into the error of excusing him on the grounds that it was far better to enjoy life than to be a sour Puritan such as myself who finds a perverse pleasure in gloom.

"It was this, in fact, that was my Uncle Haskell's defense when I remonstrated with him on one occasion when what might have seemed to himself and to others to have been a glorious spree ended with himself in jail and possessing a mild concussion to boot.

"He said to me, 'What do you know of life, you such-and-such Puritan? You don't drink, you don't smoke, you don't swear, you don't—'

"Well, I will spare you the list of pleasures in which he found me lacking. You can, undoubtedly, imagine each one. It may seem sad to you, too, that I miss out on such routes to elevation of the spirit, but my Uncle Haskell, if he knew a dozen ladies of doubtful virtue, had never known the quiet heart-filling of love. He did not know the pleasurable serenity of quiet contemplation, of reasoned discourse, of communion with the great souls who have left their thoughts behind them. He knew my feelings in this respect but scorned them.

"He may have done so the more vehemently because he knew what he had lost. While I was in college—in the days when I first came to know my Uncle Haskell and to love him—he was writing a dissertation on Restoration England. At times he spoke as though he were planning to write a novel, at times a historical exposition. He had a home in Leonia, New Jersey, then—still had, I should say, for he had been born there, as had his ancestors and mine back to the Quaker days in colonial times. —Well, he lost it, along with everything else.

"Now, where was I? —Yes, in his Leonia home, he built up a library of material on Restoration England, in which he found, I honestly believe, more pleasure than in any of the sensualities that eventually claimed him.

"It was his addiction to gambling that did the real damage. It was the first of the passions he called pleasures that he took to extremes. It cost him his home and his library. It cost him his work, both that in which he made his living as an antique dealer, and that in which he found his joy as an amateur historian.

"His sprees, however rowdily joyful, left him in the hospital, the jail, or the gutter, and I was not always there to find and extricate him at once.

"What kept him going was the erratic nature of his chief vice, for occasionally he made some fortunate wager or turned up a lucky card and then, for a day or for a month, he would be well to do. At those times he was always generous. He never valued money for itself nor clung to it in the face of another's need—which would have been a worse vice than any he possessed—so that the good times never lasted long nor served as any base for the renewal of his former, worthier life.

"And, as it happened, toward the end of his life, he made the killing of a lifetime. I believe it is called a 'killing,' which is reasonable since the language of vice has a peculiar violence of its own. I do not pretend to understand how it was done, except that several horses, each unlikely to win, nevertheless won, and my Uncle Haskell so arranged his bets that each winning horse greatly multiplied what had already been multiplied.

"He was left, both by his standards and mine, a wealthy man, but he was dying and knew he would not have time to spend the money in his usual fashion. What occurred to him, then, was to leave the world in the company of a huge joke— a joke in which the humor rested in what he conceived to be my corruption, though I'm sure he didn't look upon it that way.

"He called me to his bedside and said to me something which, as nearly as I can remember, was this:

" 'Now, Ralph, my boy, don't lecture me. You see for yourself that I am virtuous now. Lying here, I can't do any of the terrible things you deplore—except perhaps to swear a little. I can only find time and occasion now to be as virtuous as you and my reward is that I am to die.

" 'But I don't mind, Ralph, because I've got more money

now than I've ever had at one time for many years and I will be able to throw it away in a brand-new fashion. I am willing it to you, nephew.'

"I began to protest that I preferred his health and his true reform to his money, but he cut me off.

" 'No, Ralph, in your twisted way you have tried your best for me and have helped me even though you disapproved of me so strongly and could have no hope of a reasonable return either in money or in conversion. On top of that, you're my only relative and you should get the money even if you had done nothing at all for me.'

"Again I tried to explain that I had helped him as a human being and not as a relative, and that I had not done so as a kind of business investment, but again he cut me off. He was having difficulty speaking and I did not wish to prolong matters unduly.

"He said, 'I will leave you fifty thousand dollars, free and clear. Matters will be so arranged that all legal expenses and all taxation will be taken care of. I have already discussed this with my lawyer. With your way of life, I don't know what you can possibly do with the money other than stare at it, but if that gives you pleasure, I'll leave you to it.'

"I said gently, 'Uncle Haskell, a great deal of good can be done with fifty thousand dollars and I will spend it in ways that the Disciples of Holiness will find fitting and useful. If this displeases you, then do not leave the money to me.'

"He laughed then, a feeble effort, and fumbled for my hand in a way that made it clear how weak he had grown. I had not seen him for a year and in that interval he had gone downhill at an incredible pace.

"The doctors said that a combination of diabetes and cancer, treated inadequately, had advanced too rapidly across the bastions of his pleasure-riddled body, heaven help him, and left him with nothing but the hope of a not too prolonged time of dying. It was on himself and the horse races that he had made a simultaneous killing.

"He clutched my hand weakly and said, 'No, do whatever you want with the money. Hire someone to sing psalms. Give it away, a penny at a time, to five million bums. That's your business; I don't care. But, Ralph, there's a catch to all this, a very amusing catch.'

" 'A catch? What kind of catch?' It was all I could think of to ask.

" 'Why, Ralph, my boy, I'm afraid you will have to gamble for the money.' He patted my hand and laughed again. 'It will be a good, straight gamble with the odds five to one against you.

" 'My lawyer,' he went on, 'has an envelope in which is located the name of a city—a nice, sealed envelope, which he won't open till you come to him with the name of a city. I will give you six cities to choose from and you will select one of these. One! If the city you select matches the one in the envelope, you get fifty thousand dollars. If it does not match, you get nothing, and the money goes to various charities. *My* kind of charities.'

" 'This is not a decent thing to do, Uncle,' I said, rather taken aback.

" 'Why not, Ralph? All you have to do is guess the city and you have a great deal of money. And if you guess wrong, you lose nothing. You can't ask better than that. My suggestion is that you number the cities from one to six, then roll a dice and pick the city corresponding to the number you roll. A sporting chance, Ralph!'

"His eyes seemed to glitter, perhaps at the picture of myself rolling dice for money. I felt that sharply and I said, shaking my head, 'Uncle Haskell, it is useless to place this condition on me. I will not play games with the universe or abdicate the throne of conscience in order to allow chance to make my decisions for me. Either leave me the money, if that pleases you, or do not leave it, if *that* pleases you.'

"He said, 'Why do you think of it as playing games with the universe? Don't you accept what men call chance to be really God's will? You have said that often enough. Well then, if He thinks you worthy, you will get the money. Or don't you trust Him?'

"I said, 'God is not a man that He may be put to the test.'

"My Uncle Haskell was growing feebler. He withdrew his arm and let it rest passively on the blanket. He said in a while, 'Well, you'll have to. If you don't supply my lawyer with your choice within thirty days of my death, it will all go to my charities. Come, thirty days gives you enough time.'

"We all have our weaknesses, gentlemen, and I am not always free of pride. I could not allow myself to be forced to dance to my Uncle Haskell's piping merely in order to get the money. But then I thought that I could use the money—not for myself but for the Church—and perhaps I had no right to throw it away out of pride in my virtue, when so much would be lost in the process.

"But pride won. I said, 'I'm sorry, Uncle Haskell, but in that case, the money will have to go elsewhere. I will not gamble for it.'

"I rose to go but his hand motioned and I did not yet turn away. He said, 'All right, my miserable nephew. I want you to have the money, I really do; so if you lack sporting blood and can't take your honest chance with fate, I will give you one hint. If you penetrate it, you will know which city it is—beyond doubt, I think—and you will not be gambling when you hand in that name.'

"I did not really wish to prolong the discussion and yet I hated to abandon him and leave him desolate if I could avoid doing so. I said, 'What is this hint?'

"He said, 'You will find the answer in the one and only east—the one and only east.'

" 'The one and only east,' I repeated. 'Very well, Uncle Haskell, I will consider it. Now let us talk of other things.'

"I made as though to sit down again, but the nurse entered and said it was time for my Uncle Haskell to rest. And, indeed, I thought it was; he seemed worn to the last thread.

"He said, 'Saved a sermon, by the Almighty,' and laughed in a whisper.

"I said, 'Good-by, Uncle Haskell. I will come again.'

"When I reached the door he called out, 'Don't jump too soon, nephew. Think it over carefully. The one and only east.'

"That is the story, gentlemen. My uncle died twenty-seven days ago. Within three days, by this coming Monday, I must give my choice to the lawyer. I suspect I will not give that choice, for my Uncle Haskell's clue means nothing to me and I will not choose a city as a mere gamble. I will not."

There was a short silence after Murdock had finished his tale. James Drake puffed thoughtfully on his cigarette. Tom Trumbull scowled at his empty brandy glass. Roger Halsted doodled on his napkin. Geoffrey Avalon sat bolt upright and looked blank. Emmanuel Rubin shook his head slowly from side to side.

Gonzalo broke the silence uneasily, perhaps thinking it his duty to do so, as the host. He said, "Do you mind telling us the names of the six cities, Mr. Murdock?"

"Not at all, Mr. Gonzalo. Since you asked me to come here in order that I might possibly be helped—and since I agreed to come—I obviously seek help. With that in view, I must answer any honorable question. The names of the cities, as I received them from the lawyer on the day of my Uncle Haskell's death, are on this paper. You'll notice it is on the lawyer's stationery. It is the paper he gave me."

He passed it on to Gonzalo. Aside from the lawyer's letter-head, it contained only the typed list of six cities in alpha-betical order:

> ANCHORAGE, ALASKA
> ATHENS, GEORGIA
> AUGUSTA, MAINE
> CANTON, OHIO
> EASTON, PENNSYLVANIA
> PERTH AMBOY, NEW JERSEY

Gonzalo passed it around. When he received it back he called, "Henry!" Then, to Murdock, "Our waiter is a mem-ber of the club. "You have no objection to his seeing the list, I hope?"

"I have no objection to anyone seeing it," said Murdock.

Avalon cleared his throat. "Before we launch ourselves into speculation, Mr. Murdock, it is only fair to ask if you have given the matter some thought yourself."

Murdock's sorrowful face grew thoughtful. His lips pressed together and his eyes blinked. He said in a soft, almost shamefaced voice, "Gentlemen, I would like to tell you that I have resisted temptation completely, but the fact is I have not. I have thought at times and tried to convince myself that one city or another fits my Uncle Haskell's hint so that I can offer it to the lawyer on Monday with a clear con-science. On occasion I have settled on one or another of the cities on the list but each time it was merely a case of fooling myself, of compromising, of pretending I was not gambling when I was."

Rubin said, with a face innocently blank, "Have you prayed, Mr. Murdock? Have you sought divine guidance?"

For a moment it seemed as though Murdock's careful armor had been pierced, but only for a moment. After that slight pause he said, "If that were appropriate in this case, I would have seen a solution without prayer. In God's eyes, it is my needs that count and not my desires, and He knows my needs without my having to inform Him."

Rubin said, "Have you tried to approach the problem using the inferior weapon of reason?"

"I have, of course," said Murdock. "In a casual way. I have tried to resist being drawn into it too deeply. I mistrust myself, I fear."

Rubin said, "And have you come to any favorite conclusion? You've said that you have been unable to settle on any one city definitely, to the point where you would consider its choice as no longer representing a gamble—but do you lean in one direction or another?"

"I have leaned in one direction at one time and in another direction at another. I cannot honestly say that any one of the cities is my favorite. With your permission, I will not tell you the thoughts that have struck me since it is *your* help I seek and I would prefer you to reach your conclusions, or hypotheses, uninfluenced by my thoughts. If you miss anything I have thought of, I will tell you."

"Fair enough," said Gonzalo, smoothing down one collar of his blazer with an air of absent self-satisfaction. "I suppose we have to consider whether any of those cities is the one and only east."

Murdock said, "I would think so."

"In that case," said Gonzalo, "pardon me for mentioning the obvious, but the word 'east' occurs only in Easton. It is the one and only east."

"Oddly enough," said Murdock dryly, "I had not failed to notice that, Mr. Gonzalo. It strikes me as obvious enough to be ignored. My Uncle Haskell also said, 'Don't jump too soon.'"

"Ah," said Gonzalo, "but that might just be to throw you off. The real gambler has to know when to bluff and your uncle could well have been bluffing. If he had a real rotten kind of humor, it would have seemed fun to him to give you the answer, let it lie right there, and then scare you out of accepting it."

Murdock said, "That may be so, but that sort of thing would mean I would have to penetrate my Uncle Haskell's mind and see whether he was capable of a double cross or something like that. It would be a gamble and I won't gamble. Either the hint, properly interpreted, makes the matter so plain that it is no longer a gamble, or it is worthless. In short, Easton may be the city, but if so, I will believe it only for some reason stronger than the mere occurrence of 'east' in its name."

Halsted, leaning forward toward Murdock, said, "I think no gambler worth his salt would set up a puzzle with so easy a solution as the connection between east and Easton. That's just misdirection. Let me point out something a little more reasonable, and a little more compelling. Of the six cities mentioned, I believe Augusta is easternmost. Certainly it is in the state of Maine, which is the easternmost of the fifty states. Augusta has to be the one and only east, and beyond any doubt."

Drake shook his head violently. "Quite wrong, Roger, quite wrong. It's just a common superstition that Maine is the easternmost state. Not since 1959. Once Alaska became the fiftieth state, *it* became the easternmost state."

Halsted frowned. "Westernmost, you mean, Jim."

"Westernmost *and* easternmost. And northernmost too. Look, the 180° longitude line passes through the Aleutian Islands. The islands west of the line are in the Eastern Hemisphere. They are the *only* part of the fifty states that are in the Eastern Hemisphere and that makes Alaska the easternmost state, the one and only east."

"What about Hawaii?" asked Gonzalo.

"Hawaii does not reach the 180° mark. Even Midway Island, which lies to the west of the state, does not. You can look it up on the map if you wish, but I know I'm right."

"It doesn't matter whether you're right or not," said Halsted hotly. "Anchorage isn't on the other side of the 180° line, is it? So it's west, not east. In the case of Augusta, the *city* is the easternmost of the six mentioned."

Murdock interrupted. "Gentlemen, it is not worth arguing the matter. I had thought of the eastern status of Maine but did not find it compelling enough to convert it into a bid. The fact that one can argue over the matter of Alaska versus Maine—and I admit that the Alaska angle had not occurred to me—removes either from the category of the one and only east."

Rubin said, "Besides, from the strictly geographic point, east and west are purely arbitrary terms. North and south are absolute since there is a fixed point on Earth that is the North Pole and another that is the South Pole. Of any two spots on Earth, the one closer to the North Pole is farther north, the other farther south, but of those same two spots, neither is farther east or farther west, for you can go from one to the other, or from the other to the one, by traveling either eastward or westward. There is no absolute eastern point or western point on Earth."

"Well then," said Trumbull, "where does that get you, Manny?"

"To the psychological angle. What typifies east to us in the United States is the Atlantic Ocean. Our nation stretches from sea to shining sea and the only city on the list which is on the Atlantic Ocean is Perth Amboy. Augusta may be farther east geographically, but it is an inland town."

Trumbull said, "That's a bunch of nothing at all, Manny. The Atlantic Ocean symbolizes the east to us right now, but through most of the history of Western civilization it represented the west, the *far* west. It wasn't till after Columbus sailed westward that it became the east to the colonists of the New World. If you want something that's east in the Western tradition, and always has been east, it's China. The first Chinese city to be opened to Western trade was Canton and the American city of Canton was actually named for the Chinese city. Canton *has* to be the one and only east."

Avalon lifted his hand and said with majestic severity, "I don't see that at all, Tom. Even if Canton typifies the east by its recall of a Chinese city, why is that the one *and only* east? Why not Cairo, Illinois, or Memphis, Tennessee, each of which typifies the ancient Egyptian east?"

"Because those cities aren't on the list, Jeff."

"No, but Athens, Georgia, is, and if there is one city in all the world that is the one and only east, it is Athens, Greece—the source and home of all the humanistic values we hold dear today, the school of Hellas and of all the west—"

"Of all the *west*, you idiot," said Trumbull with sudden ferocity. "Athens was never considered the east either by itself or by others. The first great battle between east and west was Marathon in 490 B.C. and Athens represented the west."

Murdock interrupted. "Besides, my Uncle Haskell could scarcely have thought I would consider Athens unique, when it has purely secular value. Had he included Bethlehem, Pennsylvania, on his list, I might have chosen it at once with no sense of gamble. As it is, however, I can only thank you, gentlemen, for your efforts. The mere fact that you come to different conclusions and argue over them shows that each of you must be wrong. If one of you had the real answer it would be compelling enough to convince the others—and myself as well—at once. It may be, of course, that my Uncle Haskell deliberately gave me a meaningless clue for his own posthumous pleasure. If so, that does not, of course, in the least diminish my gratitude to you all for your hospitality, your company, and your efforts."

He would have risen to leave but Avalon, on his left, put a courteous but nonetheless authoritative hand on his shoulder. "One moment, Mr. Murdock, one member of our little band has not yet spoken. —Henry, have you nothing to add?"

Murdock looked surprised. "Your waiter?"

"A Black Widower, as we said earlier. Henry, can you shed any light on this puzzle?"

Henry said solemnly, "It may be that I can, gentlemen. I was impressed by Mr. Murdock's earlier argument that reason is sometimes inadequate to reach the truth. Nevertheless, suppose we start with reason. Not ours, however, but that of Mr. Murdock's uncle. I have no doubt that he deliberately chose cities that each represented the east in some ambiguous fashion, but where would he find in that list an unambiguous and compelling reference? Perhaps we would know the answer if we remembered his special interests—Mr. Murdock did say that at one time he was working on a book concerning Restoration England. I believe that is the latter half of the seventeenth century."

"Charles II," said Rubin, "reigned from 1660 to 1685."

"I'm sure you are correct, Mr. Rubin," said Henry. "All the cities named are in the United States, so I wondered whether we might find something of interest in American history during the Restoration period."

"A number of colonies were founded in Charles II's reign," said Rubin.

"Was not Carolina one of them, sir?" asked Henry.

"Sure. Carolina was named for him, in fact. Charles is Carolus, in Latin."

"But later on Carolina proved unwieldy and was split into North Carolina and South Carolina."

"That's right. But what has that got to do with the list? There are no cities in it from either Carolina."

"True enough, but the thought reminded me that there is also a North Dakota and a South Dakota, and for that matter a West Virginia, but there is no American state that has East in its title. Of course, we might speak of East Texas or of East Kansas or East Tennessee but—"

"More likely to say 'eastern,' " muttered Halsted.

"Either way, sir, there would not be a one and only east, but—"

Gonzalo exploded in sudden excitement. "Wait a minute, Henry. I think I see what you're driving at. If we have the state of West Virginia—the one and only west—then we can consider Virginia to be East Virginia—the one and only east."

"No, you can't," said Trumbull, with a look of disgust on his face. "Virginia has been Virginia for three and a half centuries. Calling it East Virginia doesn't make it so."

"It would not matter if one did, Mr. Trumbull," said Henry, "since there is no Virginian city on the list. —But before abandoning that line of thought, however, I remembered that Mr. Murdock's uncle lived in New Jersey and that his ancestors had lived there since colonial times. Memories of my grade school education stirred, for half a century ago we were much more careful about studying colonial history than we are today.

"It seems to me, and I'm sure Mr. Rubin will correct me if I'm wrong, that at one time in its early history New Jersey was divided into two parts—East Jersey and West Jersey, the two being separately governed. This did not last a long time, a generation perhaps, and then the single state of New Jersey was reconstituted. East Jersey, however, is the only section of what are now the United States that had 'east' as part of its official name as colony or state."

Murdock looked interested. His lips lifted in what was almost a smile. "The one and only east. It could be."

"There is more to it than that," said Henry. "Perth Amboy was, in its time, the capital of East Jersey."

Murdock's eyes opened wide. "Are you serious, Henry?"

"I am quite certain of this and I think it is the compelling factor. It was the capital of the one and only east in the list of colonies and states. I do not think you will lose the inheritance if you offer that name on Monday; nor do I think you will be gambling."

Rubin said, scowling, "I *said* Perth Amboy."

"For a non-compelling reason," said Drake. "How do you do it, Henry?"

Henry smiled slightly. "By abandoning reason for something more certain as Mr. Murdock suggested at the start."

"What are you talking about, Henry?" said Avalon. "You worked it out very nicely by a line of neat argument."

"After the fact, sir," said Henry. "While all of you were applying reason, I took the liberty of seeking authority and turned to the reference shelf we use to settle arguments. I looked up each city in Webster's Geographical Dictionary. Under Perth Amboy, it is clearly stated that it was once the capital of East Jersey."

He held out the book and Rubin snatched it from his hands, to check the matter for himself.

"It is easy to argue backward, gentlemen," said Henry.

8 Afterword

"The One and Only East," which appeared in the March 1975 issue of *Ellery Queen's Mystery Magazine*, was, like "The Iron Gem," written on board ship, longhand. On this occasion I was visiting Great Britain for the first time in my life—by ocean liner both ways, since I don't fly.

It was a little difficult in one way because I didn't have my reference library with me. (I must admit that one of the reasons that my Black Widowers sound so erudite on so many different subjects is that the man who writes the words has put together a very good reference library in his lifetime.) The result was that I had to play my cities back and forth out of what knowledge I had in my head. As it happened, though, I got it nearly all correct.

9

Earthset and Evening Star

Emmanuel Rubin, whose latest mystery novel was clearly proceeding smoothly, lifted his drink with satisfaction and let his eyes gleam genially through his thick-lensed glasses.

"The mystery story," he pontificated, "has its rules which, when broken, make it an artistic failure, whatever success it may have in the market place."

Mario Gonzalo, whose hair had been recently cut to allow a glimpse of the back of his neck, said, as though to no one, "It always amuses me to hear a writer describe something he scrawls on paper as art." He looked with some complacency at the cartoon he was making of the guest for that month's banquet session of the Black Widowers.

"If what you do is the definition of art," said Rubin, "I withdraw the term in connection with the writer's craft. —One thing to avoid, for instance, is the idiot plot."

"In that case," said Thomas Trumbull, helping himself to another roll and buttering it lavishly, "aren't you at a disadvantage?"

Rubin said loftily, "By 'an idiot plot,' I mean one in which the solution would come at once if an idiot investigator would but ask a logical question, or in which an idiot witness would but tell something he knows and which he has no reason to hide."

Geoffrey Avalon, who had left a neatly cleaned bone on his plate as the only witness of the slab of roast beef that had once rested there, said, "But no skilled practitioner would do that, Manny. What you do is set up some reason to prevent the asking or telling of the obvious."

"Exactly," said Rubin. "For instance, what I've been writing is essentially a short story if one moves in a straight line. The trouble is the line is so straight, the reader will see its end before I'm halfway. So I have to hide one crucial piece of evidence, and do it in such a way that I don't make an idiot plot out of it. So I invent a reason to hide that piece, and in order to make the reason plausible I have to build a supporting structure around it—and I end with a novel, and a damn good one." His sparse beard quivered with self-satisfaction.

Henry, the perennial waiter at the Black Widowers' banquets, removed the plate from in front of Rubin with his usual dexterity. Rubin, without turning, said, "Am I right, Henry?"

Henry said softly, "As a mystery reader, Mr. Rubin, I find it more satisfying to have the piece of information delivered to me and to find that I have been insufficiently clever and did not notice."

"I just read a mystery," said James Drake in his softly hoarse smoker's voice, "in which the whole point rested on character 1 being really character 2, because the *real* character 1 was dead. I was put on to it at once because, in the list of characters at the start, character 1 was not listed. Ruined the story for me."

"Yes," said Rubin, "but that wasn't the author's fault. Some flunky did that. I once wrote a story which was accompanied by one illustration that no one thought to show me in advance. It happened to give away the point."

The guest had been listening quietly to all this. His hair was just light enough to be considered blond and it had a careful wave in it that looked, somehow, as though it belonged there. He turned his rather narrow but clearly good-humored face to Roger Halsted, his neighbor, and said, "Pardon me, but since Manny Rubin is my friend, I know he is a mystery writer. Is this true of the rest of you as well? Is this a mystery writer organization?"

Halsted, who had been looking with somber approval at the generous slab of Black Forest torte that had been placed before him as dessert, withdrew his attention with some difficulty and said, "Not at all. Rubin is the only mystery writer here. I'm a mathematics teacher myself; Drake is a chemist; Avalon is a lawyer; Gonzalo is an artist; and Trumbull is a code expert with the government.

"On the other hand," he went on, "we do have an interest in this sort of thing. Our guests often have problems they bring up for discussion, some sort of mystery, and we've been rather lucky—"

The guest leaned back with a small laugh. "Nothing of the sort here, alas. Of the mystery, the murder, the fearful hand clutching from behind the curtain, there is nothing in my life. It is all very straightforward, alas; very dull. I am not even married." He laughed again.

The guest had been introduced as Jean Servais and Halsted, who had attacked the torte with vigor, and who felt a friendly glow filling him in consequence, said, "Does it matter to you if I call you John?"

"I would not strike you, sir, if you did, but I pray you not to. It is not my name. Jean, please."

Halsted nodded. "I'll try. I can manage that *zh* sound, but getting it properly nasal is another thing. Zhohng," he said.

"But that is excellent. Most formidable."

"You speak English very well," said Halsted, returning the politeness.

"Europeans require linguistic talent," said Servais. "Besides, I have lived in the United States for nearly ten years now. You are all Americans, I suppose. Mr. Avalon looks British somehow."

"Yes, I think he likes to look British," said Halsted. And with a certain hidden pleasure he said, "And it's Avalon. Accent on the first syllable and nothing nasal at the end."

But Servais only laughed. "Ah yes, I will try. When I first knew Manny, I called him 'roo-bang' with the accent on the last syllable and a strong nasalization. He corrected me very vigorously and at great length. He is full of pepper, that one."

The conversation had grown rather heated by this time over a general dispute concerning the relative merits of Agatha Christie and Raymond Chandler, with Rubin maintaining a rather lofty silence as though he knew someone who was better than either but would not mention the name out of modesty.

Rubin seemed almost relieved when, with the coffee well in progress and Henry ready to supply the postprandial brandy, the time came for him to tap the water glass with his spoon and say, "Cool it, cool it, gentlemen. We are coming now to the time when our guest, Jean Servais, is to pay for his dinner. Tom, it's all yours."

Tom scowled and said, "If you don't mind, Mr. Servais," giving the final *s* just enough of a hiss to make his point, "I'm not going to try to display my French accent and make the kind of jackass of myself that my friend Manny Rubin does. —Tell me, sir, how do you justify your existence?"

"Why, easily," said Servais pleasantly. "Did I not exist, you would be without a guest today."

"Please leave us out of it. Answer in more general terms."

"In general, then, I build dreams. I design things that cannot be built, things I will never see, things that may never be."

"All right," said Trumbull, looking glum, "you're a science fiction writer like Manny's pal what's-his-name—uh—Asimov."

"No friend of mine," said Rubin swiftly. "I just help him out now and then when he's stuck on some elementary scientific point."

Gonzalo said, "Is he the one you once said carried the Columbia Encyclopedia around with him because he was listed there?"

"It's worse now," said Rubin. "He's bribed someone at the Britannica to put him into the new 15th edition and these days he drags the whole set with him wherever he goes."

"The new 15th edition—" began Avalon.

"For God's sake," said Trumbull, "will you let our guest speak?"

"No, Mr. Trumbull," said Servais, as though there had been no interruption at all, "I am no science fiction writer, though I read it sometimes. I read Ray Bradbury, for instance, and Harlan Ellison." (He nasalized both names.) "I don't think I have ever read Asimov."

"I'll tell him that," muttered Rubin, "he'll love it."

"But," continued Servais, "I suppose you might call me a science fiction engineer."

"What does that mean?" asked Trumbull.

"I do not write of Lunar colonies. I design them."

"You *design* them!"

"Oh yes, and not Lunar colonies only, though that is our major task right now. We work in every field of imaginative design for private industry, Hollywood, even NASA."

Gonzalo said, "Do you really think people can live on the Moon?"

"Why not? It depends on what mankind is willing to do, how large an initial investment it is ready to make. The environment on the Moon can be engineered to the precise equivalent of Earth, over restricted underground areas, except for gravity. We must be content with a Lunar gravity that is one sixth our own. Except for that, we need only allow for original supplies from Earth and for clever engineering—and that is where we come in, my partner and I."

"You're a two-man firm?"

"Essentially. —While my partner remains my partner, of course."

"Are you breaking up?"

"No, no. But we quarrel over small points. It is not surprising. It is a bad time for him. But no, we will not break up. I have made up my mind to give in to him, perhaps. Of course, I am entirely in the right and it is a pity to lose what I would have."

Trumbull leaned back in his chair, folded his arms, and said, "Will you tell us what the argument is all about? We can then state our own preferences, whether for you or for your partner."

"It would not be a hard choice, Mr. Trumbull, for the sane," said Servais. "I swear it. —This is the way it is. We are designing a full Lunar colony, in complete detail. It is for a motion picture company and it is for a good fee. They will make use of some of it in a grand science fiction spectacle they are planning. We naturally supply far more than they can use but the idea is that if they have a totally self-consistent picture of what may be—and for a wonder they want it as scientifically accurate as possible—they can choose what they wish of it for use."

"I'll bet they bollix it up," said Drake pessimistically, "no matter how careful you are. They'll give the Moon an atmosphere."

"Oh, no," said Seravis, "not after six Lunar landings. That error we need not fear. Yet I have no doubt they will make mistakes. They will find it impossible to handle low-gravity effects properly throughout and the exigencies of the plot will force some infelicities.

"Still that cannot be helped and our job is merely to supply them with material of the most imaginative possible. This is my point, as you will see in a moment. —We plan a city, a small city, and it will be against the inner lip of a crater. This is unavoidable because the plot of the movie demands it. However, we have our choice as to the identity and location of the crater, and my partner, perhaps because he is an American, goes for the obvious with an American directness. He wishes to use the crater Copernicus.

"He says that it is a name that is familiar; that if the city is called Camp Copernicus that alone will breathe the Moon, exotic adventure, and so on. Everyone knows, he says, the name of the astronomer who first placed the Sun at the center of the planetary system and it is a name, moreover, that sounds impressive.

"I, on the other hand, am not impressed with this. As seen from Copernicus, the Earth is high in the sky and stays there. As you all know, the Moon faces one side always to the Earth, so that from any spot on the Moon's surface the Earth is always more or less in the same spot in the sky."

Gonzalo said suddenly, "If you want the Lunar city to be on the other side of the Moon so that the Earth *isn't* in the sky, you're crazy. The audience will absolutely want the Earth there."

Servais held up his hand in agreement. "Absolutely! I agree. But if it is always there, it is almost as though it is *not* there. One gets too used to it. No, I choose a more subtle approach. I wish the city to be in a crater that is on the boundary of the visible side. From there, of course, you will see the Earth at the horizon.

"Consider what this introduces. The Moon does not keep the same side to the Earth exactly. It swings back and forth by a very small amount. For fourteen days it swings one way and then for fourteen days it swings back. This is called 'libration' "—he paused here as though to make sure he was pronouncing it correctly in English—"and it comes about because the Moon does not move in a perfect circle about the Earth.

"Now, you see, if we establish Camp Bahyee in the crater

of that name, the Earth is not only at the horizon but it moves up and down in a twenty-eight-day cycle. Properly located, the Lunar colonists will see the Earth rise and set, slowly, of course. This lends itself to imaginative exploitation. The characters can arrange for some important action at Earthset, and the different positions of the Earth can indicate the passage of time and raise the suspense. Some terrific special effects are possible, too. If Venus is near the Earth and Earth is in a fat crescent stage, Venus will then be at its brightest; and when Earth sets, we can show Venus, in the airless sky of the Moon, to be a very tiny crescent itself."

"Earthset and evening star, and one clear call for me," muttered Avalon.

Gonzalo said, "Is there really a crater called Bahyee?"

"Absolutely," said Servais. "It is, in fact, the largest crater that can be seen from the Earth's surface. It is 290 kilometers across—180 miles."

"It sounds like a Chinese name," said Gonzalo.

"French!" said Servais solemnly. "A French astronomer of that name was mayor of Paris in 1789 at the time of the Revolution."

"That wasn't a good time to be mayor," said Gonzalo.

"So he discovered," said Servais. "He was guillotined in 1793."

Avalon said, "I am rather on your side, Mr. Servais. Your proposal lends scope. What was your partner's objection?"

Servais shrugged in a gesture that was more Gallic than anything he had yet said or done. "Foolish ones. He says that it will be too complicated for the movie people. They will confuse things, he says. He also points out that the Earth moves too slowly in the Moon's sky. It would take days for the Earth to lift its entire globe above the horizon, and days for it to lower entirely below the horizon."

"Is that right?" asked Gonzalo.

"It's right, but what of that? It will still be interesting."

Halsted said, "They can fudge that. Make the Earth move a little faster. So what?"

Servais looked discontented. "That's no good. My partner says this is precisely what the movie people will do and this alteration of astronomical fact will be disgraceful. He is very violent about it, finding fault with everything, even with the name of the crater, which he says is ridiculous and laughable so that he will not endure it in our report. We have never had arguments like this. He is like a madman."

"Remember," said Avalon, "you said you would give in."

"Well, I will have to," said Servais, "but I am not pleased. Of course, it is a bad time for him."

Rubin said, "You've said that twice now, Jean. I've never met your partner, so I can't judge the personalities involved. Why is it a bad time?"

Servais shook his head. "A month ago, or a little more, his wife killed herself. She took sleeping pills. My partner was a devoted husband, most uxorious. Naturally, it is terrible for him and, just as naturally, he is not himself."

Drake coughed gently. "Should he be working?"

"I would not dare suggest he not work. The work is keeping him sane."

Halsted said, "Why did she kill herself?"

Servais didn't answer in words but gestured with his eyebrows in a fashion that might be interpreted in almost any way.

Halsted persisted. "Was she incurably ill?"

"Who can say?" said Servais, sighing. "For a while, poor Howard—" He paused in embarrassment. "It was not my intention to mention his name."

Trumbull said, "You can say anything here. Whatever is mentioned in this room is completely confidential. —Our waiter, too, before you ask, is completely trustworthy."

"Well," said Servais, "his name doesn't matter in any case. It is Howard Kaufman. In a way, work has been very good for him. Except at work, he is almost dead himself. Nothing is any longer important to him."

"Yes," said Trumbull, "but now something *is* important to him. He wants his crater, not your crater."

"True," said Servais. "I have thought of that. I have told myself it is a good sign. He throws himself into something. It is a beginning. And perhaps all the more reason, then, that I should give in. Yes, I will. —It's settled, I will. There's no reason for you gentlemen to try to decide between us. The decision is made, and in his favor."

Avalon was frowning. "I suppose we should go on to question you further on the work you do and I suppose, moreover, that we should not intrude on a private misfortune. Here at the Black Widowers, however, no questions are barred, and there is no Fifth Amendment to plead. I am dissatisfied, sir, with your remarks concerning the unfortunate woman who committed suicide. As a happily married man, I am puzzled at the combination of love and suicide. You said she wasn't ill?"

"Actually, I didn't," said Servais, "and I am uncomfortable at discussing the matter."

Rubin struck the empty glass before him with his spoon. "Host's privilege," he said vigorously. There was silence.

"Jean," he said, "you are my guest and my friend. We can't force you to answer questions, but I made it clear that the price of accepting our hospitality was the grilling. If you have been guilty of a criminal act and don't wish to discuss it, leave now and we will say nothing. If you will talk, then, whatever you say, we will still say nothing."

"Though if it is indeed a criminal act," said Avalon, "we would certainly strongly advise confession."

Servais laughed rather shakily. He said, "For one minute there, for one frightened minute, I thought I had found myself in a Kafka novel and would be tried and condemned for some crime you would drag out of me against my will. Gentlemen, I have committed no crime of importance. A speeding ticket, a bit of creative imagination on my tax return—all that is, so I hear it said, as American as apple pie. But if you're thinking I killed that woman and made it look like suicide—please put it out of your heads at once. It *was* suicide. The police did not question it."

Halsted said, "Was she ill?"

"All right, then, I will answer. She was not ill as far as I know. But after all, I am not a doctor and I did not examine her."

Halsted said, "Did she have chlidren?"

"No. No children. —Ah, Mr. Halsted, I suddenly remember that you spoke earlier that your guests had problems which they brought up for discussion, and I said I had none. I see you have found one anyway."

Trumbull said, "If you're so sure it was suicide, I suppose she left a note."

"Yes," said Servais, "she left one."

"What did it say?"

"I couldn't quote it exactly. I did not myself see it. According to Howard, it was merely an apology for causing unhappiness but that she could not go on. It was quite banal and I assure you it satisfied the police."

Avalon said, "But if it was a happy marriage, and there was no illness and no complications with children, then— Or were there complications with children? Did she want children badly and did her husband refuse—"

Gonzalo interposed. "No one kills themselves because they don't have kids."

"People kill themselves for the stupidest reasons," said Rubin. "I remember—"

Trumbull cried out with stentorian rage, "Damn it, you guys, Jeff has the floor."

Avalon said, "Was the lack of children a disturbing influence?"

"Not as far as I know," said Servais. "Look, Mr. Avalon, I am careful in what I say, and I did *not* say it was a happy marriage."

"You said your partner was devoted to his wife," said Avalon gravely, "and you used that fine old word 'uxorious' to describe him."

"Love," said Servais, "is insufficient for happiness if it flows but one way. I did not say that *she* loved *him*."

Drake lit another cigarette. "Ah," he said, "the plot thickens."

Avalon said, "Then it is your opinion that that had something to do with the suicide."

Servais looked harassed. "It is more than my opinion, sir. I *know* it had something to do with the suicide."

"Would you tell us the details?" asked Avalon, unbending just slightly from his usual stiff posture as though to convert his question into a courtly invitation.

Servais hesitated, then said, "I remind you that you have promised me all is confidential. Mary—Madame Kaufman and my partner were married for seven years and it seemed a comfortable marriage, but who can tell in affairs of this sort?

"There was another man. He is older than Howard and to my eyes not as good-looking—but again, who can tell in affairs of this sort? What she found in him is not likely to be there on the surface for all to see."

Halsted said, "How did your partner take *that*?"

Servais looked up and flushed distinctly. "He never knew. Surely, you are not of the opinion that I told him this? I am not the type, I assure you. It is not for me to interfere between husband and wife. And frankly, if I had told Howard, he would not have believed me. It is more likely he would have attempted to strike me. And then what was I to do? Present proof? Was I to arrange matters so as to have them caught under conditions that could not be mistaken? No, I said nothing."

"And he really didn't know?" asked Avalon, clearly embarrassed.

"He did not. It had not been going on long. The pair were excessively cautious. The husband was blindly devoted. What would you?"

"The husband is always the last to know," said Gonzalo sententiously.

Drake said, "If the affair was so well hidden, how did you find out, Mr. Servais?"

"Purest accident, I assure you," said Servais. "An incredible stroke of misfortune for her in a way. I had a date for the evening. I did not know the girl well and it did not, after all, work out. I was anxious to be rid of her, but first— what would you have, it would not be gentlemanly to abandon her—I took her home in an odd corner of the city. And, having said good-by in a most perfunctory manner, I went into a nearby diner to have a cup of coffee and recover somewhat. And there I saw Mary Kaufman and a man.

"Alas, it jumped to the eye. It was late; her husband, I remembered at once, was out of town, her attitude toward the man— Accept my assurances that there is a way a woman has of looking at a man that is completely unmistakable, and I saw it then. And if I were at all unsure, the expression on her face, when she looked up and saw me frozen in surprise, gave it all away.

"I left at once, of course, with no greeting of any kind, but the damage was done. She called me the next day, in agony of mind, the fool, fearful that I would carry stories to her husband, and gave me a totally unconvincing explanation. I assured her that it was a matter in which I did not interest myself in the least, that it was something so unimportant that I had already forgotten it. —I am glad, however, I did not have to face the man. Him, I would have knocked down."

Drake said, "Did you know the man?"

"Slightly," said Servais. "He moved in our circles in a very distant way. I knew his name; I could recognize him.

—It didn't matter, for I never saw him after that. He was wise to stay away."

Avalon said, "But why did she commit suicide? Was she afraid her husband would find out?"

"Is one ever afraid of that in such a case?" demanded Servais, with a slight lifting of his lip. "And if she were, surely she would end the affair. No, no, it was something far more common than that. Something inevitable. In such an affair, gentlemen, there are strains and risks which are great and which actually add an element of romance. I am not entirely unaware of such things, I assure you.

"But the romance does not continue forever, whatever the story books may say, and it is bound to fade for one faster than for the other. Well then, it faded for the man in this case before it did for the woman—and the man took the kind of action one sometimes does in such affairs. He left—went—disappeared. And so the lady killed herself."

Trumbull drew himself up and frowned ferociously. "For what reason?"

"I assume for that reason, sir. It has been known to happen. I did not know of the man's disappearance, you understand, till afterward. After the suicide I went in search of him, feeling he was in some way responsible, and rather promising myself to relieve my feelings by bloodying his nose—I have a strong affection for my partner, you understand, and I felt his sufferings—but I discovered the fine lover had left two weeks before and left no forwarding address. He had no family and it was easy for him to leave, that blackguard. I could have tracked him down, I suppose, but my feelings were not strong enough to push me that far. And yet, I feel the guilt—"

"What guilt?" asked Avalon.

"It occurred to me that when I surprised them—quite unintentionally, of course—the element of risk to the man became unacceptably high. He knew I knew him. He may have felt that sooner or later it would come out and he did not wish to await results. If I had not stumbled into that diner they might still be together, she might still be alive, who knows?"

Rubin said, "That is farfetched, Jean. You can't deal rationally with the ifs of history. —But I have a thought."

"Yes, Manny?"

"After the suicide your partner was very quiet, nothing

is important to him. I think you said that. But now he's quarreling with you violently, though he has never done that before, I gather. Something may have happened in addition to the suicide. Perhaps *now* he has discovered his wife's infidelity and the thought drives him mad."

Servais shook his head. "No, no. If you think I have told him, you are quite wrong. I admit I think of telling him now and then. It is difficult to see him, my dear friend, wasting away over a woman who, after all, was not worthy of him. It is not proper to pine away for one who was not faithful to him in life. Ought I not tell him this? Frequently, it seems to me that I should and even must. He will face the truth and begin life anew. —But then I think and even *know* that he will not believe me, that our friendship will be broken, and he will be worse off than before."

Rubin said, "You don't understand me. Might it not be that someone *else* has told him? How do you know you were the only one who knew?"

Servais seemed a bit startled. He considered it and said, "No. He would, in that case, certainly have told me the news. And I assure you, he would have told it to me with the highest degree of indignation and informed me that he at once attempted to strike the villain who would so malign his dead angel."

"Not," said Rubin, "if he had been told that *you* were his wife's lover. Even if he refused to believe it, even if he beat the informant to the ground, could he tell *you* the tale under such circumstances? And could he be entirely certain? Would he not find it impossible to avoid picking fights with you in such a case?"

Servais seemed still more startled. He said slowly, "It was, of course, not I. No one could possibly have thought so. Howard's wife did not in the least appeal to me, you understand." He looked up and said fiercely, "You must accept the fact that I am telling you the truth about this. It was *not* I, and I will *not* be suspected. If anyone had said it was I, it could only be out of deliberate malice."

"Maybe it was," said Rubin. "Might it not be the real lover who would make the accusation—out of fear you would give him away? By getting in his story first—"

"Why should he do this? He is away. No one suspects him. No one pursues him."

"He might not know that," said Rubin.

"Pardon me." Henry's voice sounded softly from the direction of the sideboard. "May I ask a question?"

"Certainly," said Rubin, and the odd silence fell that always did when the quiet waiter, whose presence rarely obtruded on the festivities, made himself heard.

Servais looked startled, but his politeness held. He said, "Can I do anything for you, waiter?"

Henry said, "I'm not sure, sir, that I quite understand the nature of the quarrel between yourself and your partner. Surely there must have been decisions of enormous complexity to make as far as the technical details of the colony were concerned."

"You don't know even a small part of it," said Servais indulgently.

"Did your partner and you quarrel over all those details, sir?"

"N-no," said Servais. "We did not quarrel. There were discussions, of course. It is useless to believe that two men, each with a strong will and pronounced opinions, will agree everywhere, or even anywhere, but it all worked out reasonably. We discussed, and eventually we came to some conclusion. Sometimes I had the better of it, sometimes he, sometimes neither or both."

"But then," said Henry, "there was this one argument over the actual location of the colony, over the crater, and there it was all different. He attacked even the name of the crater fiercely and, in this one case, left no room for the slightest compromise."

"No room at all. And you are right. Only in this one case."

Henry said, "Then I am to understand that at this time, when Mr. Rubin suspects that your partner is being irritated by suspicion of you, he was completely reasonable and civilized over every delicate point of Lunar engineering, and was wildly and unbearably stubborn only over the single matter of the site—over whether Copernicus or the other crater was to be the place where the colony was to be built?"

"Yes," said Servais with satisfaction. "That is precisely how it was and I see the point you are making, waiter. It is quite unbelievable to suppose that he would quarrel with me over the site out of ill-humor over suspicion that I have placed horns on him, when he does not quarrel with me on any other point. Assuredly, he does not suspect me of ill-dealing. I thank you, waiter."

Henry said, "May I go a little further, sir?"

"By all means," said Servais.

"Earlier in the evening," said Henry, "Mr. Rubin was kind enough to ask my opinion over the techniques of his profession. There was the question of deliberate omission of details by witnesses."

"Yes," said Servais, "I remember the discussion. But I did not deliberately omit any details."

"You did not mention the name of Mrs. Kaufman's lover."

Servais frowned. "I suppose I didn't, but it wasn't deliberate. It is entirely irrelevant."

"Perhaps it is," said Henry, "unless his name happens to be Bailey."

Servais froze in his chair. Then he said anxiously, "I don't recall mentioning it. Sacred— I see your point again, waiter. If it slips out now without my remembering it, it is possible to suppose that, without quite realizing it, I may have said something that led Howard to suspect—"

Gonzalo said, "Hey, Henry, I don't recall Jean giving us any name."

"Nor I," said Henry. "You did not give the name, sir."

Servais relaxed slowly and then said, frowning, "Then how did you know? Do you know these people?"

Henry shook his head. "No, sir, it was just a notion of mine that arose out of the story you told. From your reaction, I take it his name *is* Bailey?"

"Martin Bailey," said Servais. "How did you know?"

"The name of the crater in which you wished to place the site is Bahyee; the name of the city would be Camp Bahyee."

"Yes."

"But that is the French pronunciation of the name of a French astronomer. How is it spelled?"

Servais said, "B-a-i-l-ly. —Great God, *Bailly!*"

Henry said, "In English pronunciation, pronounced like the not uncommon surname Bailey. I am quite certain American astronomers use the English pronunciation, and that Mr. Kaufman does too. You hid that piece of information from us, Mr. Servais, because you never thought of the crater in any other way than Bahyee. Even looking at it, you would hear the French sound in your mind and make no connection with Bailey, the American surname."

Servais said, "But I still don't understand."

"Would your partner wish to publicize the name, and place the site of a Lunar colony in Bailly? Would he want to have the colony called Camp Bailly, after what a Bailey has done to him?"

"But he didn't *know* what Bailey had done to him," said Servais.

"How do you know that? Because there's an old saw that says the husband is always the last to know? How else can you explain his utterly irrational opposition to this one point, even his insistence that the name itself is horrible? It is too much to expect of coincidence."

"But if he knew—if he knew— He didn't tell me. Why fight over it? Why not explain?"

"I assume," said Henry, "he didn't know you knew. Would he shame his dead wife by telling you?"

Servais clutched at his hair. "I never thought— Not for a moment."

"There is more to think," said Henry sadly.

"What?"

"One might wonder how Bailey came to disappear, if your partner knew the tale. One might wonder if Bailey is alive? Is it not conceivable that Mr. Kaufman, placing all the blame on the other man, confronted his wife to tell her he had driven her lover away, even killed him, perhaps, and asked her to come back to him—and the response was suicide?"

"No," said Servais. "That is impossible."

"It would be best, then, to find Mr. Bailey and make sure he is alive. It is the one way of proving your partner's innocence. It may be a task for the police."

Servais had turned very pale. "I can't go to the police with a story like that."

"If you do not," said Henry, "it may be that your partner, brooding over what he has done—if indeed he has done it— will eventually take justice into his own hands."

"You mean kill himself?" whispered Servais. "Is that the choice you are facing me with: accuse him to the police or wait for him to kill himself?"

"Or both," said Henry. "Life is cruel."

9 Afterword

I got the idea for this one when I was in Newport, Rhode Island, attending a seminar on space and the future, sponsored by NASA. It got in the way, too.

I was listening, in all good faith, to someone who was delivering an interesting speech. Since I was slated to give a talk too, I had every reason for wanting to listen. And yet, when the craters of the Moon were mentioned, my brain, quite involuntarily, began ticking, and after some fifteen minutes had passed I had "Earthset and Evening Star" in my mind in full detail and had missed the entire last half of the speech.

Ellery Queen's Mystery Magazine, alas, thought that the business with the craters was a little too recondite to carry the story and sent it back. I then took the chance that the craters might be just science-fictionish enough to interest Ed Ferman. I sent it to him, he took it, and it appeared in the October 1975 issue of F & SF.

10

Friday the Thirteenth

Mario Gonzalo unwound a long crimson scarf and hung it up beside his coat with an air of discontent.

"Friday the thirteenth," he said, "is a rotten day for the banquet and I'm cold."

Emmanuel Rubin, who had arrived earlier at the monthly banquet of the Black Widowers, and who had had a chance to warm up both externally and internally, said, "This isn't cold. When I was a kid in Minnesota, I used to go out and milk cows when I was eight years old—"

"And by the time you got home the milk was frozen in the pail. I've heard you tell that one before," said Thomas Trumbull. "But what the devil, this was the only Friday we could use this month, considering that the Milano is closing down for two weeks next Wednesday, and—"

But Geoffrey Avalon, staring down austerely from his seventy-four inches of height, said in his deep voice, "Don't explain, Tom. If anyone is such a superstitious idiot as to think that Friday is unluckier than any other day of the week, or that thirteen is unluckier than any other number, and that the combination has some maleficent influence on us all—then I say leave him in the outer darkness and let him gnash his teeth." He was host for the banquet on this occasion and undoubtedly felt a proprietary interest in the day.

Gonzalo shook back his long hair and seemed to have grown more content now that most of a very dry martini was inside him. He said, "That stuff about Friday the thirteenth is common knowledge. If you're too ignorant to know that, Jeff, don't blame me."

Avalon bent his formidable eyebrows together and said, "To hear the ignorant speak of ignorance is always amusing. Come, Mario, if you'll pretend to be human for a moment, I'll introduce you to my guest. You're the only one he hasn't met yet."

Speaking to James Drake and Roger Halsted at the other end of the room was a slender gentleman with a large-bowled pipe, a weedy yellow mustache, thin hair that was almost colorless, and faded blue eyes set deeply in his head. He wore a tweed jacket and a pair of trousers that seemed to have been comfortably free of the attentions of a pressing iron for some time.

"Evan," said Avalon imperiously, "I want you to meet our resident artist, Mario Gonzalo. He will make a caricature of you, after a fashion, in the course of our meal. Mario, this is Dr. Evan Fletcher, an economist at the University of Pennsylvania. There, Evan, you've met us all."

And as though that were a signal, Henry, the perennial waiter at all the Black Widowers' banquets, said softly, "Gentlemen," and they seated themselves.

"Actually," said Rubin, attacking the stuffed cabbage with gusto, "this whole business about Friday the thirteenth is quite modern and undoubtedly arose over the matter of the Crucifixion. That took place on a Friday and the last Supper, which had taken place earlier, was, of course, a case of thirteen at the table, the twelve Apostles and—"

Evan Fletcher was trying to stem the flow of words rather ineffectively and Avalon said loudly, "Hold on, Manny, I think Dr. Fletcher wishes to say something."

Fletcher said, with a rather apologetic smile, "I just wondered how the subject of Friday the thirteenth arose."

"Today is Friday the thirteenth," said Avalon.

"Yes, I know. When you invited me to the banquet for this evening, it was the fact that it was Friday the thirteenth that made me rather eager to attend. I would have raised the point myself, and I am surprised that it came up independently."

"Nothing to be astonished about," said Avalon. "Mario raised the point. He's a triskaidekaphobe."

"A what?" said Gonzalo in an outraged voice.

"You have a morbid fear of the number thirteen."

"I do *not*," said Gonzalo. "I just believe in being cautious."

Trumbull helped himself to another roll and said, "What do you mean, Dr. Fletcher, in saying that you would have raised the point yourself? Are you a triskai-whatever too?"

"No, no," said Fletcher, shaking his head gently, "but I have an interest in the subject. A personal interest."

Halsted said in his soft, somewhat hesitant voice, "Actually, there's a very good reason why thirteen should be considered unlucky and it has nothing to do with the Last Supper. That explanation was just invented after the fact.

"Consider that early, unsophisticated people found the number twelve very handy because it could be divided evenly by two, three, four, and six. If you sold objects by the dozen, you could sell half a dozen, a third, a fourth, or a sixth of a dozen. We still sell by the dozen and the gross today for that very reason. Now imagine some poor fellow counting his stock and finding he has thirteen items of something. You can't divide thirteen by anything. It just confuses his arithmetic and he says, 'Oh, damn, thirteen! What rotten luck!'—and there you are."

Rubin's sparse beard seemed to stiffen, and he said, "Oh, that's a lot of junk, Roger. That sort of reasoning should make thirteen a lucky number. Any tradesman would offer to throw in the thirteenth to sweeten the trade. —That's good steak, Henry."

"Baker's dozen," said James Drake in his hoarse smoker's voice.

"The baker," said Avalon, "threw in a thirteenth loaf to make up a baker's dozen in order to avoid the harsh penalties meted out for short weight. By adding the thirteenth, he was sure to go over weight even if any of the normal twelve loaves were skimpy. He might consider the necessity to be unlucky."

"The customer might consider it lucky," muttered Rubin.

"As for Friday," said Halsted, "that is named for the goddess of love, Freya in the Norse myths. In the Romance languages the name of the day is derived from Venus; it is *vendredi* in French, for instance. I should think it would be considered a lucky day for that reason. Now you take Saturday, named for the dour old god, Saturn—"

Gonzalo had completed his caricature and passed it around the table to general approval and to a snicker from Fletcher himself. He seized the opportunity to finish his potato puffs and said, "All you guys are trying to reason out something that lies beyond reason. The fact is that people *are* afraid of Friday and are afraid of thirteen and are especially afraid of the combination. The fear itself could make bad things happen. I might be so concerned that this place will catch fire, for instance, because it's Friday the thirteenth, that I won't be thinking and I'll stick my fork in my cheek."

"If that would shut you up, it might be a good idea," said Avalon.

"But I won't," said Gonzalo, "because I have my eye on my fork and I know that Henry will get us all out if the place catches on fire, even if it means staying behind himself and dying in agony. —Right, Henry?"

"I hope that the contingency will not arise, sir," said Henry, placing the dessert dishes dexterously before each diner. "Will you be having coffee, sir?" he asked Fletcher.

"May I have cocoa? Is that possible?" said Fletcher.

"Certainly it is," interposed Avalon. "Go, Henry, negotiate the matter with the chef."

And it was not long thereafter, with the coffee (or cocoa, in Fletcher's case) steaming welcomely before them, that Avalon tapped his water glass with his spoon and said, "Gentlemen, it is time to turn our attention to our guest. Tom, will you initiate the matter?"

Trumbull put down his coffee cup, scowled his face into a cross-current of wrinkles, and said, "Ordinarily, Dr. Fletcher, I would ask you to justify your existence, but having sat through an extraordinarily foolish discussion of superstition, I want to ask you whether you have anything to add to the matter. You implied early in the meal that you would have raised the matter of Friday the thirteenth yourself if it had not come up otherwise."

"Yes," said Fletcher, holding his large ceramic cup of cocoa within the parentheses of his two hands, "but not as a matter of superstition. Rather it is a serious historic puzzle that concerns me and that hinges on Friday the thirteenth. Jeff said that the Black Widowers were fond of puzzles and this is the only one I have for you—with the warning, I'm afraid, that there is no solution."

"As you all know," said Avalon, with resignation, "I'm against turning the club into a puzzle-solving organization, but I seem to be a minority of one in this matter, so I try to go along with the consensus." He accepted the small brandy glass from Henry with a look compounded of virtue and martyrdom.

"May we have this puzzle?" said Halsted.

"Yes, of course. I thought for a moment, when Jeff invited me to attend your dinner, that it was to be held on Friday the thirteenth in my honor, but that was a flash of megalomania. I undersand that you always hold your dinners on a Friday evening and, of course, no one knows about my work but myself and my immediate family."

He paused to light his pipe, then, leaning back and puffing gently, he said, "The story concerns Joseph Hennessy, who was executed in 1925 for an attempt on the life of President Coolidge.* He was tried on this charge, convicted, and hanged.

"To the end, Hennessy proclaimed his innocence and advanced a rather strong defense, with a number of people giving evidence for his absence from the scene. However, the emotional currents against him were strong. He was an outspoken labor leader, and a Socialist, at a time when fear of Socialism ran high. He was foreign-born, which didn't help. And those who gave evidence in his favor were also foreign-born Socialists. The trial was a travesty and, once he was hanged and passions had time to cool, many people realized this.

"After the execution, however, long after, a letter was produced in Hennessy's handwriting that seemed to make him a moving figure behind the assassination plot beyond a doubt. This was seized on by all those who had been anxious to see him hanged, and it was used to justify the verdict. Without the letter, the verdict must still be seen as a miscarriage of jusice."

Drake squinted from behind the curling smoke of his

* Joseph Hennessy never existed and, as far as I know, there was never an assassination attempt on Calvin Coolidge. All other historical references in the story, not involving Hennessy, are accurate—I.A.

cigarette and said, "Was the letter a forgery?"

"No. Naturally, those who felt Hennessy was innocent thought it was at first. The closest study, however, seemed to show that it was indeed in his handwriting, and there were things about it that seemed to mark it his. He was a grandiosely superstitious man, and the note was dated Friday the thirteenth and nothing more."

"Why 'grandiosely' superstitious?" asked Trumbull. "That's an odd adjective to use."

"He was a grandiose man," said Fletcher, "given to doing everything in a flamboyant manner. He researched his superstitions. In fact, the discussion at the table as to the significance of Friday and of thirteen reminded me of the sort of man he was. He probably would have known more about the matter than any of you."

"I should think," said Avalon gravely, "that investigating superstitions would militate against his being victimized by them."

"Not necessarly," said Fletcher. "I have a good friend who drives a car frequently but won't take a plane because he's afraid of them. He has heard all the statistics that show that on a man-mile basis airplane travel is safest and automobile travel most dangerous, and when I reminded him of that, he replied, 'There is nothing either in law or in psychology that commands me to be rational at every point.' And yet in most things he is the most rational man I know.

"As for Joe Hennessy, he was far from an entirely rational man and none of his careful studies of superstition prevented him in the least from being victimized by them. And his fear of Friday the thirteenth was perhaps the strongest of all his superstitious fears."

Halsted said, "What did the note say? Do you remember?"

"I brought a copy," said Fletcher. "It's not the original, of course. The original is in the Secret Service files, but in these days of Xeroxing, that scarcely matters."

He took a slip of paper out of his wallet and passed it to Halsted, who sat on his right. It made the rounds of the table and Avalon, who received it last, automatically passed it to Henry, who was standing at the sideboard. Henry read it with an impassive countenance and handed it back to Fletcher, who seemed slightly surprised at having the waiter take part, but said nothing.

The note, in a bold and easily legible handwriting, read:

Friday the 13th

Dear Paddy,

It's a fool I am to be writing you this day when I should be in bed in a dark room by rights. I must tell you, though, the plans are now completed and I dare not wait a day to begin implementing them. The finger of God has touched that wicked man and we will surely finish the job next month. You know what you must do, and it must be done even at the cost of every drop of blood in our veins. I thank God's mercy for the forty-year miracle that will give us no Friday the 13th next month.

Joe

Avalon said, "He doesn't really say anything."

Fletcher shook his head. "On the contrary, he says too much. If this were the prelude to an assassination attempt, would he have placed anything at all in writing? Or if he had, would the reference not have been much more dark and Aesopic?"

"What did the prosecution say it meant?"

Fletcher put the note carefully back into his wallet. "As I told you, the prosecution never saw it. The note was uncovered only some ten years after the hanging, when Patrick Reilly, to whom the note was addressed, died and left it among his effects. Reilly was not implicated in the assassination attempt, though of course he would have been if the note had come to light soon enough.

"Those who maintain that Hennessy was rightly executed say that the note was written on Friday, June 13, 1924. The assassination attempt was carried through on Friday, July 11, 1924. It would have made Hennessy nervous to have made the attempt on any Friday, but for various reasons involving the presidential schedule that was the only possible day for a considerable period of time, and Hennessy would be understandably grateful that it was not the thirteenth at least.

"The remark concerning the finger of God touching the wicked man is said to be a reference to the death of President Warren G. Harding, who died suddenly on August 2, 1923, less than a year before the assassination attempt was to 'finish the job' by getting rid of the Vice-President who had succeeded to the presidency."

Drake, with his head cocked to one side, said, "It sounds like a reasonable interpretation. It seems to fit."

"No, it doesn't," said Fletcher. "The interpretation is accepted only because anything else would highlight a miscarriage of justice. But to me—" He paused and said, "Gentlemen, I will not pretend to be free of bias. My wife is Joseph Hennessy's granddaughter. But if the relationship exposes me to bias, it also gives me considerable personal information concerning Hennessy by way of my father-in-law, now dead.

"Hennessy had no strong feelings against either Harding or Coolidge. He was not for them, of course, for he was a fiery Socialist, supporting Eugene Debs all the way—and that didn't help him at the trial, by the way. There was no way in which he could feel that the assassination of Coolidge would have accomplished anything at all. Nor would he have felt Harding to be a 'wicked man' since the evidence concerning the vast corruption that had taken place during his administration came to light only gradually, and the worst of it well after the note was written.

"In fact, if there was a President whom Hennessy hated furiously, it was Woodrow Wilson. Hennessy had been born in Ireland and had left the land a step ahead of English bayonets. He was furiously anti-British and therefore, in the course of World War I, was an emphatic pacifist, opposing American entry on the side of Great Britain. —That didn't help him at the trial either."

Rubin interposed, "Debs opposed entry also, didn't he?"

"That's right," said Fletcher, "and in 1918 Debs was jailed as a spy in consequence. Hennessy avoided prison, but he never referred to Wilson after American entry into war by any term other than 'that wicked man.' He had voted for Wilson in 1916 as a result of the 'He-kept-us-out-of-war' campaign slogan, and he felt betrayed, you understand, when the United States went to war the next year."

"Then you think he's referring to Wilson in that note," said Trumbull.

"I'm sure of it. The reference to the finger of God touching the wicked man doesn't sound like death to me, but something else—just the touch of the finger, you see. As you probably all know, Wilson suffered a stroke on October 2,

1919, and was incapacitated for the remainder of his term. That was the finger of God, if you like."

Gonzalo said, "Are you saying Hennessy was going to finish the job by assassinating Wilson?"

"No, no, there was no assassination attempt on Wilson."

"Then what does he mean, 'finish the job,' and doing it 'even at the cost of every drop of blood in our veins'?"

"That was his flamboyance," said Fletcher. "If he was going out for a bucket of beer he would say, 'I'll bring it back if it costs me every drop of blood in my veins.'"

Avalon leaned back in his chair, twirled his empty brandy glass, and said, "I don't blame you, Evan, for wanting to clear your grandfather-in-law, but you'll need something better than what you've given us. If you can find another Friday the thirteenth on which the letter could have been written, if you can figure out some way of pinpointing the date to something other than June 13, 1924—"

"I realize that," said Fletcher, rather glumly, "and I've gone through his life. I've worked with his correspondence and with newspaper files and with my father-in-law's memory, until I think I could put my finger on where he was and what he did virtually every day of his life. I tried to find events that could be related to some nearby Friday the thirteenth, and I even think I've found some—but how do I go about proving that any of them are *the* Friday the thirteenth? —If only he had been less obsessed by the fact of Friday the thirteenth and had dated the letter in the proper fashion."

"It wouldn't have saved his life," said Gonzalo thoughtfully.

"The letter couldn't then have been used to besmirch his memory and give rise to the pretense that the trial was fair. —As it is, I don't even know that I've caught every Friday the thirteenth there might be. The calendar is so dreadfully irregular that there's no way of knowing when the date will spring out at you."

"Oh no," said Halsted with a sudden soft explosiveness. "The calendar is irregular, but not as irregular as all that. You can find every Friday the thirteenth without trouble as far back or as far forward as you want to go."

"You can?" said Fletcher with some astonishment.

"I don't believe that," said Gonzalo, almost simultaneously.

"It's very easy," said Halsted, drawing a ball-point pen

out of his inner jacket pocket and opening a napkin on the table before him.

"Oh, no," said Rubin, in mock terror. "Roger teaches math at a junior high school, Dr. Fletcher, and you had better be ready for some complicated equations."

"No equations at all necessary," said Halsted loftily. "I'll bring it down to your level, Manny. —Look, there are 365 days in a year, which comes out to fifty-two weeks and one day. If the year were 364 days long, it would be just fifty-two weeks long, and the calendar would repeat itself each year. If January 1 were on a Sunday one year, it would be on a Sunday the next year and every year.

"That extra day, however, means that each year the weekday on which a particular date falls is shoved ahead by one. If January 1 is on a Sunday one year, it will fall on Monday the next year, and on Tuesday the year after.

"The only complication is that every four years we have a leap year in which a February 29 is added, making 366 days in all. That comes to fifty-two weeks and *two* days, so that a particular date is shoved ahead by two in the list of weekdays. It leaps over one, so to speak, to land on the second, which is why it is called leap year. That means that if January 1 falls on, say, a Wednesday in leap year, then the next year January 1 falls on a Friday, having leaped over the Thursday. And this goes for *any* day of the year and not just January 1.

"Of course, February 29 comes after two months of a year have passed so that dates in January and February make their leap the year after leap year, while the remaining months make their leap in leap year itself. In order to avoid that complication, let's pretend that the year begins on March 1 of the year before the calendar year and ends on February 28 of the calendar year—or February 29 in leap year. In that way, we can arrange to have every date leap the weekday in the year after what we call leap year.

"Now let's imagine that the thirteenth of some month falls on a Friday—it doesn't matter which month—and that it happens to be a leap year. The date leaps and lands on Sunday the next year. That next year is a normal 365-day year and so are the two following, so the thirteenth progresses to Monday, Tuesday, and Wednesday, but the year in which it is Wednesday is a leap year again and the next year it falls on a Friday. In other words, if the thirteenth of some months is on a Friday of leap year, by our definition, then it is on a Friday again five years later—"

Gonzalo said, "I'm not following you at all."

Halsted said, "Okay, then, let's make a table. We can list the years as L, 1, 2, 3, L, 1, 2, 3 and so on where L stands for leap year, coming every four years. We can label the days of the week from A to G, A for Sunday, B for Monday through to G for Saturday. That will, at least, give us the pattern. Here it is—"

He scribbled furiously, then passed the napkin round. On it was written:

```
L 1 2 3 L 1 2 3 L 1 2 3 L 1 2 3
A C D E F A B C D F G A B D E F


L 1 2 3 L 1 2 3 L 1 2 3 L
G B C D E G A B C E F G A
```

"You see," said Halsted, "on the twenty-ninth year after you start, A falls on leap year again and the whole pattern starts over. That means that this year's calendar can be used again twenty-eight years from now and then again twenty-eight years after that, and twenty-eight years after that, and so on.

"Notice that each letter occurs four times in the twenty-eight-year cycle, which means that any date can fall on any day of the week with equal probability. That means that Friday the thirteenth must come every seven months on the average. Actually, it doesn't because the months are of different lengths, irregularly spaced, so that there can be any number of Friday the thirteenths in any given year from 1 to 3. It is impossible to have a year with no Friday the thirteenths at all, and equally impossible to have more than three."

"Why is there a twenty-eight-year cycle?" asked Gonzalo.

Halsted said, "There are seven days in the week and a leap year every fourth year and seven times four is twenty-eight."

"You mean that if there were a leap year every two years the cycle would last fourteen years?"

"That's right, and if it were every three years it would last twenty-one years and so on. As long as there are seven days a week and a leap year every *x* years, with *x* and 7 mutually prime—"

Avalon interrupted. "Never mind that, Roger. You've got your pattern. How do you use it?"

"The easiest thing in the world. Say the thirteenth falls on a Friday in a leap year, where you remember to start the leap year on March 1 before the actual leap year. Then you represent it by A, and you will see that the thirteenth of that same month will fall whenever the A shows up, five years later and six years after that, and then eleven years after that.

"Now this is December 13, 1974, and by our convention of leap years this is the year before leap year. That means that it can be represented by the letter E, whose first appearance is under 3, the year before L. Well then, by following the E's we see that there will be another Friday the thirteenth in December eleven years from now, then in six more years, then in five years. That is, there will be a Friday the thirteenth in December 1985, in December 1991, and in December 1996.

"You can do that for any date for any month, using that little series I've just written out, and make up a perpetual calendar that runs for twenty-eight years and then repeats itself over and over. You can run it forward or backward and catch every Friday the thirteenth as far as you like in either direction, or at least as far back as 1752. In fact, you can find such perpetual calendars in reference books like the World Almanac."

Gonzalo said, "Why 1752?"

"That's an unusual year, at least for Great Britain and what were then the American colonies. The old Julian calendar which had been used since Julius Caesar's time had gained on the season because there were a few too many leap years in it. The Gregorian calendar, named for Pope Gregory XIII, was adopted in 1582 in much of Europe, and by that time the calendar was ten days out of synchronization with the seasons, so that ten days were dropped from the calendar, and every once in a while thereafter a leap year was omitted to keep the same thing from happening again. Great Britain and the colonies didn't go along till 1752, by which time another day had been added, so they had to drop eleven days."

"That's right," said Rubin. "And for a while they used

both calendars, referring to a particular date as O.S. or N.S. for Old Style and New Style. George Washington was born on February 11, 1732 O.S., but instead of keeping the date, as many people did, he switched to February 22, 1732 N.S. I've won considerable money by betting that George Washington wasn't born on Washington's birthday."

Halsted said, "The reason Great Britain hesitated so long was that the new calendar was initiated by the papacy, and Great Britain, being Protestant, preferred going against the Sun than along with the Pope. Russia didn't switch till 1923, and the Russian Orthodox Church is on the Julian calendar to this day, which is why the Orthodox Christmas comes on January 7 now, since the number of accumulated days' difference is thirteen.

"Great Britain went from September 2, 1752, directly to September 14, dropping the days in between. There were riots against that, with people shouting, 'Give us back our eleven days.' "

Rubin said indignantly, "That wasn't as crazy as you might think. Landlords charged the full quarter's rent, without giving an eleven-day rebate. I'd have rioted too."

"In any case," said Halsted, "that's why the perpetual calendar only goes back to 1752. Those eleven missing days mess everything up and you have to set up a different arrangement for days before September 14, 1752."

Fletcher, who had listened to everything with evident interest, said, "I must say I didn't know any of this, Mr. Halsted. I don't pretend that I followed you perfectly, or that I can duplicate what you've just done, but I didn't know that I could find a perpetual calendar in the World Almanac. It would have saved me a lot of trouble—but of course, knowing where all the Friday the thirteenths are wouldn't help me determine which Friday the thirteenth might be *the* Friday the thirteenth."

Henry interposed suddenly and said in his soft, polite voice, "I'm not sure of that, Mr. Fletcher. May I ask you a few questions?"

Fletcher looked startled and, for a short moment, was silent.

Avalon said quickly, "Henry is a member of the club, Evan. I hope you don't mind—"

"Of course not," said Fletcher at once. "Ask away, Henry."

"Thank you, sir. —What I want to know is whether Mr.

Hennessy knew of this pattern of date variations that Mr. Halsted has so kindly outlined for us."

Fletcher looked thoughtful. "I can't say for certain; I certainly haven't heard of it, if he did. —Still, it's very likely he would have. He prided himself, for instance, on being able to cast a horoscope and, for all the nonsense there is in astrology, casting a proper horoscope takes a bit of mathematics, I understand. Hennessy did not have much of a formal education, but he was fearfully intelligent, and he was interested in numbers. In fact, as I think of it, I am sure he couldn't possibly have been as interested in Friday the thirteenth as he was, without being impelled to work out the pattern."

"In that case, sir," said Henry, "if I ask you what Mr. Hennessy was doing on a certain day, could you call up someone to check your notes on the matter, and tell us?"

Fletcher looked uncertain. "I'm not sure. My wife is home, but she wouldn't know where to look, and it's not likely I'll be able to give her adequate directions. —I could try, I suppose."

"In that case, do you suppose you could tell me what Mr. Hennessy was doing on Friday, March 12, 1920?"

Fletcher's chair scraped backward and for a long moment Fletcher stared openmouthed. "What makes you ask that?"

"It seems logical, sir," said Henry softly.

"But I *do* know what he was doing that day. It was one of the important days of his life. He swung the labor organization of which he was one of the leaders into supporting Debs for the presidency. Debs ran that year on the Socialist ticket even though he was still in jail, and he polled over 900,000 votes—the best the Socialists were ever able to do in the United States."

Henry said, "Might not the labor organization have ordinarily supported the Democratic candidate for that year?"

"James M. Cox, yes. He was strongly supported by Wilson."

"So to swing the vote away from Wilson's candidate might be, in Mr. Hennessy's flamboyant style, the finishing of the job that the finger of God had begun."

"I'm sure he would think of that in that fashion."

"In which case the letter would have been written on Friday, February 13, 1920."

"It's a possibility," said Fletcher, "but how can you prove it?"

"Dr. Fletcher," said Henry, "in Mr. Hennessy's note he thanks God that there is no Friday the thirteenth the month after and even considers it a miracle. If he knew the perpetual calendar pattern he certainly wouldn't think it a miracle. There are seven months that have thirty-one days, and are therefore four weeks and three days long. If a particular date falls on a particular weekday in such a month, it falls on a weekday three past it the next month. In other words, if the thirteenth falls on a Friday in July, then it will fall on a Monday in August. Is that not so, Mr. Halsted?"

"You're perfectly right, Henry. And if the month has thirty days it moves two weekdays along, so that if the thirteenth falls on a Friday in June it falls on a Sunday in July," said Halsted.

"In that case, in any month that has thirty or thirty-one days, there cannot possibly be a Friday the thirteenth followed the next month by another Friday the thirteenth, and Hennessy would know that and not consider it a miracle at all.

"*But*, Mr. Fletcher, there is one month that has only twenty-eight days and that is February. It is exactly four weeks long, so that March begins on the same day of the week that February does, and repeats the weekdays for every date, at least up to the twenty-eighth. If there is a Friday the thirteenth in February, there must be a Friday the Thirteenth in March as well—*unless it is leap year.*

"In leap year, February has twenty-nine days and is four weeks and one day long. That means that every day in March falls one weekday later. If the thirteenth falls on a Friday in February, it falls on a Saturday in March, so that, though February has a Friday the thirteenth, March has a Friday the twelfth.

"My new appointment book has calendars for both 1975 and 1976. The year 1976 is a leap year and, in it, I can see that there is a Friday, February 13, and a Friday, March 12. Mr. Halsted has pointed out that calendars repeat every twenty-eight years. That means that the 1976 calendar would also hold for 1948 and for 1920.

"It is clear that once every twenty-eight years there is a Friday the thirteenth in February that is not followed by one in March, and Mr. Hennessy, knowing that the meeting of his labor group was scheduled for the second Friday in March, something perhaps maneuvered by his opposition to keep him at home, was delighted and relieved at the fact that it was at least not a second Friday the thirteenth."

There was a silence all about the table and then Avalon said, "That's very nicely argued. It convinces me."

But Fletcher shook his head. "Nicely argued, I admit, but I'm not sure—"

Henry said, "There is, possibly, more. I couldn't help wonder why Mr. Hennessy called it a 'forty-year miracle.' "

"Oh well," said Fletcher indulgently, "there's no mystery about that, I'm sure. Forty is one of those mystic numbers that crops up in the Bible all the time. You know, the Flood rained down upon the Earth for forty days and forty nights."

"Yes," said Rubin eagerly, "and Moses remained forty days on Mount Sinai, and Elijah was fed forty days by the ravens, and Jesus fasted forty days in the wilderness, and so on. Talking about God's mercy would just naturally bring the number forty to mind."

"Perhaps that is so," said Henry, "but I have a thought. Mr. Halsted, in talking about the conversion of the Julian to the Gregorian calendar, said that the new Gregorian calendar omitted a leap year occasionally."

Halsted brought his fist down on the table. "Good God, I forgot. Manny, if you hadn't made that stupid joke about equations, I wouldn't have been so anxious to simplify and I wouldn't have forgotten. —The Julian calendar had one leap year every four years without fail, which would have been correct if the year were exactly 365¼ days long, but it's a tiny bit shorter than that. To make up for that tiny falling-short, three leap years have to be omitted every four centuries, and by the Gregorian calendar those omissions come in any year ending in 00 that is *not* divisible by 400, even though such a year would be leap in the Julian calendar.

"That means," and he pounded his fist on the table again, "that 1900 was *not* a leap year. There was *no* leap year between 1896 and 1904. There were seven consecutive years of 365 days each, instead of three."

Henry said, "Doesn't that upset the perpetual calendar that you described?"

"Yes, it does. The perpetual calendar for the 1800s meets the one for the 1900s in the middle, so to speak."

"In that case, what was the last year before 1920 in which a Friday the thirteenth in February fell in a leap year?"

"I'll have to figure it out," said Halsted, his pen racing over a new napkin. "Ah, ah," he muttered, then threw his pen down on the table and said, "In 1880, by God."

"Forty years before 1920," said Henry, "so that on the day that Hennessy wrote his note, an unlucky day in February was *not* followed by an unlucky day in March for the first time in forty years, and it was quite fair for him to call it, flamboyantly, a forty-year miracle. It seems to me that February 13, 1920, is the only possible day in his entire lifetime on which that note could have been written."

"And so it does to me," said Halsted.

"And to me," said Fletcher. "I thank you, gentlemen. And especially you, Henry. If I can argue this out correctly now—"

"I'm sure," said Henry, "that Mr. Halsted will be glad to help out."

10 Afterword

I *had* to write this one. On Friday, December 13, 1974, I was co-host for that month's meeting of the Trap Door Spiders. (The Trap Door Spiders have *two* hosts and twice the membership of the Black Widowers, you see.) I had picked a new restaurant and was particularly anxious that everything go well.

I had guaranteed that twelve to fifteen members would show up and I feared that we might not make the number and that I would have a bad time with the restaurant. I counted them as they came in and when number twelve arrived I was relieved. (And the restaurant was pleased too. We were served an excellent meal with superb service—though, of course, no Henry.)

Then, just as the cocktail hour was over and we sat down to dinner, in came member number thirteen. Personally, I think it's a credit to the membership that not one person present seemed the least bit concerned that we were thirteen at the table on Friday the thirteenth (and as far as I know, nothing has happened as a result).

I must admit *I* was concerned, because I could not let such an event pass without beginning to work on a Black Widower plot at once. Again *Ellery Queen's Mystery Magazine* felt this to be too complicated a situation, and I passed it on to *F & SF*, which took it. It appeared in the January 1976 issue.

11

The Unabridged

Roger Halsted, normally an equable person (as one would have to be to survive the teaching of mathematics at a junior high school), arrived at the monthly banquet of the Black Widowers in a highly apparent state of the sulks.

"I'll have a bloody Mary, Henry," he said. "Light on the blood and an extra slug of Mary."

Silently and deftly, Henry produced the drink, complete with slug, and James Drake, who was the host for the evening, stared at him over the smoke of his cigarette and let his inconsiderable gray mustache twitch. "What's the matter, Rog?" he asked in his soft, hoarse voice.

Roger said, "I'm late."

"So?" said Drake, who had to come in from New Jersey and had been known to be late himself. "Drink fast and catch up."

"It's *why* I'm late that bothers me," said Halsted. His high forehead had turned pink past the place where the vanished hairline had once been. "I was looking for my cuff links. My favorite pair. —My only pair, actually. I spent twenty minutes. I looked everywhere."

"Did you find them?"

"No! Have you got any idea how many hiding places there are in a two-story three-bedroom house? I could have spent twenty hours and ended with nothing."

Geoffrey Avalon drifted over, with the second drink at the halfway mark. "You don't have to look through the *whole* house, Rog. You didn't paste them over the molding or inside the drainpipe, did you? Where do you usually keep them?"

"In a little box I've got in the drawer. I looked there first. They weren't there."

His voice had risen past its usual quiet pitch and Emmanuel Rubin called out from the other side of the banquet table, "You left them in your shirt the last time you wore them and they got sent to the laundry and you'll never see them again."

"That's not so," said Halsted, clenching his left hand into a fist and waving it. "This is the only darned shirt I've got with French cuffs and I haven't worn it in three months and I saw the cuff links in the box just the other night when I was looking for something else."

"Then look for something else again," said Rubin, "and they'll turn up."

"Ha-ha," said Halsted grimly, and finished his drink.

Mario Gonzalo said, "Is that shirt you're wearing the one with the French cuffs, Rog?"

"Yes, it is."

"Well then, if that's the only shirt you've got with French cuffs, and you couldn't find your only pair of cuff links, what are you using to hold the cuffs together?"

"Thread," said Halsted bitterly, shooting his cuffs for inspection. "I had Alice tie them with white thread."

Gonzalo, himself an example of faultless sartorial splendor, with a predominant bluish touch in shirt and jacket, shading into the darker tints of his tie, winced. "Why didn't you put on a different shirt?"

"My blood was up," said Halsted, "and I wasn't going to be forced into changing the shirt."

Drake said, "Well, if you'll cool down a bit, Rog, I'll introduce my guest. Jason Leominster, this is Roger Halsted, and coming up the stairs for a scotch and soda is the final member, Thomas Trumbull."

Leominster smiled dutifully. He was not quite as tall as Avalon's six feet two, but he was thinner. He was clearly in his forties though he looked younger, and under his tan jacket he wore a black turtleneck sweater which managed to seem not out of place. He had high and pronounced cheekbones over a narrow and pointed chin.

He said, "I'm afraid you're not getting much sympathy, Mr. Halsted, but you may have mine for what it's worth. When it comes to not finding things, my heart bleeds."

Before Halsted could express what gratitude he felt for that, Henry signaled the beginning of dinner, the Black Widowers took their seats, and Trumbull loudly and rapidly, proclaimed the ritualistic toast to Old King Cole.

Rubin, staring hard at what was before him, lifted his straggly beard skyward in an access of indignation and said to Henry, "This thing looks like an egg roll. What is it, Henry?"

"It's an egg roll, sir."

"What's it doing here?"

Henry said, "The chef has put together a Chinese meal for the club this month."

"In an Italian restaurant?"

"I believe he considers it a challenge, sir."

Trumbull said, "Shut up and eat, Manny, will you? It's good."

Rubin bit into it, then reached for the mustard. "It's all right," he said discontentedly, "for an egg roll."

Even Rubin melted with the birds' nest soup, and when the first of the seven platters proved to be Peking duck, he grew positively mellow.

"Actually," he said, "it's not that you lose things. You *forget* them. It's that way with me. It's that way with everyone. You're holding something, and put it down with your mind on something else. Two minutes later you can't for the life of you tell where that something you put down is. Even if, by sheer accident, you find it, you still can't remember putting it down there. Roger hasn't lost his cuff links. He *put* them somewhere and he doesn't remember where."

Gonzalo, who was daintily picking out a black mushroom in order to experience its unaccompanied savor, said, "Much as it pains me to agree with Manny—"

"Much as it pains you to be right for one rare occasion, you mean."

"—I've got to admit there's something to what he has just said. By accident, I'm sure. The worst thing anyone can do is to put something away where he knows it will be safe from a burglar's hand. The burglar will find it right away, but the owner will never see it again. I once put a bankbook away and didn't find it for five years."

"You hid it under the soap," said Rubin.

"Does that work with you?" asked Gonzalo sweetly. "It doesn't with me."

"Where was it after you found it, Mario?" asked Avalon.

"I've forgotten again," said Gonzalo.

"Of course," interposed Leominster agreeably, "it is possible to put something in one place, shift it to another for still safer keeping, then remember only the first place—where it isn't."

"Has that happened to you, Mr. Leominster?" asked Trumbull.

"In a manner of speaking," said Leominster, "but I don't really know if it happened at all."

Henry arrived with the platter of fortune cookies and said in a low voice to Halsted, "Mrs. Halsted has just called, sir. She wants me to tell you that the cuff links were found."

Halsted turned sharply. "Found? Did she say where?"

"Under the bed, sir. She says they had presumably fallen there."

"I *looked* under the bed."

"Mrs. Halsted says they were near one of the feet of the bed. Quite invisible, sir. She had to feel around. She said to tell you that it has happened before."

"Open your fortune cookie, Rog," said Avalon indulgently. "It will tell you that you are about to find something of great importance."

Halsted did so, and said, "It says, 'Let a smile be your umbrella,'" and chafed visibly.

Rubin said, "I'm not sure that it's proper for a Black Widower to be receiving a message from a woman while a stag meeting is actually in session."

Gonzalo said, "Electric impulses have no sex, though I don't suspect you would know that, Manny, any more than you know anything else about the subject."

But Henry was bringing the brandy and Drake headed off the inevitable furious (and possibly improper) response by tapping a rapid tattoo on his water glass.

Drake said, "Let me introduce Jason Leominster, a somewhat distant neighbor of mine. He's a genealogist and I don't think there's a single member of the Black Widowers —always excepting Henry—with a genealogy that would bear looking into, so let's be cautious."

Leominster said, "Not really. No one has ever been disappointed in a genealogy. The number of ancestors increases geometrically with each generation, minus the effect of intermarriage. If we explore the siblings, the parents and their siblings, the grandparents and their siblings; all the attachments by marriage and *their* siblings; and the parents and grandparents that enter in with the cases of remarriage, we have hundreds of individuals to play with when we go back only a single century.

"By emphasizing the flattering connections and ignoring the others, we can't lose. To the professional genealogist, of course, there can be items of historic value uncovered, often minor, and sometimes surprisingly important. I discovered, for instance, a collateral descendant of Martha Washington who—"

Trumbull, having raised his hand uselessly in the course of these remarks, now said, "Please, Mr. Leominster— Look, Jim, this is out of order. It's got to be question-and-answer. Will you indicate a griller?"

Drake stubbed out his cigarette and said, "It sounded interesting to me as it was. But go ahead. You be the griller."

Trumbull scowled. "I just want everything in order, Mr. Leominster, I apologize for interrupting you. It *was* interesting, but we must proceed according to tradition. My first question would have been that of asking you to justify your existence, but your remarks have already indicated how your answer would be framed. Let me, therefore, go on to the next question. Mr. Leominster, you said in the course of the dinner that a person might hide something in one place, switch it to another, then remember only the first. You also said that it happened to you only in a manner of speaking and may never have happened at all. Could you elaborate on this? I am curious to know what was in your mind."

"Nothing, really. My aunt died last month," and here Leominster raised his hand, "but spare me the formalities of regrets. She was eighty-five and bedridden. The point is that she left me her house and its contents, which had been her brother's till he died ten years ago, and Mr. Halsted's affair with the cuff links reminded me of what went on when my aunt inherited the house."

"Good," said Trumbull, "what went on then?"

"Why, she was convinced something was hidden in the house; something of value. It was never found and that's all there is to it."

Trumbull said, "Then whatever it is is still there, isn't it?"

"If it was ever there in the first place, then I suppose so."

"And it's yours now?"

"Yes."

"And what do you intend to do about it?"

"I don't see that I can do anything. We didn't find it when we looked for it, and I probably won't find it now. Still—"

"Yes?"

"Well, I intend in time to put the house up for sale and auction off its contents. I have no use for them as things and a reasonable use for the cash equivalents. It would be, however, annoying to auction off something for a hundred dollars and find that it contains an item worth, let us say, twenty-five thousand dollars."

Trumbull sat back and said, "With the host's permission, Mr. Leominster, I'm going to ask you to tell the story in some reasonable order. What is the thing that is lost? How did it come to be lost? And so on."

"Hear, hear!" said Gonzalo approvingly. He had finished his sketch, making Leominster's face a triangle, point-down, without in the least losing its perfect recognizability.

Leominster looked at the sketch stoically and nodded, sipping at his brandy, while Henry noiselessly cleared the table.

Leominster said, "I am from what is called an old New England family. The family made its money two centuries ago in textile mills and, I believe, in some of the less cheerful aspects of trade in those days—slaves and rum. The family has kept its money since, investing it conservatively and so on. We're not tycoons, but we're all well off—those of us who are left: myself and a cousin. I am divorced, by the way, and have no children.

"The family history is what makes me interested in genealogy, and the family finances make it possible for me to humor myself in this respect. It is not exactly a remunerative pursuit—at least, not in the fashion in which I pursue it—but I can afford it, you see.

"My Uncle Bryce—my father's older brother—retired fairly early in life after the death of his wife. He built a rather fussy house in Connecticut and involved himself in collecting things. I myself don't see the pleasure in accumulation, but I imagine it gave rise in him to the same pleasures that are given me by genealogical research."

"What did he collect?" asked Avalon.

"Several types of items, but nothing unusual. He was a rather plodding sort of fellow, without much imagination. He collected old books to begin with, then old coins, and finally stamps. The fever never got to him so badly that he would invest really large sums, so that his collections are not what you might call first class. They're the kind that appraisers smile condescendingly over. Still, it gave him pleasure, and his thousand-book library isn't entirely worthless. Nor is the rest. And of course even a minor collector may sometimes get his hands on a good item."

"And your uncle had done so?" asked Trumbull.

"My Aunt Hester—she was the third child, two years younger than my Uncle Bryce and five years older than my father, who died fourteen years ago— My Aunt Hester *said* that my uncle had a valuable item."

"How did she know?"

"My Aunt Hester was always close to my uncle. She lived in Florida, but after my uncle was widowed she took to spending some of the summer months with him in Connecticut each year. She had never married and they grew closer with age, since there was almost no one else. My uncle had a son but he has been in South America for a quarter century. He has married a Brazilian girl and has three children. He and his father were not on good terms at all, and neither seemed to exist as far as the other was concerned. There was myself, of course, and they entertained me often out of a sense of duty and distant liking; and I was rather fond of them.

"Aunt Hester was a prim old lady, terribly self-conscious about the family position; to a ridiculous and outmoded extent, of course. She was precise and stiff in her speech, and was convinced that she was living in a hostile world of thieves and Socialists. She never wore her jewelry, for instance. She kept it in a safe-deposit box at all times.

"It was natural, then, that my uncle would leave the house to my aunt, and that she would in turn leave it to me. I'm genealogical enough, however, to remember that my Uncle Bryce has a son who is the direct heir and more deserving, by ties of blood, to have the house. I've written to my cousin asking him if he is satisfied with the will, and I received a letter from him three days ago telling me I was welcome to the house and contents. Actually, he said, rather bitterly, that as far as he was concerned I could burn the house and contents."

Trumbull said, "Mr. Leominster, I wonder if you could get back to the lost object."

"Ah, I'm sorry. I had forgotten. Aunt Hester, considering her views, was not happy over my uncle's cavalier treatment of his collection. Aunt Hester had a totally exaggerated idea of its value. 'These items and sundries,' she would say to me, 'are of peerless worth.' "

"Is that what she called them? Items and sundries?" asked Avalon, smiling.

"That was a pet phrase of hers. I assure you I remember it correctly. She had an archaic way of speaking—a deliberately cultivated one, I'm sure. She felt that language was a great mark of social status—"

"Shaw thought so too," interrupted Rubin. "Pygmalion."

"Never mind, Manny," said Trumbull. "Won't you please proceed, Mr. Leominster?"

"I was just going to say that Aunt Hester's fetish of verbal complication was something which she felt, I think, set her off from the lower classes. If I were to tell her that she ought to ask someone about something, she was quite certain to say something like, 'But of whom, exactly, dear, ought I to inquire?' She would never say 'ask' if she could say 'inquire'; she never ended a sentence with a preposition or split an infinitive. In fact, she was the only person I ever met who consistently used the subjunctive mood. She once said to me, 'Would you be so gracious, my dear Jason, as to ascertain whether it be raining or no,' and I almost failed to understand her.

"But I am wandering from the point again. As I said, she had an exaggerated idea of the value of my uncle's collection and she was always after him to do something about it. At her insistence, he put in an elaborate burglar alarm system and had a special signal installed that would sound in the local police station."

"Was it ever used?" asked Halsted.

"Not as far as I know," said Leominster. "There was never any burglary. My uncle didn't exactly live in a high-crime area—though you could never convince my aunt of that—and I wouldn't be surprised if prospective burglars had a more accurately disappointing notion of the worth of my uncle's collection than my aunt had. After my uncle's death, Aunt Hester had some of his belongings appraised. When they told her that his stamp collection was worth, perhaps, ten thousand dollars, she was horrified. 'They are thieves,' she told me. 'Having remitted ten thousand dollars, they would then certainly proceed to retail the collection for a million at the very least.' She would allow no further appraisals, and held onto everything with an unbreakable clutch. Fortunately, she had plenty to live on and didn't have to sell anything. To her dying day, though, I am sure she was convinced that she was leaving me possessions equivalent to an enormous fortune. —No such thing, unfortunately.

"My Uncle Bryce was hardheaded enough in this respect. He knew that the collections were of only moderate value. He said so to me on several occasions, though he also said he had a few items that were worthwhile. He did not specify. According to Aunt Hester, he went into more detail with her. When she urged him to put his stamp collection in a vault, he said, 'What, and never be able to look at it? It would have no value to me at all, then. Besides, it isn't worth much, except for one item, and I've taken care of that.' "

Avalon said, "That one item in the stamp collection that your uncle said he had taken care of—is that what is now lost? Was it some stamp or other?"

"Yes, so Aunt Hester said at the time of my uncle's death. He had left her the house and its contents, which meant that stamp too. She called me soon after the funeral to say that she could not find the stamp and was convinced it had been stolen. I had attended the funeral, of course, and was still in Connecticut, having taken the occasion to track down some old gravestones, and I came over for dinner the day after she called me.

"It was a hectic meal, for Aunt Hester was furious over not having found the stamp. She was convinced it was worth millions and that the servants had taken it—or perhaps the funeral people had. She even had a little suspicion left over for me. She said to me over dessert, 'Your Uncle, I presume, never discoursed on the matter of its location with you, did he?'

"I said he did not—which was true. He had never done so."

Trumbull said, "Did she have any idea at all where he hid it?"

"Yes, indeed. That was one of her grounds for annoyance. He had told her, but had not been specific enough, and she had not thought to pin him down exactly. I suppose she was satisfied that he had taken care of it and didn't think further. He told her he had placed it in one of his unabridged volumes, where he could get it easily enough to look at it whenever he wished, but where no casual thief would think to find it."

"In one of his unabridged volumes?" said Avalon in astonishment. "Did he mean in his collection?"

"Aunt Hester quoted him as saying 'one of my unabridged volumes.' We assumed he meant in his collection."

Rubin said, "It's a foolish place to put it. A book can be stolen as easily as a stamp. It can be stolen for itself and the stamp would go along as a side reward."

Leominster said, "I don't suppose my uncle seriously thought of it as a place of safety; merely as a way of satisfying my aunt. In fact, if she had not nagged him, I'm sure that Uncle Bryce would have left it right in the collection, which is, was, and has always been safe and sound. Of course, I never said this to my aunt."

Rubin said, "When people speak of 'the Unabridged,' they usually mean Webster's Unabridged Dictionary. Did your uncle have one?"

"Of course. On a small stand of its own. My aunt had thought of that and had looked there and hadn't found it. That was when she called me. We went into the library after dinner and I went over the Unabridged again. My uncle kept his better stamps in small, transparent envelopes and one of them might have been placed among the pages. Still, it would have been quite noticeable. It was an onionskin edition, and there would certainly have been a tendency for the dictionary to open to that page. Aunt Hester said it would be just like Uncle Bryce to hide it in such a foolish manner as to make it easily stolen.

"That was quite impossible, however. I had used the Unabridged myself now and then in my uncle's last years and I'm sure there was nothing in it. I inspected the binding to make sure he hadn't hid it behind the backstrip. I was even tempted to pull the entire volume apart, but it didn't seem likely that Uncle Bryce had gone to elaborate lengths. He had slipped it between the pages of a book—but not the Unabridged.

"I said as much to Aunt Hester. I told her that it might be among the pages of another book. I pointed out that the fact that he had referred to 'one of the unabridged volumes' was a sure sign that it was not in *the* Unabridged."

"I agree," said Rubin, "but how many unabridged volumes did he have?"

Leominster shook his head. "I don't know. I know nothing about books—at least from a collector's point of view. I asked Aunt Hester if she knew whether he had any items that were unabridged—an unabridged Boswell, for instance, or an unabridged Boccaccio—but she knew less about such matters than I did."

Gonzalo said, "Maybe 'unabridged' means something special to a book collector. Maybe it means having a book jacket—just as an example—and it's between the book and its jacket."

Avalon said, "No, Mario. I know something about books, and unabridged has no meaning but the usual one of a complete version."

"In any case," said Leominster, "it doesn't matter, for I suggested that we ought to go through all the books."

"A thousand of them?" asked Halsted doubtfully.

"As it turned out there were well over a thousand and it was a task indeed. I must say that Aunt Hester went about it properly. She hired half a dozen children from town—all girls, because she said girls were quieter and more reliable than boys. They were each between ten and twelve, old enough to work carefully and young enough to be honest. They came in each day for weeks and worked for four or five hours.

"Aunt Hester remained in the library at all times, handing out the books in systematic order, receiving them back, handing out another, and so on. She allowed no short cuts; no shaking the books to see if anything fell out, or flipping the pages, either. She made them turn each page individually."

"Did they find anything?" asked Avalon.

"Numerous things. Aunt Hester was too shrewd to tell them exactly what she was looking for. She just asked them to turn every single page and bring her any little thing they found, any scrap of paper, she said, or anything. She promised them a quarter for anything they found, in addition to a dollar for every hour they worked, and fed them all the milk and cake they could hold. Before it was over, each girl had gained five pounds, I'm sure. They located dozens of miscellaneous items. There were bookmarks, for instance, though I'm sure they were not my uncle's, for he was no reader; postcards, pressed leaves, even an occasional naughty photograph that I suspect my uncle had hidden for occasional study. They shocked my aunt but seemed to delight the little girls. In any case they did not find any stamp."

"Which must have been a great disappointment to your aunt," said Trumbull.

"It certainly was. She had immediate dark suspicions that one of the little girls had walked off with it, but even she couldn't maintain that for long. They were perfectly unsophisticated creatures and there was no reason to suppose that they would have thought a stamp was any more valuable than a bookmark. Besides, Aunt Hester had had her eye on them at every point."

"Then she never found it?" asked Gonzalo.

"No, she never did. She kept on looking through books for a while—you know, those that weren't in the library. She even went up into the attic to find some old books and magazines, but it wasn't there. It occurred to me that Uncle Bryce may have changed the hiding place in his later years and had told her of the new one—and that she had forgotten the new place and remembered only the old one. That's why I said what I did during dinner about two hiding places. You see, if that were true, and I have a nagging suspicion that it is, then the stamp could be anywhere in the house— or out of it, for that matter—and frankly, a search is hopeless in my opinion.

"I think Aunt Hester gave up too. These last couple of years, when her arthritis had made it almost impossible for her to move around, she never mentioned it. I was afraid that when she left the house to me, as he had made it quite plain she would, it would be on condition that I find the stamp—but no such thing was mentioned in her will."

Avalon twirled the brandy glass by its stem and said rather portentously, "See here, there's no real reason to think that there was such a stamp at all, is there? It may be that your uncle amused himself with the belief he had a valuable item, or may just have been teasing your aunt. Was he the kind of

nan capable of working up a rather malicious practical
oke?"

"No, no," said Leominster, with a definite shake of his
head. "He did not have that turn of mind at all. Besides,
Aunt Hester said she had seen the stamp. On one occasion,
he had been looking at it and he called in Hester and
showed it to her. He said, 'You are looking at thousands of
dollars, dear.' But she did not know where he had gotten it,
or to what hiding place he had returned it. All she had
thought at the time was that it was unutterably foolish for
grown men to pay so much money for a silly bit of paper—
and I rather agreed with her when she told me. She said
there wasn't anything attractive about it."

"Does she remember what it looked like? Could you recognize it if you found it?" asked Avalon. "For instance, suppose
that shortly before the time of your uncle's death he had
placed the stamp with the rest of his collection for some
reason—perhaps because your aunt was in Florida and could
not nag him, if he wanted it available for frequent gloating.
—Was she in Florida at the time of his death, by the way?"

Leominster looked thoughtful. "Yes, she was, as a matter
of fact."

"Well then," said Avalon. "The stamp may have been in
the collection all along. It may still be. Naturally, you wouldn't
find it anywhere else."

Trumbull said, "That can't be, Jeff. Leominster has already
told us that the stamp collection was appraised at ten
thousand dollars, total, and I gather that this one stamp
would have raised that mark considerably higher."

Leominster said, "According to Aunt Hester, Uncle Bryce
once told her that the stamp in question was worth his entire
remaining collection twice over."

Avalon said, "Uncle Bryce may have been kidding himself
or the appraisers may have made a mistake."

"No," said Leominster, "it was not in the collection. My
aunt remembered its appearance and it was unusual enough
to be identifiable. She said it was a triangular stamp, with
the narrow edge downward—something like my face as drawn
by Mr. Gonzalo."

Gonzalo cleared his throat and looked at the ceiling, but
Leominster, smiling genially, went on. "She said it had the
face of a man on it, and a bright orange border and that
my uncle referred to it as a New Guinea Orange. That is a

distinctive stamp, you must admit, and while it never occurred to me that it might be in the collection itself, so that I did not search for it specifically, I did go through the collection out of curiosity, and I assure you I didn't see the New Guinea Orange. In fact, I saw no triangular stamps at all—merely versions of the usual rectangle.

"Of course, I did wonder whether my uncle was wrong about the stamp's value, and whether he might not have found out he was wrong toward the end and sold the stamp or otherwise disposed of it. I consulted a stamp dealer and he said there were indeed such things as New Guinea Orange. He said some of them were very valuable and that one of them, which might be in my uncle's collection because it was not recorded elsewhere, was worth twenty-five thousand dollars."

"Well, look," said Drake. "I have an idea. You've mentioned your cousin, the one in Brazil. He was your uncle's son, and he was disinherited. Isn't it possible that he wasn't entirely disinherited; that your uncle mailed him the stamp, told him its value, and let that be his inheritance? He could then leave the house and its contents to his sister with a clear conscience, along with whatever else he had in his estate."

Leominster thought for a while. He said, "That never ocurred to me. I don't think it's likely, though. After all, his son was in no way in financial trouble and I was always given to understand he was very well to do. And there was hard feelings between father and son, too; very hard. It's a family scandal of which I do not have the details. I don't think Uncle Bryce would have mailed him the stamp."

Gonzalo said eagerly, "Could your cousin have come back to the United States and—"

"And stolen the stamp? How could he have known where it was? Besides, I'm sure my cousin has not been out of Brazil in years. No, heaven only knows where the stamp is, or whether it exists at all. I wish I could get a phone call, as Mr. Halsted did, that would tell me it's been located under the bed, but there's no chance of that."

Leominster's eye fell to his still unopened Chinese fortune cookie and he added whimsically, "Unless this can help me." He cracked it open, withdrew the slip of paper, looked at it, and laughed.

"What does it say?" asked Drake.

"It says, 'You will come into money,' " said Leominster. "It doesn't say how."

Gonzalo sat back in his chair and said, "Well then, Henry will tell you how."

Leominster smiled like one going along with a joke. "If you could bring me the stamp on your tray, Henry, I'd appreciate it."

"I'm not joking," said Gonzalo. "Tell him, Henry."

Henry, who had been listening quietly from his place at the sideboard, said, "I am flattered by your confidence, Mr. Gonzalo, but of course I cannot locate the stamp for Mr. Leominster. I might ask a few questions, however, if Mr. Leominster doesn't mind."

Leominster raised his eyebrows and said, "Not at all, if you think it will help."

"I cannot say as to that, sir," said Henry, "but you said your uncle was no reader. Does that mean he did not read the books in his library?"

"He didn't read much of anything, Henry, and certainly not the books in his library. They weren't meant to be read, only collected. Dry, impossible stuff."

"Did your uncle do anything to them—rebind them, or in any way modify them? Did he paste pages together, for instance?"

"To hide the stamp? Bite your tongue, Henry. If you do anything to any of those books, you reduce their value. No, no, your collector always leaves his collection exactly as he receives it."

Henry thought a moment, then said, "You told us your aunt affected an elegant vocabulary."

"Yes, she did."

"And that if you said 'ask,' for instance, she would change it to 'inquire.' "

"Yes."

"Would she have been aware of having made the change? —I mean, if she had been asked under oath to repeat your exact words, would she have said 'inquire' and honestly have thought you had said it?"

Leominster laughed. "I wouldn't be surprised if she would. She took her false elegance with enormous seriousness."

"And you only know of your uncle's hiding place by your aunt's report. He never told you, personally, of his hiding place, did he?"

"He never told me, but I'm bound to say that I don't for a minute believe Aunt Hester would lie. If she said he told her, then he did."

"She said that your uncle said he had hidden it in one of his unabridged volumes. That was exactly what she said?"

"Yes. Exactly. In one of his unabridged volumes."

Henry said, "But might not your aunt have translated his actual statement into her own notion of elegance, a short word into a long one? Isn't that possible?"

Leominster hesitated. "I suppose so, but what short word?"

"I cannot say with absolute certainty," said Henry, "but is not an abridged volume one that has been cut, and is not an unabridged volume therefore one that is uncut. If your uncle had said 'in one of my uncut volumes,' might not that have been translated in your aunt's mind to 'in one of my unabridged volumes'?"

"And if so, Henry?"

"Then we must remember that 'uncut' has a secondary meaning with respect to books that 'unabridged' does not. An uncut volume may be one with its pages uncut, rather than its contents. If your uncle collected books which he did not read, and with which he did not tamper, some of them may have been bought with their pages uncut and would have kept their pages *still* uncut to this day. Does he, in fact, have uncut books in his library?"

Leominster frowned and said hesitantly, "I think I remember one definitely, and there may have been others."

Henry said, "Every pair of adjacent pages in such a book would be connected at the margin, and perhaps at the top, but would be open at the bottom, so that they would form little bags. And if that is so, sir, then the young girls who went through the books would have turned the pages without paying any attenion to the fact that some of them might be uncut, and inside the little bag—one of them—a stamp in its transparent envelope may easily have been affixed with a bit of transparent tape. The pages would have bellied slightly as they were turned and would have given no signs of the contents. Nor would the girls think to look inside if their specific instructions were merely to turn the pages."

Leominster rose and looked at his watch. "It sounds good to me. I'll go to Connecticut tomorrow." He almost stuttered as he spoke. "Gentlemen, this is very exciting and I hope that once I am settled you will all come and have dinner with me to celebrate. —You especially, Henry. The reasoning was so simple that I'm amazed none of the rest of us saw it."

"Reasoning is always simple," said Henry, "and also always incomplete. Let us see if you really find your stamp. Without that, of what use is reason?"

11 *Afterword*

I sometimes feel faintly embarrassed over the slightness of the points on which the solution to a Black Widowers story rests, but that's silly. These are, frankly, puzzle stories, and the size of the puzzle doesn't matter as long as it's a sufficient challenge to the mind.

And as for myself, I have the double pleasure of thinking of the puzzle point first, and then of hiding it under layers of plot without being unfair to the reader.

"The Unabridged" I didn't submit anywhere, but saved it for this collection.

12

The Ultimate Crime

"The Baker Street Irregulars," said Roger Halsted, "is an organization of Sherlock Holmes enthusiasts. If you don't know that, you don't know anything."

He grinned over his drink at Thomas Trumbull with an air of the only kind of superiority there is—insufferable.

The level of conversation during the cocktail hour that preceded the monthly Black Widowers' banquet had remained at the level of a civilized murmur, but Trumbull, scowling, raised his voice at this point and restored matters to the more usual unseemliness that characterized such occasions.

He said, "When I was an adolescent I read Sherlock Holmes stories with a certain primitive enjoyment, but I'm not an adolescent any more. The same, I perceive, cannot be said for everyone."

Emmanuel Rubin, staring owlishly through his thick glasses, shook his head. "There's no adolescence to it, Tom. The Sherlock Holmes stories marked the occasion on which the mystery story came to be recognized as a major branch of literature. It took what had until then been something that *had* been confined to adolescents and their dime novels and made of it adult entertainment."

Geoffrey Avalon, looking down austerely from his seventy-four inches to Rubin's sixty-four, said, "Actually, Sir Arthur

Conan Doyle was not, in my opinion, an exceedingly good mystery writer. Agatha Christie is far better."

"That's a matter of opinion," said Rubin, who, as a mystery writer himself, was far less opinionated and didactic in that one field than in all the other myriad branches of human endeavor in which he considered himself an authority. "Christie had the advantage of reading Doyle and learning from him. Don't forget, too, that Christie's early works were pretty awful. Then, too"—he was warming up now—"Agatha Christie never got over her conservative, xenophobic prejudices. Her Americans are ridiculous. They were all named Hiram and all spoke a variety of English unknown to mankind. She was openly anti-Semitic and through the mouths of her characters unceasingly cast her doubts on anyone who was foreign."

Halsted said, "Yet her detective was a Belgian."

"Don't get me wrong," said Rubin. "I love Hercule Poirot. I think he's worth a dozen Sherlock Holmeses. I'm just pointing out that we can pick flaws in anyone. In fact, all the English mystery writers of the twenties and thirties were conservatives and upper-class-oriented. You can tell from the type of puzzles they presented—baronets stabbed in the libraries of their manor houses—landed estates—independent wealth. Even the detectives were often gentlemen—Peter Wimsey, Roderick Alleyn, Albert Campion—"

"In that case," said Mario Gonzalo, who had just arrived and had been listening from the stairs, "the mystery story has developed in the direction of democracy. Now we deal with ordinary cops, and drunken private eyes and pimps and floozies and all the other leading lights of modern society." He helped himself to a drink and said, "Thanks, Henry. How did they get started on this?"

Henry said, "Sherlock Holmes was mentioned, sir."

"In connection with you, Henry?" Gonzalo looked pleased.

"No, sir. In connection with the Baker Street Irregulars."

Gonzalo looked blank. "What are—"

Halsted said, "Let me introduce you to my guest of the evening, Mario. He'll tell you. —Ronald Mason, Mario Gonzalo. Ronald's a member of BSI, and so am I, for that matter. Go ahead, Ron, tell him about it."

Ronald Mason was a fat man, distinctly fat, with a glistening bald head and a bushy black mustache. He said, "The Baker Street Irregulars is a group of Sherlock Holmes enthusiasts. They meet once a year in January, on a Friday near the great man's birthday, and through the rest of the year engage in other Sherlockian activities."

"Like what?"

"Well, they—"

Henry announced dinner, and Mason hesitated. "Is there some special seat I'm supposed to take?"

"No, no," said Gonzalo. "Sit next to me and we can talk."

"Fine." Mason's broad face split in a wide smile. "That's exactly what I'm here for. Rog Halsted said that you guys would come up with something for me."

"In connection with what?"

"Sherlockian activities." Mason tore a roll in two and buttered it with strenuous strokes of his knife. "You see, the thing is that Conan Doyle wrote numerous Sherlock Holmes stories as quickly as he could because he hated them—"

"He did? In that case, why—"

"Why did he write them? Money, that's why. From the very first story, 'A Study in Scarlet,' the world caught on fire with Sherlock Holmes. He became a world-renowned figure and there is no telling how many people the world over thought he really lived. Innumerable letters were addressed to him at his address in 221b Baker Street, and thousands came to him with problems to be solved.

"Conan Doyle was surprised, as no doubt anyone would be under the circumstances. He wrote additional stories and the prices they commanded rose steadily. He was not pleased. He fancied himself as a writer of great historical romances and to have himself become world-famous as a mystery writer was displeasing—particularly when the fictional detective was far the more famous of the two. After six years of it he wrote 'The Final Problem,' in which he deliberately killed Holmes. There was a world outcry at this and after several more years Doyle was forced to reason out a method for resuscitating the detective, and then went on writing further stories.

"Aside from the value of the sales as mysteries, and from the fascinating character of Sherlock Holmes himself, the stories are a diversified picture of Great Britain in the late Victorian era. To immerse oneself in the sacred writings is to live in a world where it is always 1895."

Gonzalo said, "And what's a Sherlockian activity?"

"Oh well. I told you that Doyle didn't particularly like writing about Holmes. When he did write the various stories, he wrote them quickly and he troubled himself very little about mutual consistency. There are many odd points, therefore, unknotted threads, small holes, and so on, and the game is never to admit that anything is just a mistake or error. In fact, to a true Sherlockian, Doyle scarcely exists—it was Dr. John H. Watson who wrote the stories."

James Drake, who had been quietly listening from the other side of Mason, said, "I know what you mean. I once met a Holmes fan—he may even have been a Baker Street Irregular—who told me he was working on a paper that would prove that both Sherlock Holmes and Dr. Watson were fervent Catholics and I said, 'Well, wasn't Doyle himself a Catholic?' which he was, of course. My friend turned a very cold eye on me and said, 'What has *that* to do with it?'"

"Exactly," said Mason, "exactly. The most highly regarded of all Sherlockian activities is to prove your point by quotations from the stories and by careful reasoning. People have written articles, for instance, that are supposed to prove that Watson was a woman, or that Sherlock Holmes had an affair with his landlady. Or else they try to work out details concerning Holmes's early life, or exactly where Watson received his war wound, and so on.

"Ideally, every member of the Baker Street Irregulars should write a Sherlockian article as a condition of membership, but that's clung to in only a slipshod fashion. I haven't written such an article yet, though I'd like to." Mason looked a bit wistful. "I can't really consider myself a true Irregular till I do."

Trumbull leaned over from across the table. He said, "I've been trying to catch what you've been saying over Rubin's monologue here. You mentioned 221b Baker Street."

"Yes," said Mason, "that's where Holmes lived."

"And is that why the club is the Baker Street Irregulars?"

Mason said, "That was the name Holmes gave to a group of street urchins who acted as spies and sources of information. They were his irregular troops as distinguished from the police."

"Oh well," said Trumbull, "I suppose it's all harmless."

"And it gives us great pleasure," said Mason seriously. "Except that right now it's inflicting agony on me."

It was at this point, shortly after Henry had brought in the veal cordon bleu, that Rubin's voice rose a notch. "Of course," he said, "there's no way of denying that Sherlock Holmes was derivative. The whole Holmesian technique of detection was invented by Edgar Allen Poe; and his detective, Auguste Dupin, is the original Sherlock. However, Poe only wrote three stories about Dupin and it was Holmes who really caught the imagination of the world.

"In fact, my own feeling is that Sherlock Holmes performed the remarkable feat of being the first human being, either real or fictional, ever to become a world idol entirely because of his character as a reasoning being. It was not his military victories, his political charisma, his spiritual leadership—but simply his cold brain power. There was nothing mystical about Holmes. He gathered facts and deduced from them. His deductions weren't always fair; Doyle consistently stacked the deck in his favor, but every mystery writer does that. I do it myself."

Trumbull said, "What you do proves nothing."

Rubin was not to be distracted. "He was also the first believable super-hero in modern literature. He was always described as thin and aesthetic, but the fact that he achieved his triumphs through the use of brain power mustn't mask the fact that he is also described as being of virtually super-human strength. When a visitor, in an implicit threat to Holmes, bends a poker to demonstrate his strength, Holmes casually straightens it again—the more difficult task. Then, too—"

Mason nodded his head in Rubin's direction and said to Gonzalo, "Mr. Rubin sounds like a Baker Street Irregular himself—"

Gonzalo said, "I don't think so. He just knows everything—but don't tell him I said so."

"Maybe he can give me some Sherlockian pointers, then."

"Maybe, but if you're in trouble, the real person to help you is Henry."

"Henry?" Mason's eye wandered around the table as though trying to recall first names.

"Our waiter," said Gonzalo. "He's *our* Sherlock Holmes."

"I don't think—" began Mason doubtfully.

"Wait till dinner is over. You'll see."

Halsted tapped his water glass and said, "Gentlemen, we're

going to try something different this evening. Mr. Mason has a problem that involves the preparation of a Sherlockian article, and that means he would like to present us with a purely literary puzzle, one that has no connection with real life at all. —Ron, explain."

Mason scooped up some of the melted ice cream in his dessert plate with his teaspoon, put it in his mouth as though in a final farewell to the dinner, then said, "I've got to prepare this paper because it's a matter of self-respect. I love being a Baker Street Irregular, but it's difficult to hold my head up when every person there knows more about the canon than I do and when thirteen-year-old boys write papers that meet with applause for their ingenuity.

"The trouble is that I don't have much in the way of imagination, or the kind of whimsey needed for the task. But I know what I want to do. I want to do a paper on Dr. Moriarty."

"Ah, yes," said Avalon. "The villain in the case."

Mason nodded. "He doesn't appear in many of the tales, but he is the counterpart of Holmes. He is the Napoleon of crime, the intellectual rival of Holmes and the great detective's most dangerous antagonist. Just as Holmes is the popular prototype of the fictional detective, so is Moriarty the popular prototype of the master villain. In fact, it was Moriarty who killed Holmes, and was killed himself, in the final struggle in 'The Final Problem.' Moriarty was not brought back to life."

Avalon said, "And on what aspect of Moriarty did you wish to do a paper?" He sipped thoughtfully at his brandy.

Mason waited for Henry to refill his cup and said, "Well, it's his role as a mathematician that intrigues me. You see, it is only Moriarty's diseased moral sense that makes him a master criminal. He delights in manipulating human lives and in serving as the agent for destruction. If he wished to bend his great talent to legitimate issues, however, he could be world famous—indeed, he *was* world famous, in the Sherlockian world—as a mathematician.

"Only two of his mathematical feats are specifically mentioned in the canon. He was the author of an extension of the binomial theorem, for one thing. Then, in the novel, *The Valley of Fear*, Holmes mentions that Moriarty had written a thesis entitled *The Dynamics of an Asteroid*, which was filled with mathematics so rarefied that there wasn't a scientist in Europe capable of debating the matter."

"As it happened," said Rubin, "one of the greatest mathematicians alive at the time was an American, Josiah Willard Gibbs, who—"

"That doesn't matter," said Mason hastily. "In the Sherlockian world only Europe counts when it comes to matters of science. The point is this, nothing is said about the contents of *The Dynamics of an Asteroid*; nothing at all; and no Sherlockian has ever written an article taking up the matter. I've checked into it and I know that."

Drake said, "And *you* want to do such an article?"

"I want to very much," said Mason, "but I'm not up to it. I have a layman's knowledge of astronomy. I know what an asteroid is. It's one of the small bodies that circles the Sun between the orbits of Mars and Jupiter. I know what dynamics is; it's the study of the motion of a body and of the changes in its motion when forces are applied. But that doesn't get me anywhere. What is *The Dynamics of an Asteroid* about?"

Drake said thoughtfully, "Is that all you have to go by, Mason? Just the title? Isn't there any passing reference to anything that is in the paper itself?"

"Not one reference anywhere. There's just the title, plus the indication that it is a matter of a highly advanced mathematics."

Gonzalo put his sketch of a jolly, smiling Mason—with the face drawn as a geometrically perfect circle—on the wall next to the others and said, "If you're going to write about how planets move, you need a lot of fancy math, I should think."

"No, you don't," said Drake abruptly. "Let me handle this, Mario. I may be only a lowly organic chemist, but I know something about astronomy too. The fact of the matter is that all the mathematics needed to handle the dynamics of the asteroids was worked out in the 1680s by Isaac Newton.

"An asteroid's motion depends entirely upon the gravitational influences to which it is subjected and Newton's equation makes it possible to calculate the strength of that influence between any two bodies if the mass of each body is known and if the distance between them is also known. Of course, when many bodies are involved and when the distances among them are constantly changing, then the mathematics gets tedious—not difficult, just tedious.

"The chief gravitational influence on any asteroid is that originating in the Sun, of course. Each asteroid moves around the Sun in an elliptical orbit, and if the Sun and asteroid were all that existed, the orbit could be calculated, exactly, by Newton's equation. Since other bodies also exist, their gravitational influences, much smaller than that of the Sun, must be taken into account as producing much smaller effects. In general, we get very close to the truth if we just consider the Sun."

Avalon said, "I think you're oversimplifying, Jim. To duplicate your humility, I may be only a lowly patent lawyer, and I won't pretend to know any astronomy at all, but haven't I heard that there's no way of solving the gravitational equation for more than two bodies?"

"That's right," said Drake, "if you mean by that, a general solution for all cases involving more than two bodies. There just isn't one. Newton worked out the general solution for the two-body problem but no one, to this day, has succeeded in working out one for the three-body problem, let alone for more bodies than that. The point is, though, that only theoreticians are interested in the three-body problem. Astronomers work out the motion of a body by first calculating the dominant gravitational influence, then correcting it one step at a time with the introduction of other lesser gravitational influences. It works well enough." He sat back and looked smug.

Gonzalo said, "Well, if only theoreticians are interested in the three-body problem and if Moriarty was a high-powered mathematician, then that must be just what the treatise is about."

Drake lit a new cigarette and paused to cough over it. Then he said, "It could have been about the love life of giraffes, if you like, but we've got to go by the title. If Moriarty had solved the three-body problem, he would have called the treatise something like, *An Analysis of the Three-Body Problem*, or *The Generalization of the Law of Universal Gravitation*. He would *not* have called it *The Dynamics of an Asteroid*."

Halsted said, "What about the planetary effects? I've heard something about that. Aren't there gaps in space where there aren't any asteroids?"

"Oh, sure," said Drake. "We can find the dates in the

Columbia Encyclopedia, if Henry will bring it over."

"Never mind," said Halsted. "You just tell us what you know about it and we can check the dates later, if we have to."

Drake said, "Let's see now." He was visibly enjoying his domination of the proceedings. His insignificant gray mustache twitched and his eyes, nested in finely wrinkled skin, seemed to sparkle.

He said, "There was an American astronomer named Kirkwood and I think Daniel was his first name. Sometime around the middle 1800s he pointed out that the asteroids' orbits seemed to cluster in groups. There were a couple of dozen known by then, all between the orbits of Mars and Jupiter, but they weren't spread out evenly, as Kirkwood pointed out. He showed there were gaps in which no asteroids circled.

"By 1866 or thereabouts—I'm pretty sure it was 1866— he worked out the reason. Any asteroid that would have had its orbit in those gaps would have circled the Sun in a period equal to a simple fraction of that of Jupiter."

"If there's no asteroid there," said Gonzalo, "how can you tell how long it would take it to go around the Sun?"

"Actually, it's very simple. Kepler worked that out in 1619 and it's called Kepler's Third Law. May I continue?"

"That's just syllables," said Gonzalo. "What's Kepler's Third Law?"

But Avalon said, "Let's take Jim's word for it, Mario. I can't quote it either, but I'm sure astronomers have it down cold. Go ahead, Jim."

Drake said, "An asteroid in a gap might have an orbital period of six years or four years, let us say, where Jupiter has a period of twelve years. That means an asteroid, every two or three revolutions, passes Jupiter under the same relative conditions of position. Jupiter's pull is in some particular direction each time, always the same, either forward or backward, and the effect mounts up.

"If the pull is backward, the asteroidal motion is gradually slowed so that the asteroid drops in closer toward the Sun and moves out of the gap. If the pull is forward, the asteroidal motion is quickened and the asteroid swings away from the Sun, again moving out of the gap. Either way nothing stays in the gaps, which are now called 'Kirkwood gaps.' You get the same effect in Saturn's rings. There are gaps there too."

Trumbull said, "You say Kirkwood did this in 1866?"

"Yes."

"And when did Moriarty write his thesis, supposedly?"

Mason interposed. "About 1875, if we work out the internal consistency of the Sherlockian canon."

Trumbull said, "Maybe Doyle was inspired by the news of the Kirkwood gaps, and thought of the title because of it. In which case, we can imagine Moriarty playing the role of Kirkwood and you can write an article on the Moriarty gaps."

Mason said uneasily, "Would that be enough? How important was Kirkwood's work? How difficult?"

Drake shrugged. "It was a respectable contribution, but it was just an application of Newtonian physics. Good second-class work; not first class."

Mason shook his head. "For Moriarty, it would have to be first class."

"Wait, wait!" Rubin's sparse beard quivered with growing excitement. "Maybe Moriarty got away from Newton altogether. Maybe he got onto Einstein. Einstein revised the theory of gravity."

"He extended it," said Drake, "in the General Theory of Relativity in 1916."

"Right. Forty years after Moriarty's paper. That's got to be it. Suppose Moriarty had anticipated Einstein—"

Drake said, "In 1875? That would be before the Michelson-Morley experiment. I don't think it could have been done."

"Sure it could," said Rubin, "if Moriarty were bright enough—and he was."

Mason said, "Oh yes. In the Sherlockian universe, Professor Moriarty was brilliant enough for anything. Sure he would anticipate Einstein. The only thing is that, if he had done so, would he not have changed scientific history all around?"

"Not if the paper were suppressed," said Rubin, almost chattering with excitement. "It all fits in. The paper was suppressed and the great advance was lost till Einstein rediscovered it."

"What makes you say the paper was suppressed?" demanded Gonzalo.

"It doesn't exist, does it?" said Rubin. "If we go along with the Baker Street Irregular view of the universe, then

Professor Moriarty *did* exist and the treatise *was* written, and it *did* anticipate General Relativity. Yet we can't find it anywhere in the scientific literature and there is no sign of the relativistic view penetrating scientific thought prior to Einstein's time. The only explanation is that the treatise was suppressed because of Moriary's evil character."

Drake snickered. "There'd be a lot of scientific papers suppressed if evil character were cause enough. But your suggestion is out anyway, Manny. The treatise couldn't possibly involve General Relativity; not with that title."

"Why not?" demanded Rubin.

"Because revising the gravitational calculations in order to take relativity into account wouldn't do much as far as asteroidal dynamics are concerned," said Drake. "In fact, there was only one item known to astronomers in 1875 that could be considered, in any way, a gravitational puzzle."

"Uh-oh," said Rubin, "I'm beginning to see your point."

"Well, I don't," said Avalon. "Keep on going, Jim. What was the puzzle?"

Drake said, "It involved the planet Mercury, which revolves about the Sun in a pretty lopsided orbit. At one point in its orbit it is at its closest to the Sun (closer than any other planet, of course, since it is nearer to the Sun in general than the others are) and that point is the 'perihelion.' Each time Mercury completes a revolution about the Sun, that perihelion has shifted very slightly forward.

"The reason for the shift is to be found in the small gravitational effects, or perturbations, of the other planets on Mercury. But after all the known gravitational effects are taken into account, the perihelion shift isn't completely explained. This was discovered in 1843. There is a very tiny residual shift forward that can't be explained by gravitational theory. It isn't much—only about 43 seconds of arc per century, which means the perihelion would move an unexplained distance equal to the diameter of the full Moon in about forty-two hundred years, or make a complete circle of the sky"—he did some mental calculations—"in about three million years.

"It's not much of a motion, but it was enough to threaten Newton's theory. Some astronomers felt that there must be an unknown planet on the other side of Mercury, very close to the Sun. Its pull was not taken into account, since it was unknown, but it was possible to calculate how large a planet would have to exist, and what kind of an orbit it must have, to account for the anomalous motion of Mercury's perihelion. The only trouble was that they could never find that planet.

"Then Einstein modified Newton's theory of gravitation, made it more general, and showed that when the new, modified equations were used the motion of Mercury's perihelion was exactly accounted for. It also did a few other things, but never mind that."

Gonzalo said, "Why couldn't Moriarty have figured that out?"

Drake said, "Because then he would have called his treatise, *On the Dynamics of Mercury*. He couldn't possibly have discovered something that solved this prime astronomical paradox that had been puzzling astronomers for thirty years and have called it anything else."

Mason looked dissatisfied. "Then what you're saying is that there isn't anything that Moriarty could have written that would have had the title *On the Dynamics of an Asteroid* and still have represented a first-class piece of mathematical work?"

Drake blew a smoke ring. "I guess that's what I'm saying. What I'm also saying, I suppose, is that Sir Arthur Conan Doyle didn't know enough astronomy to stuff a pig's ear, and that he didn't know what he was saying when he invented the title. But I suppose that sort of thing is not permitted to be said."

"No," said Mason, his round face sunk in misery. "Not in the Sherlockian universe. There goes my paper, then."

"Pardon me," said Henry, from his post at the sideboard. "May I ask a question?"

Drake said, "You know you can, Henry. Don't tell me you're an astronomer."

"No, sir. At least, not beyond the average knowledge of an educated American. Still, am I correct in supposing that there are a large number of asteroids known?"

"Over seventeen hundred have had their orbits calculated, Henry," said Drake.

"And there were a number known in Professor Moriarty's time, too, weren't there?"

"Sure. Several dozen."

"In that case, sir," said Henry, "why does the title of the treatise read *The Dynamics of an Asteroid*? Why *an* asteroid?"

Drake thought a moment, then said, "That's a good point. I don't know—unless it's another indication that Doyle didn't know enough—"

"Don't say that," said Mason.

"Well—leave it at I don't know, then."

Gonzalo said, "Maybe Moriarty just worked it out for one asteroid, and that's all."

Drake said, "Then he would have named it *The Dynamics of Ceres* or whatever asteroid he worked on."

Gonzalo said stubbornly, "No, that's not what I mean. I don't mean he worked it out for one particular asteroid. I mean he picked an asteroid at random, or just an ideal asteroid, maybe not one that really exists. Then he worked out its dynamics."

Drake said, "That's not a bad notion, Mario. The only trouble is that if Moriarty worked out the dynamics of an asteroid, the basic mathematical system, it would hold for all of them, and the title of the paper would be *The Dynamics of Asteroids*. And besides, whatever he worked out in that respect would be only Newtonian and not of prime value."

"Do you mean to say," said Gonzalo, reluctant to let go, "that not one of the asteroids had something special about its orbit?"

"None known in 1875 did," said Drake. "They all had orbits between those of Mars and Jupiter and they all followed gravitational theory with considerable exactness. We know some asteroids with unusual orbits *now*. The first unusual asteroid to be discovered was Eros, which has an orbit that takes it closer to the Sun than Mars ever goes and brings it, on occasion, to within fourteen million miles of Earth, closer to Earth than any other body its size or larger, except for the Moon.

"That, however, wasn't discovered till 1898. Then, in 1906, Achilles was discovered. It was the first of the Trojan asteroids and they are unusual because they move around the Sun in Jupiter's orbit though well before or behind that planet."

Gonzalo said, "Couldn't Moriarty have anticipated those discoveries, and worked out the unusual orbits?"

"Even if he had anticipated them, the orbits are unusual only in their position, not in their dynamics. The Trojan asteroids did offer some interesting theoretical aspects, but that had already been worked out by Lagrange a century before."

There was a short silence and then Henry said, "The title is, however, so definite, sir. If we accept the Sherlockian premise that it must make sense, can it possibly have referred to some time when there was only a single body orbiting between Mars and Jupiter?"

Drake grinned. "Don't try to act ignorant, Henry. You're talking about the explosion theory of the origin of the asteroids."

For a moment, it seemed as though Henry might smile. If the impulse existed, he conquered it, however, and said, "I have come across, in my reading, the suggestion that there had once been a planet between Mars and Jupiter and that it had exploded."

Drake said, "That's not a popular theory any more, but it certainly had its day. In 1801, when the first asteroid, Ceres, was discovered, it turned out to be only about 450 miles across, astonishingly small. What was far more astonishing, though, was that over the next three years three other asteroids were discovered, with very similar orbits. The notion of an exploded planet was brought up at once."

Henry said, "Couldn't Professor Moriarty have been referring to that planet before its explosion, when speaking of *an* asteroid?"

Drake said, "I suppose he could have, but why not call it a planet?"

"Would it have been a large planet?"

"No, Henry. If all the asteroids are lumped together, they would make up a planet scarcely a thousand miles in diameter."

"Might it not be closer to what we now consider an asteroid, then, rather than to what we consider a planet? Mightn't that have been even more true in 1875 when fewer asteroids were known and the original body would have seemed smaller still?"

Drake said, "Maybe. But why not call it *the* asteroid, then?"

"Perhaps Professor Moriarty felt that to call the paper *The Dynamics of the Asteroid* was too definite. Perhaps he felt the explosion theory was not certain enough to make it possible to speak of anything more than *an* asteroid. However unscrupulous Professor Moriarty might have been in the world outside science, we must suppose that he was a most careful and rigidly precise mathematician."

Mason was smiling again. "I like that, Henry. It's a great idea." He said to Gonzalo, "You were right."

"I told you," said Gonzalo.

Drake said, "Hold on, let's see where it takes us. Moriarty can't be just talking about the dynamics of the original asteroid as a world orbiting about the Sun, because it would be following gravitational theory just as all its descendants are.

"He would have to be talking about the explosion. He would have to be analyzing the forces in planetary structure that would make an explosion conceivable. He would have to discuss the consequences of the explosion, and all that would not lie within the bounds of gravitational theory. He would have to calculate the events in such a way that the explosive forces would give way to gravitational effects and leave the asteroidal fragments in the orbits they have today."

Drake considered, then nodded, and went on. "That would not be bad. It would be a mathematical problem worthy of Moriarty's brain, and we might consider it to have represented the first attempt of any mathematician to take up so complicated an astronomical problem. Yes, I like it."

Mason said, "I like it too. If I can remember everything you've all said, I have my article. Good Lord, this is wonderful."

Henry said, "As a matter of fact, gentlemen, I think this hypothesis is even better than Dr. Drake has made it sound. I believe that Mr. Rubin said earlier that we must assume that Professor Moriarty's treatise was suppressed, since it cannot be located in the scientific annals. Well, it seems to me that if our theory can also explain that suppression, it becomes much more forceful."

"Quite so," said Avalon, "but can it?"

"Consider," said Henry, and a trace of warmth entered his quiet voice, "that over and above the difficulty of the problem, and of the credit therefore to be gained in solving it, there is a peculiar appeal in the problem to Professor Moriarty in view of his known character.

"After all, we are dealing with the destruction of a world. To a master criminal such as Professor Moriarty, whose diseased genius strove to produce chaos on Earth, to disrupt and corrupt the world's economy and society, there must have been something utterly fascinating in the vision of the actual *physical* destruction of a world.

"Might not Moriarty have imagined that on that original asteroid another like himself had existed, one who had not only tapped the vicious currents of the human soul but had even tampered with the dangerous forces of a planet's interior? Moriarty might have imagined that this super-Moriarty of the original asteroid had deliberately destroyed his world, and all life on it, including his own, out of sheer joy in malignancy, leaving the asteroids that now exist as the various tombstones that commemorate the action.

"Could Moriarty even have envied the deed and tried to work out the necessary action that would have done the same on Earth? Might not those few European mathematicians who could catch even a glimpse of what Moriarty was saying in his treatise have understood that what it described was not only a mathematical description of the origin of the asteroids but the beginning of a recipe for the ultimate crime—that of the destruction of Earth itself, of all life, and of the creation of a much larger asteroid belt?

"It is no wonder, if that were so, that a horrified scientific community suppressed the work."

And when Henry was done, there was a moment of silence and then Drake applauded. The others quickly joined in.

Henry reddened. "I'm sorry," he murmured when the applause died. "I'm afraid I allowed myself to be carried away."

"Not at all," said Avalon. "It was a surprising burst of poetry that I was glad to have heard."

Halsted said, "Frankly, I think that's perfect. It's exactly what Moriarty would do and it explains everything. Wouldn't you say so, Ron?"

"I will say so," said Mason, "as soon as I get over being speechless. I ask nothing better than to prepare a Sherlockian paper based on Henry's analysis. How can I square it with my conscience, however, to appropriate his ideas?"

Henry said, "It is yours, Mr. Mason, my free gift, for initiating a very gratifying session. You see, I have been a devotee of Sherlock Holmes for many years, myself."

12 Afterword

Let me confess.

I am a member of Baker Street Irregulars. *I* got in despite the fact that I had never written a Sherlockian article. *I* was the one who thought it would be easy to write one if I had to and then found to my horror that every member of the Baker Street Irregulars was infinitely more knowledgeable in the sacred writings than I was and that I couldn't possibly compete. (Nevertheless, Ronald Mason in this story is not I and does not look anything like me.)

It was only under the urgings of fellow BSI-ers Michael Harrison and Banesh Hoffman that I finally stirred out of my paralysis, and then only after Harrison had suggested I take up the matter of *The Dynamics of an Asteroid*. I wrote a 1,600-word article with great enthusiasm and fell so deeply in love with my own clever analysis of the situation that I could not bear to think that only a few hundred other BSI-ers would ever see it.

I therefore converted it into "The Ultimate Crime" and made a Black Widowers story out of it for a wider audience.

And at last I feel like a real Baker Street Irregular.

And once again, now that I have come to the conclusion of the book, I will have to repeat what I said at the end of the first book. I *will* write more Black Widowers. For one thing, I have fallen in love with all the characters. For another, I can't help myself. It's gotten to the point where almost everything I see or do gets run through some special pipeline in my mind, quite automatically and involuntarily, to see if a Black Widowers plot might not come out the other end.

Isaac Asimov

- [ ] BEFORE THE GOLDEN AGE, Book I   22913-0   1.95
- [ ] BEFORE THE GOLDEN AGE, Book II   Q2452   1.50
- [ ] BEFORE THE GOLDEN AGE, Book III   23593-9   1.95
- [ ] THE BEST OF ISAAC ASIMOV   23653-6   1.95
- [ ] BUY JUPITER AND OTHER STORIES   23062-7   1.50
- [ ] THE CAVES OF STEEL   Q2858   1.50
- [ ] THE CURRENTS OF SPACE   23507-6   1.50
- [ ] EARTH IS ROOM ENOUGH   23383-9   1.75
- [ ] THE END OF ETERNITY   23704-4   1.75
- [ ] THE GODS THEMSELVES   23756-7   1.95
- [ ] I, ROBOT   Q2829   1.50
- [ ] THE MARTIAN WAY   23783-4   1.75
- [ ] THE NAKED SUN   23805-9   1.75
- [ ] NIGHTFALL AND OTHER STORIES   23188-7   1.75
- [ ] NINE TOMORROWS   Q2688   1.50
- [ ] PEBBLE IN THE SKY   23423-1   1.75
- [ ] THE STARS, LIKE DUST   23595-5   1.75
- [ ] WHERE DO WE GO FROM HERE?—Ed.   X2849   1.75

Buy them at your local bookstores or use this handy coupon for ordering:

FAWCETT BOOKS GROUP
P.O. Box C730, 524 Myrtle Ave., Pratt Station, Brooklyn, N.Y. 11205

Please send me the books I have checked above. Orders for less than 5 books must include 75¢ for the first book and 25¢ for each additional book to cover mailing and handling. I enclose $_____ in check or money order.

Name_____
Address_____
City_____State/Zip_____
Please allow 4 to 5 weeks for delivery.